Captivating Captains

THE CAPTAIN AND THE BAKER

CATHERINE CURZON &
ELEANOR HARKSTEAD

The Captain and the Baker
ISBN # 978-1-83943-917-9
©Copyright Catherine Curzon and Eleanor Harkstead 2020
Cover Art by Louisa Maggio ©Copyright August 2020
Interior text design by Claire Siemaszkiewicz
Pride Publishing

THE CAPTAIN AND THE BAKER

Dedication

CC – to Chrissy,
because there's always time for doughnuts.

EH – to Deborah,
who knows a grumpy chef or two.

Chapter One

Jake, immaculate in his chef whites but his hair just ruffled enough to look careless, tried to smile into the television camera.

There wasn't much to smile about because, although the set of *Saturday Breakfast* was more than familiar to him, he hadn't had to share it with Locryn Trevorrow before.

Locryn, as sugary sweet as the cakes and delicacies he baked, was as far as it was possible to be from Jake, a chef who'd made a name for himself swearing on the telly while cooking. As he had watched Locryn across the studio that morning, all smiles and sunshine and *please* and *thank you* and *how marvelous*, he couldn't imagine the man had ever sworn in his life. He'd probably draw the line at *fiddlesticks*.

"And now it's the moment we've all been waiting for!" Katya, the host of the show, beamed, showing dazzling white teeth. "Our search for a bride and groom ends today with our very last couple, so get on the phones and get voting! You all know the rules by now. We've scoured the country and, out of thousands of applicants, we've found three couples who are competing for the chance to hold their wedding at Jake Brantham's brand-new restaurant. The twist is, even Jake doesn't know where that will be! All he knows is that it'll be in the hometown of our winning couple and we'll watch it all happen in his new series, *From Wreck to Restaurant!*"

The camera cut away to Jake, who pulled his best theatrical glower. The one all his fans went crazy for.

"Each week we've invited a couple onto *Saturday Breakfast* and paired them with a chef from their town, who's been challenged by Jake to cook one of his signature dishes. Our last couple are Zoe and David, from the gorgeous little village of Porthavel, and they're joined by Britain's favorite and loveliest baker, Locryn Trevorrow!" Across the studio crew, a loud smattering of applause sounded, which Locryn dismissed with a bashful wave of his hand. "We sent our intrepid crew off to meet Zoe and David at home in Cornwall, so let's take a look at life in one of Britain's cutest fishing villages."

The floor manager called, "And we're off."

A makeup artist dashed onto the set and immediately began dusting at Katya's face. Standing behind the worktop where he would soon do battle with Jake's recipe, Locryn called to Jake, "Morning! We haven't had a chance to meet yet, so hello!"

Plummy wasn't the word for it. Jake had wondered if that voice was a put-on for the cameras, but it didn't sound like it. Did that mean the cottage in the opening titles of *Trevorrow Treats* was real too, right down to the roses around the door and the goats on the front lawn, grazing the grass that overlooked the Atlantic Ocean on Cornwall's south coast?

"And a good fucking morning to you!" Jake unfolded one arm and waved. A sort of wave, at least. Locryn blinked at him, then gave a smile that was more like a grimace. Perhaps they didn't say *fucking* in his little corner of Cornwall.

"You ready to feel the meat?" Jake asked. He planted his hands on his hips, his eyebrow arched in challenge.

"Yes…right, meat." Locryn abandoned his designated mark as a runner began assembling the ingredients on the worktop. There were fresh herbs and juicy tomatoes, oils and spices, but none of the sugar and silliness that Locryn Trevorrow had turned into his fortune. He approached Jake and lowered his voice a little to ask, "You do know I'm a baker? I'm just slightly concerned because it doesn't look like you've set me a baking challenge."

"And you do know I'm *not* a bloody baker?" Jake sighed. "You've got to follow one of my recipes, mate — and I don't do cupcakes or croissants!"

Locryn shook his head, then ruffled one hand through his dark-blond hair. He glanced back at the worktop, where the runner had now covered the ingredients with a tea towel that bore a pattern of sunflowers.

Very bloody him.

"I'll give it my best," he decided. Then he smiled and said, "You never know, if I get it terribly wrong, Zoe and David might get the sympathy vote anyway!"

And I'll have to go to the arse end of nowhere for months.

"Do you think so?" Jake dabbed at some crumbs on the workstation in front of him. "I bet it's fucking fixed anyway. That posh couple from Hamble'll win because—and don't tell anyone I told you"—Jake revved up to unleash his secret in an unsubtle stage whisper, and he didn't care if anyone overheard—"the groom's uncle is one of *this* show's producers."

Locryn unfastened one of his cufflinks—*they wouldn't be buttons, would they*—and rolled up his sleeve as he said, "That's not true, is it? Tell me that's a fib."

A fucking fib. Is he nine?

"It's *true!*" Jake gave an emphatic nod. "Eugenia and Ptolemy have an *in*. You may as well send your two fucking home right away! It's a long way back to your foggy old smuggler country. If they leave now, they'll just about catch the next train!"

But all Locryn did was unfasten the second cufflink and serenely roll up his sleeve. Then he smiled and told Jake, "You're just as charming as I thought you'd be. Don't count me out yet, Mr. Brantham. If all else fails, I can try and fall back on this smile."

"I don't do *charming*, Trevorrow. I do simple, local, fresh." Jake emphasized each word, punching his fist against his palm. Locryn blinked then glanced toward the floor manager, who was frantically ushering everyone back into position. Across the studio all three couples were sitting on bright yellow couches around a coffee table in the mock-up of a sitting room, where guests were stationed while the cooks gave their demonstrations. Locryn gave them a thumbs-up and David and Zoe returned it, the young couple looking as nervous as he was laid-back.

That won't last.

"It's *Saturday Breakfast* and—awwww—aren't David and Zoe adorable?" Katya made a face into the camera as though she were addressing a newborn kitten. "And someone else we adore is our guest chef, or should I say guest *baker*, Locryn Trevorrow. Locryn's famous for his naughty but gorgeous cakes and bakes, and he's come all the way from Porthavel with our last couple to try and cook them to victory. Are you ready to face Jake's challenge, Locryn?"

He nodded and replied, "As I'll ever be, Katya."

"You've already met our couples and the lines are open, so get voting now. At the end of the program we'll find out which of our gorgeous couples have won their dream wedding, and Jake will find out where he's going to be turning a wreck into a restaurant in his brand-new series, *From Wreck to Restaurant*." She glanced toward Jake and grinned. "Will he be in Hamble, York or Porthavel? It's up to you at home. Jake, it's time for you to reveal to Locryn what he's going to be cooking today!"

Rubbing his hands together, Jake crossed the studio and stood beside Locryn. The man's cologne was suddenly all around Jake. Not a cloying, gassy cloud of it but a spicy scent that Jake, despite himself, found oddly enticing.

Oh, fuck that, no.

"So, Locryn, no f—fancy cupcakes for you today!" Jake said. "Instead, you'll be making one of *my* favorites, pork goujons with tomato sauce. It's simple, it's local, it's fresh, and when you get to the breadcrumbs, it's bloody close to baking."

"*Pork?*" Locryn looked down at the worktop as Katya pulled back the tea towel to reveal the ingredients. He rubbed his hands together and glanced toward the couples on the sofa. "I'm up for that. It's for Zoe and David, after all!"

"You've got your recipe, you've got your ingredients and you've got Jake to keep you on your toes." Katya grinned. "Jake, any hints or tips for Locryn before he dives in and tries to recreate one of your Michelin-starred staples?"

"Feel the meat," Jake advised. He leaned with one hand on the worktop. "Don't skate round it. It's central to the dish. You need to *feel* it and know when it's cut the right size, know when it's cooked through. That's the secret working with any f—flesh. Meat. You've got to feel it."

Oh, fiddle-fucking-sticks.

"Thanks, Jake!" Katya beamed at him and it was Jake's cue to stand aside. "So, Locryn, what do you make of all this *feeling the meat* business? Bit unusual for you?"

"It's not something I do every day. I hoped Jake might take pity on me and let me bake one of my gorgeous cakes. I wasn't expecting pork, but I'm raring to go." Locryn took a pair of spectacles from his pocket and popped them on. He picked up the recipe and scanned it.

"Is this the sort of dish you'd cook for yourself at home for dinner?" Katya asked, but before Locryn could reply, she said to camera, "Wouldn't we all love to know what Locryn cooks in his cute little cottage!"

Tiny dinners for tiny pixies, probably, Jake supposed.

"It's a myth that I live mostly on cream teas and fairy cakes." Locryn picked up a knife and cut the top off an onion. "I've shown a lot Porthavel on my program and we have the most exquisite fresh fish landed every day, so I eat a lot of seafood. You can wander down to the quay and pick something up that's straight out of the sea and into the kitchen. I don't cook with pork a lot, but that might change if I don't make too much of a hash of this."

Jakes ears alighted on Locryn's words.

Exquisite fresh fish.

His mouth began to water at the thought, and he wondered if Porthavel would really be so bad, with a quay creaking with mountains of fresh seafood.

But he'd have to share a village with the King of Twee.

No fucking way!

"Seafood? Sounds lovely!" Katya sniffed one of the small ceramic pots of herbs. "So this is, what is it, basil?"

Parsley, you abject dimwit!

But Jake could only fold his arms and shout, "Locryn, a clue! It's not angelica strands!"

"Any tips to save me from crying while I'm chopping this onion?" Locryn blinked at him from behind the lenses of his glasses. His eyes were ridiculously blue. Sparkling, even. That had to be worth a few votes, Jake knew.

"You can either man up or cut them underwater!" Jake shouted back. It's what the viewers expected of him, and he didn't like to disappoint.

"Oh, Jake, you're so naughty!" Katya expelled a theatrical attempt at an exasperated sigh. "Would you like a tissue, Locryn?"

"I'll man up." Locryn laughed. "And if we *do* win and Jake has to come down to Porthavel and give the gorgeous Zoe and dashing David the wedding of their dreams, I might have a challenge for *him*. I've always wondered what a Michelin-starred Cornish pasty would taste like!"

"F—flipping marvelous!" Jake announced.

That was a close one.

"We'll have to screen a Cornwall special!" Katya laughed. "Do you make Cornish pasties, Locryn?"

Locryn picked up the piece of pork and considered it as he said, "I do. In fact, it's the *only* savory I serve in my café. So I'm not sweet *all* the time, just most of it." He looked to Jake. "Feel the meat, right?"

When that blue gaze met his, Jake *wanted* to sneer, but couldn't. Locryn, for all that he was so bloody nice and therefore so bloody annoying, was bloody good-looking.

And Jake couldn't afford to notice.

"Yeah, feel it. Good, firm meat."

And before he went to work, Locryn quirked one mischievous eyebrow at Jake. And Jake felt a shiver run through him.

Good, firm — what was in that bloody cologne?

Jake couldn't think of anything to say.

"Nice piece of pork there, Locryn!" Katya remarked. Then looking into the camera again she said, "And all our recipes are on our website! Send in your photos of your own pork goujons and tell us how good they taste."

"They won't taste as good as mine!" Jake was under the impression that he'd only thought that, but when he saw several faces turn to him in consternation, he suddenly realized he'd said it aloud. But it wouldn't matter, would it? It was what had become expected of him.

"They'll taste *amazing!*" Katya assured viewers after a horrified second of silence.

And Locryn smiled that smile, his charm given full rein toward the camera.

"Trying something new isn't about outdoing a man with Michelin stars," Locryn said smoothly. "It's about the joy in cooking or baking or throwing a steak on a summer barbie. We all start somewhere and, Katya, you and I both know, we *all* have our culinary disasters. It's part of the fun!"

Fun? Cooking's not fun, it's business! It's keeping a roof over my head and the heads of the staff in my restaurant. Fucking fun? No, it's fucking not!

Jake cupped his hands around his mouth like a megaphone and shouted across the studio, "Come on, Locryn! There's hungry people over here! Don't tickle it, cook it!"

But Locryn continued in his usual serene manner, cutting up the pork and dipping it into the breadcrumbs with a nifty flick of his wrist. As Katya wandered across to speak to the hopeful couples, Jake watched Locryn work and heard that melodic hum that was so familiar from his baking shows.

He washed his hands then pushed up the sleeves of his dark-blue shirt again, showing off the famed forearms that his fans went mad for. Arms. Who was getting into a tizz on social media about a baker's arms, for God's sake?

They were toned, that was for sure. A manly patina of hair, too. But imagine being with the bloke. He probably had frills all over his house. You'd get into his bed and would have to fight through a mountain of scatter cushions to reach the mattress.

Would it be worth it for those arms, though?

Jake laughed to himself and shook his head. How could he even entertain the thought? They'd get on each other's nerves in seconds, and what the hell did they even have in common?

The poor sod and the grinning couple from Cornwall weren't going to win anyway. Jake chanced a look at them, holding hands and smiling nervously. They were cute, but beside them Eugenia and Ptolemy reclined with perfect confidence and self-possession, angling themselves at the camera as if they'd been practicing. The unschooled charms of Locryn's hopeful couple were refreshing compared to them, but Jake was resigned to Hamble.

Locryn was at the stove now, frying onions and tomatoes for the sauce. The camera was on the two men and Locryn asked Jake, "By the way, Jake, jam or cream first for you?"

"Jam, then cream. With butter underneath. Nice, simple, indulgent treat." Jake said. "Are you going to tell me I'm wrong?"

"Butter's a bit controversial," Locryn chuckled, tossing the contents of the pan with a flamboyant flip of his wrist, "but jam first is the only way to eat a scone for us Cornish. I know you'll get letters, Katya, but in Cornwall that's how we do it."

"So I've been eating scones like a Cornishman?"

"You sound surprised, Jake!" Katya laughed. Then she was back staring into the camera again. "How do *you* like your scones? Get in touch and let us know!" She smiled at Locryn and said, "So how are you getting on with the goujons, Locryn?"

"Making light work of the salsa and the coleslaw is in the fridge." *Ah, but is it any good?* "In a couple of minutes I'll be frying my goujons and it'll be the moment of tasting truth!"

And it's not fucking salsa.

"I like the sound of salsa!" Katya pretended to shake maracas and danced some sort of horrible, awkward jig around Locryn. That or she was having a fit, Jake wasn't sure.

"Get frying, Locryn! Come *on!*" Jake clicked his fingers. Could he flap the unflappable Locryn?

The other guest chefs had given the producers and Jake exactly what grabbed the ratings. Despite their fame they'd let his barked critiques ruffle them, dropping eggs and burning dishes, one even managing to set the grill alight. Not so Locryn, it seemed. As he approached the fryer he joked, "Pray for my breadcrumbs. I need them to cling on!"

"Don't burn your fingers, Locryn!" Jake called. "That oil's f — fearsomely hot!"

"I have a seaside café specializing in decadence," the Cornishman reminded him as he put the goujons into the oil. "I'm a dab hand with a doughnut fryer."

"I love a sugary doughnut by the sea!" Katya rubbed her stomach. "Ring doughnuts or jam?"

"Or creamy custard?" Jake asked. He could just picture Locryn sniffing a bundle of vanilla before slipping it into a jug of cream.

"Oh, all of the above and a dozen more." He smiled, nostalgia lighting up his eyes. "I love sitting out in the garden with the animals, dreaming up tempting fillings."

Jake rolled his eyes.

I don't want to spend a miserable autumn in off-season Cornwall. But he can twinkle all he likes, he's not going to win.

Locryn moved quickly now, plating up the golden goujons and bright sauce, adding a small, brightly patterned dish of the coleslaw that he'd made. He stood back and announced to Katya and Jake, "Ta-daaa!"

You bastard.

"Doesn't look as bad as I expected," Jake said.

Katya was far more effusive in her praise. "Looks great, Locryn!"

"We'll let Jake and our three happy couples be the judge." Locryn beamed. "And I know that only one couple can win but I'm a bit of a romantic—I love a wedding—so I'm going to make sure that the couples that *don't* get the big prize *do* get one of my wedding cupcake towers. Every bride needs a massive pile of cakes, don't you think?"

A cheer went up around the studio at this unexpected generosity.

Katya clapped. "Oh, that's so lovely of you! Isn't it lovely of him, everyone?"

As Jake took up his fork, he glanced sidelong at Locryn. *Is it allowed?* Did it count as bribery so that *his* couple would win?

"I'll send you all a card!" Jake laughed. "*And* luncheon vouchers!"

Katya touched her finger to her earpiece then said, "And our producers have just confirmed that *all* our guest chefs will match Locryn's prize and will provide a little something for each couple's catering! You've started a trend!"

Locryn smiled as he pushed his spectacles into his hair. The couples gathered round and, as one, the studio waited for Jake's verdict.

Jake dipped a goujon into the sauce and bit in.

It was cooked to perfection. But even though Locryn had followed Jake's recipe, Jake could taste a difference, that subtlety that only a truly gifted cook could provide.

He patted Locryn's shoulder. "Amazing goujons. Well done." And Jake went for another, this time with a dollop of Locryn's off-piste coleslaw. "That is really,

really good. Really nice. I'd serve this in my restaurant."

"Gosh!" Locryn said. *'Gosh.' A grown man.* "Will you sign something to that effect?"

"A certificate?" Jake said. "You'll have to cook more than just goujons for *that!*"

"And now our lovely couples can all try!" Katya handed out the forks. Eugenia and Ptolemy had ended up at the front, first in with their forks, while Locryn's couple wavered at the back.

Fuck's sake.

Jake speared some goujons and passed them to Zoe and David.

"There you go!" Jake said. "Get your laughing tackle round *those!*"

"And while we have a good old goujon and a chat to our lucky couples, keep voting," Katya told the audience. "In a couple of minutes we'll have the results, and I for one cannot wait to know whose wedding Jake's going to be catering. Will it be Vihaan and Preya, Ptolemy and Eugenia or David and Zoe?"

As she turned her attention to the couples and the floor manager signaled to Jake and Locryn that their microphones were off, Locryn asked in a whisper, "Surprised you, didn't I?"

"Yes, you fucking well did!" Jake replied. "By the way, sorry your couple won't win. They seem all right."

And Jake had surprised himself. *All right?* What was wrong with him?

"They deserve to win, they've been through a lot." Locryn watched the young couple chat happily with Katya. The engagement ring on Zoe's finger was the smallest of the three, but her smile was by far the widest. "But it's not all about winning, is it? I mean, it is for you, but it isn't for us."

"This is all just for fun?" Jake licked the cream from the coleslaw off his thumb. "Look, if I didn't focus on winning, I'd still be washing pots in a burger van outside a bus depot. And that, mate, was *shit*."

"Daddy didn't buy me a café to play in. It took a lot of hard work," Locryn replied, his tone still pleasant despite his words. "But for me…it's fun. No screaming and swearing in my kitchen, I leave all that to you. I don't do terrifying half so well."

"It wouldn't go with your brand, would it?" Jake affected a gentle tone like something from an advert for fabric softener. "*Oh, fiddlesticks, you belty bathbun, this meringue is a load of sugar!*"

"Oh, I don't have a brand." *And does nothing get you fucking riled up?* "I'm just me!"

"Come off it, is that cottage even real?" Jake shook his head. "*No one* lives like that! Not even you! You've probably got a sex dungeon and a house full of chrome and silver!"

Locryn blinked, then tapped his glasses so they slid back onto his nose. "Is that what you get up to in London, is it? I've got a smugglers' tunnel, if that counts."

Jake snorted with laughter and slapped the worktop. "Please tell me, is that an innuendo or what?"

"I'll let you decide." Locryn winked. "But if you *do* end up in Cornwall, I'll show it to you."

Jake's mouth fell open. "You'll show me your—?" *No, he* really *means a tunnel.* "Fuck, sorry, yes, we'll see, eh? I mean, it won't fucking happen, but still."

A gesture from the floor manager told them to rejoin the group and they gathered round in time for Katya to announce, "The results are in! The public have spoken and we've got a winner!"

Jake patted Locryn's shoulder, commiserating. "Come and say hello if you're passing Hamble!" he whispered.

"In *From Wreck to Restaurant*, Jake's going to be helping one couple celebrate their wedding, and one community celebrate coming together to open a brand-new restaurant." Katya took a deep breath. "Congratulations to our lucky couple who are…Zoe and David! Jake, you're going to Porthavel, where the Cornish pasties live!"

"Fuck me."

The words had escaped Jake before he could stop them.

Katya looked horrified and all Jake could see was the cavernous *O* of her mouth. People were clapping, cheering, Ptolemy and Eugenia were in tears, but Jake heard everything from a remove as if he wasn't really in the *Saturday Breakfast* kitchen at all and was watching it at home on television. Jake clutched the edge of the worktop, trying to stand now that his legs had turned to custard. There were voices but every word was indistinct, a muffled susurration that climbed and climbed in pitch. The polka dots on Zoe's blouse wriggled and danced, swirling and swirling, faster and faster and faster until they swallowed one another up.

This happened at the restaurant last week, Jake remembered, but before he could follow another thought in his head, all of the lights went out and every voice fell silent.

Chapter Two

Jake winced as the blood pressure cuff tightened on his upper arm. He looked away from the machine that was powering it, trying to ignore its almighty racket that sounded like a vacuum cleaner swallowing a paperclip.

"I'm not stressed," Jake said. "Everyone's making a fuss about sod — nothing."

"This says otherwise." Dr. Harris unfastened the cuff and sat back in her seat as she folded it in on itself. "One hundred and thirty-seven over eighty. That's high, Jake. That tells me you *are* stressed."

"Stressed? *Me?*" Jake patted the machine. "Are you sure this is working okay? Is it *meant* to make that God-awful noise? It might be on the blink, Doctor, haven't you thought of that?"

She shook her head. "Why don't you tell me what's going on in your life just now? Planning a Christmas getaway?"

"Sort of." Jake scratched his hand back through his hair. "I'm spending the next few months in…in…" Jake struggled for air. *Not again, no. Not now.* "Cornwall," he said huskily. "It's relaxing there, right?"

"That sounds fantastic. Just the thing to combat stress. Fresh, clean air, no career hassles. At the moment I'm keen to avoid medication if we can, but...have you considered talking therapies?"

"Talking about what?" Jake rolled his eyes. "I'm a busy man, that's all. And anyway, I've got to open a restaurant and cater a wedding while I'm in Cornwall. I can talk about *that*, maybe?"

Dr. Harris took a deep breath, then shook her head. "I'd advise you not to do that. Or if you insist, at least tell me you've got a *very* good PA to take the weight off you. What happened was your body giving you a warning, Jake. You need to heed it."

"My agent booked me in to see you." Jake wagged his finger at the doctor. "I can look after myself! My business manager runs the restaurants when I'm busy, and my PA... Well, he's actually off at the moment because he's got appendicitis and it got a bit fu—flipping dicey. I've got his clipboard, I can cope!"

"As your doctor, it's my duty to tell you that you shouldn't be doing this." Her lips thinned. "And if you insist on doing it, you could be putting your health at risk. You can't keep going at this pitch of stress forever, no matter how fit you are."

"It was bloody hot in that kitchen when I passed out. And when I keeled over in the studio, well, it was warm, and I'd got up really early." Jake's phone went off in his pocket and he took it out and muted it. "I didn't faint, I just fell asleep. Really fast."

She turned to her computer and pressed a few keys, then summarized his test results from the screen. "Your heartbeat is fine, if a little elevated. You're a healthy weight. But that's twice you've passed out. You *didn't* fall asleep. Look, I can't stop you going to Cornwall to film, but will you at least try to find some time for Jake in amongst it all?"

Jake toyed with a pen on the edge of her desk, tapping a staccato rhythm. "How do you mean? I'm Jake Brantham twenty-four-seven. I can't be more fu — Jake Brantham if I tried!"

"I mean walk on the beach, climb the cliffs, sit on the harbor and watch the waves. I mean take it easy. Slow. Down."

Chapter Three

One of the production team's people carriers collected Jake from the rented farmhouse on the edge of the village where he was staying. His phone rang three times on the journey, two calls coming through almost at once, and Jake jumped from one to the other. He switched from a call about an error on the timesheets at his restaurant in Whitstable to a call about a sackload of carrots that had gone missing from his London restaurant.

"I'm in Cornwall! I don't fucking know where the carrots are!" And with that Jake ended the call. Wasn't this what he paid his staff handsomely for? A man like him couldn't be counting every piece of cress and polishing every spoon. That was what the supposedly crack culinary teams he employed were for.

Slow down.

Fat chance.

The people carrier slowed almost to a halt. "What's the fucking hold up now? Is it rush hour already? One man and his dog walking down the middle of the street in the path of a tractor? Fuck me!"

A bicycle bell rang somewhere behind the people carrier, then a familiar figure passed the window, easily overtaking the slow-moving vehicle. The bicycle was neither sleek and highly engineered nor small and foldable, the two species that seemed to be found on every square foot in London, but a large, robust and clearly vintage model painted a rich royal blue. A wicker basket sat between the handlebars, and who should be piloting the bicycle but Locryn Trevorrow, his rainbow-knit scarf flying behind him like a pennant.

A bike with a wicker basket?

Is he for fucking real?

Jake shook his head. He was stuck here now for the next few months and that meant being in the same postcode as the most annoying man he had ever encountered. It was all an act, it had to be, because no one could be that twee. Could they?

It was bad enough that they were on the way to Locryn's café. Jake had seen it from the window of the other people carrier the day before, and the floral bunting strewn along the windows had nearly brought him out in a rash.

There would be publicity photos and a happy couple to bring into line, and that was before he laid eyes on the hellhole he was expected to convert, but that's what he was paid so handsomely for. *From Wreck to Restaurant*'s format would be simple. A pigsty would be transformed into a stylish place to dine in the space of one month.

Jake peered out of the car's tinted windows. It wasn't just a man and his dog, it was several men, several dogs and an entire market.

But he looked at his watch. There wouldn't be any time for markets today, not with the schedule so tight. He'd be lucky if he could get a cup of tea in Locryn's café, let alone wander around the stalls.

Locryn had said he could buy fresh seafood on the quay, and Jake hadn't seen any yet. But then he just hadn't had time.

He'd barely had time to see the ocean, let alone Porthavel. All he'd seen was Fionn, his producer, and a mountain of shooting schedules. All he had was a vague impression of jauntily painted cottages and a fearsome sea, but beyond that it was a blur. It wasn't easy being the name above the title.

Jake looked at his watch. The quick drive into the village had been anything but and he had five minutes to get to the café if they were going to stay on schedule. And they had to, because Jake wasn't going to let it all go tits-up.

"Unless this car grows stilts in the next three seconds, I'm getting out and I'll bloody walk!"

His phone rang, Fionn's name lighting up the display. Why couldn't he get a signal when he wanted one, but now people wanted to hassle *him*, those absent bars had returned?

"Yes!" Jake barked. He pinched the skin between his eyebrows, hoping it would lessen the ache growing there. "Fionn, what is it?"

"Sweets, everyone's here but you're not. Where are you?" In the background he could hear soft sixties pop music playing and the gentle sound of tinkling crockery. "Can't do Jake's *meet the public* moment without Jake!"

"Yeah, I know that, but it's market day!" Jake slapped the empty seat beside him. "Wish we'd fucking known. Who's the researcher on this series? Didn't they check? Right, I'm getting out! I'm fucking walking!"

Jake slid open the door and bounced onto the pavement. He knew they were heading toward the harbor, where Locryn's café stood, commanding a view of fishing boats, so he power-walked the rest of the way.

"Got that, Fionn? I'm walking!"

"Cool, cool! Don't stop for autographs and selfies. There'll be oodles of time for that," she reminded him as mobile phones were raised and pictures snapped. "You're stuck here for a couple of months, after all! Oh, Locryn's here now. I'm going to say hi. I'd love to get in on his telly stuff. Toodles, lovely, toodles!"

"Don't kiss his — " The call had ended and now Jake was slaloming between a forest of arms bearing phones. "Sorry! I'm in a rush! I'll see you all later! Coming through! Come on, guys, I'm in a fucking rush!"

Having managed to fend off most advances, Jake arrived at Locryn's café.

"Fuck me," he muttered as he ran his gaze along the bunting again. "Fuck *me!*" he repeated when the bell jingled above the door like something from a children's story. The café smelled like fresh-baked bread and cooling sponge cakes and every eye in it was turned on him, Jake Brantham, as he *fuck me'd* his way into a café that appeared to have been created by Beatrix Potter. He was confronted by gingham textiles and dressers filled with china and right in front of him, one arm in his coat and one arm out, was Locryn Trevorrow.

Jake hadn't seen him since London, when he'd blinked up from the studio floor and seen Locryn's face among the crowd that had been looking down at him.

It was better seeing Locryn in a café, that was for sure.

"This is very you," Jake said. "Very...cute."

"Am I cute?" Locryn slapped his hand to Jake's shoulder. "It's good to see you looking better. Fionn was just telling me that you had a nasty virus that day. All better now?"

Lingering beside a Welsh dresser piled with china, Fionn pursed her crimson lips. *A virus.* That was the official line, the one they were feeding interested parties. It would never do for Jake, the man who thrived on stress, to have been laid low by it.

Even if only for a few seconds.

"Yeah, yeah, I'm much better, thanks!" Jake stretched as if he'd just woken from a nap. "Tip-top form!"

"I know you've got filming to do, so I'll leave you to it." Locryn took his coat off. "Can I get you a cup of tea? A coffee? A big hot chocolate with a mountain of fresh whipped cream and handmade marshmallows on top?"

Why not?

But there was a film crew and the public to deal with and Jake couldn't drink something as outrageous as *that.*

"Black coffee, thanks," Jake said, sounding chirpy as he tried not to pretend that he didn't regret his choice. "There's my bride and groom, right? Zoe and..." *Shit. What's his bloody name?* "Daniel."

"An excellent choice! It's only traveled six miles along the coast into our grinder." Locryn smiled, then whispered, "David. And that's his dad, Petroc, and Zoe's mum, Merryn. Have you got all that? Can I take your co—leather jacket?"

"Locally grown Cornish coffee beans?" Jake laughed. "Right. Petroc, Merryn, David. Petroc, Merryn, David…and Zoe. I think that's it. And the jacket's fine, I'll keep it on for the camera." For some reason that Jake couldn't define, he raised an eyebrow at Locryn and whispered, "Y'know, for that bad-boy vibe."

"I wouldn't know." Locryn unknotted his scarf. "We don't get too many bad boys in Porthavel."

"You two can chat each other up later on your own time," Fionn told them, her smile rather chilled by her brusque tone. She slipped her arm through Jake's. "Jake, come and say hello to our winners and their gorgeous Cornish parentals!"

Jake waved as he approached the sofa they were sitting on, Zoe and David in the middle, holding hands, with Merryn beside Zoe and Petroc flanking David. Merryn was like a woman from *Dallas* or *Dynasty* with her small-town glamour look going on. Big earrings, big hair, enormous smile, with a jacket that bordered on power-dressing. Her daughter was like a miniature, calmed-down version, in a cardigan instead and frilly blouse. Petroc looked like he would rather be anywhere else and David—who had the sort of enviable cheekbones you could slice bread with—laughed nervously.

Zoe and David made a good-looking pair, and Jake announced, "Hi there, bloody hell, what a bunch of gorgeous bastards!"

"Hello!" Zoe waved, her eyes wide with excitement, her entire demeanor that of a tightly coiled spring. "Oh God, we won. How did we win? I can't believe Jake Brantham's catering our wedding! We had no idea when we ent—well, *I* entered. I didn't even tell David. I had no idea we'd get to the final!"

She took David's hand and squeezed it, exchanging a proud look with her mother.

"Yeah, I had no idea!" David's Cornish accent was so strong that it took Jake by surprise all over again. He seemed to add three extra syllables to every word he said, four if it was already a long one. "My Zoe's a naughty one! And now we're on the telly. And you've already called us *bastards*." Jake was impressed by the length of David's first vowel in that word, then was doubly impressed when David said, "When are you calling us *fuckers*?" and rolled the R from Porthavel to Bodmin.

"I'll call you a fucker every day if you like!" Jake laughed. Then he rubbed his hands together, getting down to business. "So, David and Zoe, you want your parents involved in the wedding day. Proper family occasion, right?"

"Don't say fucker on the telly, lad," Petroc chided his son gently. His accent was as strong as the younger man's, stronger if that were even possible, his ruddy cheeks suggesting a man who was more used to being outdoors than sitting in tea rooms. "Mr. Brantham, hello."

Jake held out his hand to shake. Playful, he said, "Petroc, great to meet you. Is *bastard* okay if we can't say *fucker*?"

"Well now, *you* can say whatever you please." Petroc took his hand in his bear's paw grip. His palm was coarse and weathered as they shook, but his manner was almost bashful. "It's your program, I wouldn't tell you—"

Zoe smiled gently and said, "Petroc's a bit nervous about the cameras."

"I'm bloody shitting bricks," he admitted. Then he looked to Merryn and murmured, "Sorry, sorry."

"See, he likes having a swear himself!" Merryn cackled. She'd be trouble after a few a Lambrinis. "You should hear them, the old trawlermen, jawing away on their swears! They'd make you sound like Locryn, Mr. Brantham!"

"Jake, please. Just call me Jake."

The cameras had been hovering discreetly but now came closer, one crouching in front, pointing at the group on the sofa, and one behind, fixed on Jake.

"Ignore them! You'll forget they're there soon enough," Jake whispered with a smile. "So I'm the caterer for your wedding. What does your dream wedding reception look like? Classic roast chicken or smoked salmon, or have you got something else in mind?"

"We both come from old Porthavel families," Zoe told him, linking her fingers with David's. "And we want our wedding to be exactly what you always say. Fresh and local and simple, so we thought maybe little pasties, squab pies, that sort of thing? But with a Jake Brantham spin?"

"That's just the sort of thing I was hoping for!" Jake slapped his knee as he emphasized each word. "Simple. Local. Fresh. So that's the savories dealt with. Any ideas for your cake? Traditional tiered, or a big fondant trawler? Or something else!"

She looked at Merryn, as though seeking a bit of moral support. "We wondered— I know there's the contract and everything, but I work in the café with Locryn and we wondered if maybe he could do the cake? He's ever so special to us, you see."

"He is." Merryn nodded. "He really is."

Bloody Locryn.

"Ah… Well, you see, don't worry, they'll edit this later—you see, it's part of the deal. You get me to do the food, and that includes the cake. There's a whole episode just about the cake, you see, so I...I have to do it because it's my show." Jake wasn't too sure about the rapid blinking of the two women, which seemed to signal the onset of tears. "I mean, it's not set in stone. Maybe Locryn could...?" *Line a baking tin with greaseproof paper?*

Jake glanced at Fionn. Surely she didn't want people crying on the show. Or at least, not until the last few pressured days before the wedding, when events were edited to make it look like a disaster zone, and it all turned out perfectly.

The producer swooped, stepping between Locryn and the table as he seized the break in filming to approach with Jake's coffee. She was still smiling, but there was no warmth in the expression.

"It's a no can do, I'm afraid. This show's about Jake working with the community to open a restaurant and give you your dream wedding." She laid the thick contract the couple had signed down on the gingham tablecloth. "Jake's catering the *entire* event. It's the Jake show, not the Jake and Locryn show. They're not...I don't know...*Jakryn*. This isn't TOWIE."

"But we just thought—" Zoe began, but Fionn silenced her with a shake of her head, the hair of the producer's blunt silver bob moving as one.

"No." Fionn looked Locryn up and down as he put Jake's coffee on the table. "Lovely though Loc is, it's the Jake show. We do swearing and drama, we don't do sugar strands."

David set his jaw. "But we been talking about a Mr. Trevorrow cake for an age, haven't we, angel? And I never saw no business about cake in the contract."

"It's all right," Locryn soothed. "I'll do your Christmas cake instead if you like. Let's not rock the boat."

Something about that seemed to cause a ripple of amusement around the table. Even Fionn gave a chuckle, which struck Jake as particularly worrying.

"There you go, a Locryn Trevorrow Christmas cake awaits!" Jake could picture it, a traditional cake covered in spiky royal icing with a carnival of fondant figures skating over the winter wonderland. The last Christmas cake Jake had made had been sprayed gold with a toy motorbike on top of it.

Zoe looked at her mum again, then at David. She asked, "What do you think?"

"A Christmas cake would lovely," Merryn said, her smile rather forced. "And your first Christmas together as man and wife, too. It's very special."

"Take the Christmas cake, love," Petroc advised in a curt voice. "Let's not be causing a scene now."

Jake glanced over to the cameras. "Rolling?"

The cameramen nodded, and Jake carried on as if the upset about the cake had never happened. "So what about your cake? Are you having a tiered cake with a bride and groom on top, or something completely different?"

Zoe looked over the top of his head to where Locryn was standing, then at Petroc, who nodded her on. After a moment she asked David, "What do you fancy?"

"A great big boat!" Then he roared with laughter and slapped his leg. "You'll get used to them around here, Mr. Brantham!"

"Yeah, bet I will. So, a great big boat. Well, that's certainly food for thought!"

"I think that's perfect." *And who asked you*, Jake wondered as Locryn spoke. But everyone at the table turned as one, apparently hanging on his words. "David and Petroc are trawlermen and so was Zoe's dad. They're the engine of a village like this one."

"Never a truer word spoken," Merryn said. "Though you'd never get *me* out at sea in a boat!"

Jake laughed, even though the thought of making a boat-shaped cake was less of an entertaining challenge than an insurmountable nightmare. "But you'd eat the cake version?"

"I'd definitely have a nibble!"

Zoe looked unconvinced, her gaze still lingering on Locryn as he strolled back toward the counter. She didn't say anything, but she didn't have to. Jake could recognize an unhappy bride when faced with one.

This bloody cake better not turn into an issue. Fuck's sake, some people are never happy.

That scene finished, Jake was off to shoot the next one. As he and Fionn headed out of the café, he asked her, "You *sure* about the cake? Really? Zoe's not happy about it, and I don't give a shit whether it's in the contract or not. A fucking boat cake? That's Locryn's territory, not mine. I'm not fucking up a wedding cake on telly. There'll be tears. The bride and groom are meant to look pleased, not as disappointed as someone whose fucking tent's blown away on the first day of their hols."

Fionn bundled Jake into the people carrier as she said, "Okay, if that's what you want, that's what we'll do. If you want to give away the money shot to a man who's already chasing you in the ratings *and* in book sales, who am I to tell you it's the worst idea that I've ever fucking heard? Give the wedding cake to Locryn Trevorrow? If you do that, he'll be hosting this program next year instead of you!"

Fuck that.

"I'm not having Locryn steal my show!" Jake took the blindfold from his pocket and smoothed it out on his thigh. "Imagine all those fiddlesticks and hundreds and thousands. Fuck me, it puts my teeth on edge!"

"Exactly. We'll get a few talking heads from him about what a fantastic job you're doing, grab some pickups of him peddling merrily along the quayside, and as far as I'm concerned, that's all the screen time he's getting." Fionn pulled the car door closed. "You can do a cake. How hard can it be?"

Jake nodded, although a film reel spooled through his mind showing him every cake he'd ever attempted, almost all of which had failed. Soggy bottoms, burned tops, dry buttercream, collapsing tiers. And he somehow had to make a boat out of cake.

Cake. Fuck's sake.

"Easy-fucking-peasy," Jake said. He held up the black length of cloth. "Blindfold time?"

"If you like." She shrugged. "This place is smaller than one of my handbags. Nowhere's more than a minute from anywhere else. Can you imagine living here? I'd go stir crazy in a day! Give us the city, eh? Give us the bustle and the noise and the not giving a fuck."

"Too right!" But Jake gazed out at the market stalls as they crawled by them and he saw tempting heaps of vegetables, arrays of seafood and produce he could only glimpse for a second. Were those huge jars of honey, with honeycomb? Did he see a stall full of nothing but herbs?

Imagine having all that on my doorstep.

Jake reluctantly drew on the blindfold. What awaited him? An old sail loft, maybe. He'd like that. It would definitely tie-in with the boat-shaped cake.

"Right, cameras are rolling. I'll steer you into position." He heard the car door open then Fionn took his arm and escorted him out and the noise of the market hit him, filled with laughter and chatter. "Ready?"

Jake took a deep breath. Maybe it wasn't going to be a sail loft. Was it a street food stall? *Could* anyone have a wedding reception at a stall?

"Ready!" Jake flexed his fingers.

And what a happy place Porthavel was. All around him, he heard laughter. It wasn't such a bad place to be. He could prove the doctor wrong. He'd be chill in no time.

Fionn shepherded him into position. He heard her heels clicking away then she called, "Whenever you're ready, darling!"

Jake closed his eyes, even though he was wearing a blindfold. A hush descended, disturbed only by quarreling seagulls on the harbor wall and a shout of "Shut it, you noisy gits!" from a local.

Jake tugged down the blindfold and blinked.

And there in front of him was a pirate galleon.

At least, it looked like one, moored up in the harbor.

"No. Fuck me, no. It's… It's a fucking pirate ship! What the fuck!"

He was no longer wondering if this would make great telly or not. All he could do was stare, wondering how the hell he could turn a run-down novelty pirate ship into a restaurant. And host a wedding on it without it looking like something from a cartoon.

I bet it's riddled with more woodworm than a pirate's peg leg. And seconds from sinking! With me and my career.

And so *this* was why everyone was laughing.

Jake heard the flutter of simulated camera shutters catching the moment of horrified realization. A pirate ship. In Cornwall. In autumn.

Fionn and the show's director were watching him expectantly, a camera on the deck waiting to catch him as he climbed the gangplank.

The narrow, slippery gangplank.

What if he passed out again and fell in the harbor?

Jake shook the thought out of his head. He could do this.

He marched up the gangplank and ignored the squeak of his shoes on the oozy wood, all the while unleashing a stream of swearwords as he went on deck.

"Holy crapping hell, a fucking pirate ship! What next, host a dinner in the belly of a fucking whale? Fuck me! Jesus, this is a nightmare! Ride me sideways, what the balls is *that?* A fucking fiberglass cod? What the fuck *is* this?"

Fionn gave him a thumbs-up, motioning for him to venture farther.

"Go inside!" she called. "Cameras are all rigged and ready, go and have a poke around! Isn't it brilliant? A pirate ship for the captain of London cuisine! Captain Jake!"

Jake went through the door, or perhaps *hatch* was the better word for it. Inside, he found a mottled, wonky sign saying *Please wait here to be seated, me 'earties!* Flanked by two fiberglass cods balancing on their tails, complete with pirate hats and eyepatches.

"Fucking hell, it's Cornish Disney World!"

Leading down from the entrance there was a double-width staircase with elaborate carved newel posts and bannisters depicting mermen and mermaids, starfish and seahorses. Jake ran his hand over the carvings. So what had this been, a nautical-themed Cornish restaurant?

Jake padded down the stairs into a huge dining area. Dust-heavy red velvet curtains covered the windows, which gave it a slightly 1970s bistro vibe. The walls were the wooden ribs of the ship itself, and Jake stroked the grain.

"It's naff but it has bloody potential!" Jake said through gritted teeth.

I'm going to look like a fucking joke.

Captain fucking Jake.

All the chairs were upside down on the tables, giving him a forest of chair legs to peer through until he spotted doors at the other end of the ship.

Kitchen. Has to be.

In the dim light, he noticed a large wooden panel covering the wall beside the kitchen door and he realized it could be lifted to create an open kitchen. Now that was a nice touch. Jake loved showing diners how it was done.

He opened the kitchen door and felt for the light switch inside. Suddenly, the large room was illuminated and Jake was, unusually, impressed. The whole place felt unused and abandoned, but the kitchen had been left clean. There were no horrifying gobbits of congealed fat, colonies of fungus or rotten food in sight. As Jake banged about from fridge to freezer, and peered inside the ovens—followed by a cameraman who peered inside with him—he saw that the kitchen's equipment wasn't new, but some of it didn't look too ancient. And it had at least been well looked after.

And if he got a team of good cooks, then they were off to a good start, because the food was the most crucial aspect of any restaurant. Even if there were giant, anthropomorphic fish by the front door.

Jake planted his hands on his hips and smiled.

You bastards, you thought you'd thrown me a curveball. I'll show you!

Jake was more than ready to take on the challenge. Even though, in the silence, he could hear water lapping against the hull of his new restaurant.

Captain Jake indeed.

Chapter Four

Jake was impressed by Porthavel's showing at the village hall. A chance for locals, without cameras recording every second, to be conned into thinking they were included in proceedings. Fionn would lay down the law and filming would go on happily without anyone swearing at seagulls or mooning in the background of key scenes.

But as Jake got comfortable on the stage of the village hall, with the cut-out wooden scenery for Widow Twanky's laundrette from *Aladdin* behind him, he was handed a cake. An iced bun studded with glacé cherries.

Jake glared into the milling audience. Was this Locryn's doing? What a way to troll him.

And as he surveyed the faces that were turned up to him, he spotted him. Locryn Trevorrow was sitting toward the back of the hall, engaged in happy conversation with the people around him. He knew then that he was right.

It was Locryn's bun.

And it was light as air.

Jake didn't want to enjoy it, but he did. And as he ate it, he knew he could never, ever bake its equal. Or even come close. Jake could manage a pedestrian sort of cake, a pleasant sort of bun, but nothing like this. Locryn deserved his place as a baker of renown.

Even if he is fucking annoying.

Jake held up the crumb-lined polka-dot paper case to Fionn as she joined him on the stage. "Fuck me, Locryn does good cake. Have you tried it?"

"Do I look like I eat cake?" It was a fair point. She didn't look like she ate much, despite being the queen of culinary programming. "If I get those urges I pour another wine. *Don't* get a taste for it."

But it *was* bloody good. Jake hid the empty case in his pocket.

"Standing room only," Jake whispered, jerking his thumb at the audience, which had now run out of chairs. "You'd think they'd be jaded about cookery shows, living in the same village as Locryn!"

"That's just cake, though. No Michelin stars for cake!"

Even cake as good as this.

"No Michelin stars for novelty pirate restaurants either," Jake remarked coldly. "You still haven't told me whose idea it was!"

"Your ratings need a boost before they start to dip, Cap'n Jake." She shrugged one bony shoulder. "Your boost just happens to be shaped like a pirate ship."

"Just don't make me look like an idiot," Jake replied. "Yeah, you'd get great ratings for that, especially if I do an accidentally-on-purpose pratfall into the harbor. But I'm a professional, Fionn. I don't do theme park caffs."

She blinked, her mascara-heavy lashes not so much fluttering as slamming.

"It's a Christmas special. You're lucky it's not Santa's grotto."

A keen runner with a headset and a clipboard peered over the edge of the stage. "It's seven-thirty, the hall's full to bursting. Shall we start?"

"Go on, Captain," Fionn purred, shirking the spotlight as ever, even as she was happy to reap its rewards thanks to Jake's efforts. "Your public awaits."

Only then did he realize how many people in the audience were enjoying Locryn's buns.

So to speak.

Jake got up from the chair. "Evening, Porthavel! How are you all today?"

The audience looked at him a little suspiciously. Then one of them cleared his throat. He was a white-haired man, rosy cheeks peeking out from a white beard, wearing a little blue sailor's cap balanced on his round head.

"Sure we ain't too naff for you, boy?"

Jake strained to hear him. "Sure you..." Then it dawned on him. What he'd said on the ship.

Well, I'm supposed to! It's part of my schtick!

Jake threw a quick glare behind him to Fionn, then he left his chair and dropped down onto the edge of the stage and swung his legs back and forth. "Now what's your name, sir?"

"Captain Cod," he said. *Of course. What else would it be?* "Word is you've got boats of your own?"

"I have, yes. One on the Thames, one at Whitstable, one at York." Jake rubbed his palms together and said, "And I've got to be honest with you, Mr....erm...

Captain Cod, none of them are pirate ships with giant fiberglass codfish. Wearing hats."

Captain Cod. Fiberglass cod.

Oh fuck.

"And?" He folded his arms tight across his barrel chest. "We was happy to see you, boy, but you stood on the deck of my old boat and used some very choice language in front of the market. And there're kiddies at that market. You want to be ashamed of yourself, you do!"

"Yeah, Mr. Brantham, you bloody well do, effing and jeffing like that!" A worthy lady in a mohair jumper covered in pompoms jabbed her finger at Jake. "Such shitty language! I was shocked."

"You *have* all seen my shows, haven't you?" Jake spread his hands and gazed around the room. "I don't dub the swearing in afterward!"

But the crowd looked unconvinced, and their murmurs of complaint were growing louder. Then a screwed-up ball of paper flew out of the audience and bounced off Jake's shoulder, followed by another, then a third, as he was stoned by Locryn's bright, cheery bun cases.

"Hey, come on!" Fionn stood safely out of range of the paper missiles. "Jake loves it here already and he's going to turn that boat into a restaurant to be proud of, but he needs your help. The program needs a community spirit like yours to make it work. Whether you want to help with the renovations or even train with Captain Jake in the kitchen, there're so many opportunities for everyone in Porthavel. Jake, why don't you tell the villagers about some of the trainees you've taken on after your other shows? It doesn't stop when the cameras are turned off, does it?"

"Captain Jake?" Cod shook his head, clearly not convinced. "We'll see about that!"

Jake gripped the edge of the stage and ran his gaze across the audience. "When I see potential in someone, I want to nurture it. Bring out the best in people. I've done my shows all over the country and I must have taken on twenty, twenty-five cooks and helped them into work. Some in my restaurants, some in my friends'. There was one lad, I remember, he was spinning candyfloss on Barry Island. Where is he now? He's a chef at the Dorchester. Because. He had. *Potential.*" Jake thumped his fist against his knee with each word. *Please don't chuck me into the sea.* "How many of you here tonight will end up working on...on Captain Cod's pirate ship? How many of you might go from there to — to who knows where? Maybe you'll end up swearing on the telly like me one day too! But that's not going to happen if you throw all this shit at me, is it?"

"Why don't you ask your wife why we're throwing shit?" The suggestion came from a man in a beanie hat who was sitting on the front row. "Ask her about the wicker cod!"

"Wife? Wicker cod?" Jake shook his head. Had he misheard? "Sorry, I don't know who — wife? Do you mean Fionn, the *producer?*" Jake looked over his shoulder at Fionn and suppressed a shiver.

"Ask her!" Another ball of paper hit Jake.

What has she said?

"Fionn, could you tell the good people of Porthavel that you're not my wife? And what the hell's this about a wicker cod?"

Was it some sort of nautical-themed hanging basket she'd seen in the village?

"I'm not his wife, I'm the producer of *Wreck to Restaurant*," Fionn told them. "And I didn't— it was a joke. Come on, I don't *really* think you're going to build a wicker cod, do I?"

"Standing on the harbor," said an elderly woman with ruddy cheeks and a thick gray perm, "crowing into her phone about *weird-beard yokels*. If that's what you think, you London folk, you can fuck off and take your fucking swearing with you. Bollocks to London and bollocks to the telly. You're just here to laugh at us and nobody laughs at Dave and Zoe in this village!"

Jake raised his eyebrows at Fionn and hissed, "For fuck's sake! You can't reference *The Wicker Man*. It's offensive to yokels!"

"Boo!" The jeers increased until they were deafening and the missiles began again. Then a figure rose into the hail of paper, his hands raised for calm.

Locryn Trevorrow. The voice of fucking reason.

"Please, can everybody just—" He cleared his throat then spoke again, his voice cutting through the catcalls. "Porthavelans, that's enough! Is this how we welcome our guests?"

The missiles stopped and the catcalls ended in silence. One by one the audience shook their heads.

"Sorry if we got off on the wrong feet," Jake said. "You guys in this village, you're great, and I want to be part of that." *Do I bollocks.* "Zoe and David won the competition because the people of Britain love them. They want them to have the best wedding this side of the Tamar Bridge. Yes, it's going to be on a pirate ship, and it's going to be *in your village*. I want you all to be a part of the show. *All* of you."

But maybe not the sweary lady in the pompoms.

"What Fionn said wasn't meant to cause offense," Locryn told his grumbling peers, though Jake knew better. "And we shouldn't hold it against her or Ja—Captain Jake. Instead, let's show them that Porthavel is the sort of village where we work hard and we work together. This is an amazing opportunity to be part of something wonderful, so let's start by picking up our litter, shall we?"

Chairs scraped back. Someone fetched a broom, someone else fetched a dustpan. Another fetched a bin bag. Jake watched as the village pulled together, and he hopped down from the stage to help. He saw Fionn standing with Locryn and wondered for a worrying moment exactly what they were plotting, but it didn't take long to find out.

"There'll be a sign-up form for those who want to take part in the show on the café counter from tomorrow," Locryn told the villagers. "And everybody's welcome to help Zoe and David have a wedding to remember. Nobody deserves it more than they do!"

There were nods of agreement then.

"Too right, they do!"

"Lovely young couple like that."

"Great!" Jake vaulted back onto the edge of the stage. "So, sign up, let us know what you want to help with and...let's give Zoe and David the best Porthavel wedding ever!"

This time the shouts were cheers, but Jake couldn't help shooting a warning look at Fionn. That sort of palaver, going on about wicker bloody cod, could cause havoc, and it was the last thing a man who was supposed to be relaxing needed. She met his gaze as the audience began to depart, her expression utterly unapologetic.

Jake zipped up his leather jacket, hiding inside it as if it were armor. Then he said to Fionn, "No more bad-mouthing the locals. Please, Fionn."

She turned away from the remaining villagers and dropped her voice to a whisper to tell him, "I had a hidden camera rigged up, Jake, never fear. We've got all this on tape, it's going to make for fab telly!"

Jake shook his head. "No. Oh, hell, no, Fionn, that's not going on air. I'm exec producer on this, and I'm putting my foot down. Absolutely not. They didn't know they were being filmed! That's not fair!"

And I'll look fucking ridiculous!

"But— Jake, sweetie, don't you love a redemption arc? Suspicion and distrust turns to success and the endless gratitude of the yokels?"

"Not like that." Jake shoved his hands into his pockets. "Nice old ladies swearing their cardies off. No, we can't broadcast it."

Fionn shrugged. "Probably a good call. Don't want Locryn to come out as the hero of *your* story, after all."

"No, we don't." Jake sighed. "I better have a word with him, actually. You go on, Fionn, I'm going to finish here then go home and swear at my reflection."

Then have a nice, calming bath and try not to think about being immolated by furious Porthavelans in my own pirate ship.

She awarded him with a red wine-scented air kiss on either cheek then swept from the room, her mobile already clutched in her skinny hand. Jake watched Locryn say his own goodnights to the locals as he tied his rainbow scarf into a casual knot, the now empty cake box tucked beneath one elbow.

"Erm…Locryn?" Jake crossed the room to him. "Can I have a quick word?"

"Of course." He beamed. "Sorry about all that, Captain. But I'm not sure *weird beards* was a great opening gambit, I'm afraid!"

"Yeah." Jake scrubbed his hand back through his hair. "Just wanted to say thanks for calming everyone down. Could've got hairy! And for arranging the sign-up sheet. You don't have to do all this, you know. I really fucking appreciate it, but…"

"I know you won't let your producer make Porthavel into a punchline," Locryn assured Jake with a smile. "And if there's anything I can do to help with the cake, just let me know. Happy to advise on the matter of building a convincing wedding boat cake."

Advise?

Ad-fucking-vise?

"Locryn, how can I put this? *Wreck to Restaurant* is *my* show. *I* do the food. And that includes the wedding cake. I'm a Michelin-starred chef, for fuck's sake. I'm more than capable of making a wedding cake, and that includes one shaped like a fucking boat!"

Locryn blinked, and for a second, Jake wondered if he might be about to be on the receiving end of a rant of his own. *Did* Locryn ever rant? He must. His mouth opened, then closed again, a smile playing about his lips when he said, "I suppose I *did* master your goujon recipe, so perhaps you're right. Otherwise, that might suggest that a baker like me has it in him to be a *chef* like you, mightn't it?"

"Look here, Locryn." Jake wagged his finger at him, and he had to blink to avoid the lure of Locryn's dancing blue eyes. "Have I ever gatecrashed any of *your* shows? *Have I?* Have I driven my big old London bus into the middle of Porthavel and knocked your chocolate crispie cakes flying? No! So stop trying to weedle into my program! It's getting on my tits!"

"I don't want to be on your program and I certainly don't need to be," Locryn told him. "What I want is for a very special couple to get the wedding and the cake they deserve. You should've heard what your producer was saying this morning! If you think you can come into our village and make their wedding into a punchline, you're sadly mistaken."

"That's not what I'm doing. I take my job seriously." Jake puffed out his breath in frustration. "It's not my pissing fault I've ended up with the set of *Carry On, Treasure Island*, is it? Do you think that was my idea? Then I've got Captain Birdseye's idiot brother up in my grill because I dared to suggest it was naff!"

"*Idiot*? How dare you talk about Cod like that?" Locryn shook his head, his jaw tightening. "I think you and I had better do our best to avoid one another, don't you? I don't think we're ever going to get along."

"I'll be *very* happy to avoid you." Jake turned up his collar and zipped his jacket up even farther. "I'd avoid this *entire place* if I could, but the people have decided, haven't they? Jake Brantham, condemned to Locryn Trevorrow's unfriendly little corner of Cornwall for months — *months!* I wish I'd never come here, Locryn, but I didn't have the fucking choice!"

"Perhaps you're so used to shouting and swearing that you don't recognize a friendly community when you see one." Locryn buttoned up his deep-blue overcoat. "You're not in London now. The pace of life's very different here."

"*Friendly?*" Jake's laughter boomed around the village hall. "Is that what you call friendly, is it, your fucking fan club pelting me with bits of paper?"

"After your *wife* and you called us *naff wicker cod burners!*"

Wife. Jesus.

"Why do you all think I'm married to *her?*" Jake bounced up and down on his toes in frustration. "I'm a gay man. She's hardly my type!"

"Gay?" Locryn blinked his blue eyes. "You're not — Really? Well, that's certainly a surprise!"

"I don't shout about it." Jake bit his lip before saying, "I just hoped people would guess, seeing as whenever I have to go to some event with a plus-one I take a bloke. Or my mum. Seems it didn't bloody work."

"Well, we Porthavelans don't worry about that side of things." Locryn shrugged. "I'll say goodnight, Captain."

"Goodnight, then." Jake held out his hand to shake, but it wasn't the thrusting, bold gesture that it usually was. "And don't worry, I'll keep out of your hair."

Your lovely dark-gold hair.

Jake shook his head to chase the thought away.

The handshake was brief then, with a little smile, Locryn and his cake box were gone.

Chapter Five

Jake began his walk home. The sun had set and the streets were empty, a strong breeze gusting through the lanes of the close-clustered houses.

Have I fucked everything up?

No, but now it was going to be very hard to live in Porthavel and not at every moment fear the return of the mob. And who knew what they'd throw at him next — mussel shells? Dried-up old starfish? Lobster pots?

After passing the harbor — the last thing Jake wanted to see that evening was his sodding pirate ship — he went down the concrete steps to the beach and decided to wear out his rage in a brisk walk, pushing against the wind. But the wind only grew stronger, until Jake could barely force through it, and the waves began to roll and foam, towering up like mountains before crashing on the beach.

He jumped back as a wave rushed at him, and the first spattering specks of rain began to fall.

Porthavel doesn't like me. Not even the sea likes me!

Jake abandoned the beach and began to make his way home, but he was in the dark and barely able to open his eyes in the wind, which carried sharp sand and salt.

And he lost his way.

And it wasn't as if he could ask for help.

There were no streetlamps, nobody else out walking, just Jake and the narrow, winding streets with their picturesque cottages cozy and safe against the storm. London suddenly seemed like the most welcoming place on earth. If Jake woke up in any random corner of the city, he'd have found his way home without so much as a moment's panic. Not so here, though, in the village that had already decided it loathed him. Here he was lost.

Jake managed to find a road out of the village and he was soon wandering along a lane with high hedges on either side. It looked a bit like the lane where his house was, but he could barely see a thing. And one hedge-lined lane looked much like another on a good day.

Something darted across the road ahead and Jake gasped. It was probably only a rat or something, but before he could identify it, it had vanished under a sheet of corrugated iron by the verge.

And when the wind gusted again, the iron trembled before lifting up of its own accord and flying up and over the hedge.

Jake ducked low, hoping the wind wouldn't lift him up off his feet and hurl him too, but now he saw, shivering where the sheet of metal had once been, not a rat but a small black cat with a white bib.

It looked terrified and was drenched through.

Jake battled with the wind and the rain and bent down to the cat. It made no attempt to run, so Jake scooped it up in one movement and zipped it into the front of his jacket.

Can't just leave the poor sod.

The cat wriggled against him, shivering, and Jake protectively placed one arm across his chest, groping through the darkness with the other as he tried to find his home.

And now Jake hurried, the small, wet creature his prime focus as he headed through the storm. He turned a bend and a cottage was up ahead, its lights shining their welcome.

Jake experienced a strange sense of déjà vu, just as he always did whenever he met someone in person for the first time after only ever seeing them on television before.

How could he not recognize the cottage from all those bakery programs Locryn did?

Because wasn't this Locryn's house?

Which, he realized with a miserable shudder, was nowhere near Jake's.

He couldn't just walk in, but equally Jake couldn't walk another step. He was well and truly lost.

And he had a cat in his jacket.

He battled to open the garden gate, which the wind was determined to keep shut, and once Jake had won his fight, he knocked on Locryn's front door.

Jake waited as patiently as he could, but it wasn't easy standing outside in a gale with a plaintively mewing cat fidgeting inside his jacket. He tried again, but still Locryn didn't answer.

Was he even in?

Jake walked around the perimeter of the cottage, the leaded, diamond-shaped windows staring blank and unlit back at him.

So it was all a façade, then. Locryn didn't live here at all.

Then, at the back of the house, Jake saw lights from the window, and when he pressed his face against the glass, he saw Locryn's kitchen.

And there at the table, wearing only a dressing gown, was Locryn himself.

Baking.

The wind whipped and shrieked around Jake, the falling rain rushing back and forth like a curtain of water, but he couldn't move from the spot. All he could do was gawp in wonderment.

There was no denying it, Locryn was a beautiful man. Those forearms were on show again from his rolled-up sleeves, and a very tempting expanse of firm chest, decorated with a manly layer of dark hair, peeped from the vee of his dressing gown.

And he's a bloody annoying Peter Perfect!

A fresh gust of wind battered Jake, almost knocking him off his feet. He lifted his fist and rapped on the window with his knuckles, but Locryn didn't even look up. As another heavy deluge of rain fell above him, Jake knocked again, harder this time. Locryn paused, then blinked toward the window, peering into the darkness.

Don't you dare close the bloody curtains.

Instead Locryn crossed to the kitchen door and opened it, admitting Jake to his welcome sanctuary, light spilling out from within and bringing with it warmth and the smell of baking bread.

"Locryn? I'm the last person you want to see right now, I know, but where's my house?"

Locryn frowned, then shouted against the storm, "Where's— Have you been drinking?"

"No! I went for a walk! And…I'm lost, Locryn. Will you help me, please?"

The cat struggled and Jake pulled the zip on his jacket down enough for it to pop its head out.

"And I found a cat. Is it yours?"

"You'd both better come in." Locryn stepped back into the kitchen, battling to keep the wind from snatching the door out of his hand. Not that it was much of a fight, with those broad shoulders. "Quick, before we get blown away!"

Jake plunged into the welcome safety of Locryn's kitchen. The cat sprang out of Jake's jacket and nearly knocked him backward, but once he'd steadied himself, he saw that the cat had made straight for Locryn's Aga and was soon curled up in front of the large old-fashioned oven.

"This leather jacket's not going to cut the fucking mustard down here, is it?" Jake laughed with relief to be out of the storm. "Have you got *enough* rain? Sure you don't want some more?"

"What on earth are you doing out on a night like this?" Locryn glanced at the cat, but she already looked very satisfied with her lot. "Let me fetch you a towel or you'll catch your death. Pull up a chair to the Aga, get warmed up with your kitty."

"You don't have to. I just want to know where my house has gone." Jake was dazed, and he now realized how tired he was from his hike through the storm. He dropped down onto a chair and held out his palms to the Aga. "Has it been blown away? I'm a friend of Dorothy's, but I never intended to *be* her."

"Does that make me the Wicked Witch of the West or Glinda?" He could hear Locryn bustling about in the hallway and a few seconds later he was padding back into the room on bare feet, his arms filled with fluffy bright-blue towels. "Here you go. I'll let you dry off while I get my fruit cake in the oven. I'll get you something to warm you up too. Brandy ought to do it!"

Jake placed the towels on the chair beside him. When he took off his jacket, he realized that his T-shirt underneath was soaked and had stuck to his skin. "Brandy would be *amazing*, Locryn. Thanks. I don't think I've been *this* wet through since I was dunked in that tank on telly to raise dosh for charity!"

"Oh, that was worth seeing." Locryn put the cake tin into the Aga then turned. Was Jake imagining it or did— No. Why would Locryn sweep his gaze over Jake? They didn't even like each other, and just because Locryn was a baker with an Aga and no obvious significant other, it didn't necessarily mean he was gay. Or that Jake was his type even if he *was*. "Do you want to borrow—I don't wear T-shirts, I'm afraid. Your clothes are soaked to the skin. Let me pop them in the dryer and you can borrow a huge dressing gown while you wait."

"That'd be great." Jake paused, halfway out of his T-shirt, his stomach shiny with the rain. "Are you sure? After what happened earlier?"

"You might not think much of me, but that's what we do in Porthavel when someone needs help." Locryn stroked the little cat's head then headed for the door again. "I told you, this isn't London, Jake!"

"I think a lot of you, actually." With effort, Jake pulled off his T-shirt. Then he was, surreally, topless in

Locryn's kitchen. "I had one of your little cakes earlier. It was really good. It's just—this bloody program."

Locryn threw him another glance, clearly not convinced, then was gone again, leaving Jake alone in his famed and very real kitchen.

And what a place it was. If a set designer and dresser had created this kitchen in a studio, they couldn't have made it more picture-book perfect than it was. From the vast old Aga to the scrubbed pine table and the dresser on which mismatched pieces of china were carelessly if artfully arranged, it was perfect. Cozy and homely and everything that Jake would call *twee*. But not tonight. Tonight it was heaven.

It suited Locryn to a tee.

"Here we are, Captain Jake." Locryn's gaze didn't waver from Jake's face as he strolled back into the kitchen and held out a white robe. It was huge and fluffy and as bright as freshly fallen snow. "Not quite so on-brand as a leather jacket or a Jolly Roger, but a lot more cozy."

"Right now, that dressing gown looks very appealing indeed. Just a second."

Jake turned around and took off his soggy trainers, then peeled himself out of his jeans. He was left in only his boxer shorts.

"Sorry, my jeans are soaked through too. I'm sure you don't need to see me in my shorts!" Jake turned back to Locryn and took the dressing gown, hurrying into it. He could hear Locryn pouring the drinks, tactfully giving Jake some space to change. The wind and rain battered against the little cottage but now Jake felt as cozy as the kitchen had seemed from outside, safely cosseted in the warmth and light.

Jake piled up his discarded clothes, adding his socks. What Locryn would make of their repeating pattern of cartoon fish skeletons on plates, he couldn't imagine. Then he started to rub his hair dry.

"I never thought you filmed in your *actual* kitchen, but this really is it, isn't it?"

"Of course!" Locryn put the brandy glasses down atop a sheaf of sketches on the table. He picked up the bundle of damp clothes. "Sometimes we use the bakehouse in the garden too. I don't know if I dare put these jeans in the dryer. They look rather expensive to me!"

"I've got some more in my suitcase," Jake said, but his house, wherever it had got to, seemed very far away. "I could hang them over a chair?"

Locryn was already there though, hanging the jeans over the back of a chair before he positioned it in front of the Aga. Then he asked, "What's your little chum's name? She's adorable!"

"I was hoping you'd know. She must be a local moggy." Jake crouched down next to the cat and fussed her, and a loud purr vibrated in her throat. "She was in the lane, just down from your cottage. Hiding under a sheet of metal, and when it blew away — she looked too tired to move, and I couldn't leave her, could I?"

Locryn shook his head. "Of course not. I don't recognize her from the village. Does she have a name?"

"She's not wearing a collar. Doesn't look like she's had a good meal in a long time either." Jake grinned as the cat rubbed her head against his knee. "Oh, what the hell, let's call her Dorothy, seeing as I'm her friend."

Locryn laughed. "Would you like some water, Dorothy? I've got some fresh crab in the fridge too, if it's to madam's taste?"

"She's Cornish, I bet she loves it!"

Dorothy got up from her patch by the Aga and threaded herself around Locryn's legs, peering up at him with her large emerald eyes.

Locryn's bare legs. Which Jake told himself not to look at.

"Let's see what we can do for you, Dorothy," the baker said. "There're some brownies in the tin next to your brandy, Jake. Help yourself if chocolate takes your fancy."

"Thanks, mate." Jake opened the tin and the smell of the brownies that rose up to tease his nostrils was nothing short of divine. As Jake bit into one — the flavor was even more gorgeous than the smell — he glanced at the sketches on the table.

And Jake realized that Locryn had been drawing out a design for a cake that looked very much boat-shaped. Jake helped himself to one of the glasses of brandy and took a deep gulp before returning to the chair by the Aga.

Don't be cross. Don't tell him you've seen the sketches. He could've done them ages ago. The bloke's just saved you from being washed out to sea.

But as Jake watched Dorothy follow Locryn around the kitchen, he couldn't dismiss the thought.

"So…" Jake rolled the word around his mouth before asking, "…the wedding cake?"

"Zoe and I drew up the sketches months ago," Locryn explained, clearly realizing too late that he hadn't tidied them away. He stopped and put two delicate china bowls down on the floor, one filled with crabmeat, one with water. "Zoe popped over after the meeting to collect her favorites so she could show you what she had in mind for her cake. We're not scheming, so don't start shouting and swearing at me, all right?"

Jake raised his hand. "Locryn, I'm not going to shout. I'm sat here in your dressing gown, drinking your brandy. I just…I saw how disappointed Zoe was yesterday when she was told you couldn't bake the cake, and I'm not daft. That wasn't her being Bridezilla, was it? You baking her cake really means something to her."

Finally done with feeding the cat and drying clothes and pouring brandy, Locryn settled into one of the chairs. He took his spectacles from the pocket of his dressing gown and put them on, then leafed through the sketches. Eventually he sighed, "There'll be plenty of other cakes. And yours'll be wonderful, I know that."

Jake sat quietly for a few moments, watching Dorothy gratefully hoover up the crabmeat, purring nonstop. He leaned back in the chair and sighed.

"I don't want to be an arsehole about it." Jake's bottom lip began to quiver. He wasn't sure why, but words were trying to force their way out of him, words he'd never thought he'd say. "I'm banging on about it being my television show, but I can have loads of them. This is Zoe and David's wedding. They might only have one in their lives, and… Shit, it's not fair, is it? Not having the cake you want at your wedding because of some adult baby like me whining about his precious television show."

"It's honestly fine. That producer of yours would only make some sort of awful sob story out of it, I couldn't bear that." He picked up one of the brownies and took a bite. "Just make it a really nice cake?"

"Except that I'm the executive producer." Jake sipped the brandy again. A wonderful warmth and calm was spreading through him, and he glanced at Locryn. *Handsome bloody Locryn.* "What sob story?"

But Locryn looked at him with a hint of suspicion in his eyes. "I'm not saying another word until you swear to me you won't put this in the program. Not a mention of it, Jake, I mean it."

"It's okay, I won't say anything. I've already put the brakes on Fionn trying to use hidden camera footage, so don't worry." Jake mimed zipping his mouth. "Not a word."

"This isn't the world you know." He looked down at the sketches again and shook his head. "You've seen the storm tonight. It's ferocious out there but our trawlermen still have to put to sea. We live from the land when it's out of season. Fishing, farming, we depend on it. Storms like this come out of nowhere and they can be deadly in villages like Porthavel."

"It certainly took me by surprise." Jake pictured the fishing boats he'd seen drawn up in the harbor earlier. Maybe some of them were out there now in the storm?

"All over the village tonight people are waiting for the trawlermen to come safely home." Locryn ran his hand back through his hair. "And sometimes—not often, thank the Lord— they don't. Zoe lost her dad on a night like this, Jake."

"I had no idea." Jake put his empty glass aside. Suddenly being a television chef seemed inadequate, swearing down a camera about a flat soufflé nothing short of pathetic. "And that's why the boat-shaped cake is so important?"

He nodded. "Jory and Petroc owned a trawler together. They were close as brothers. Merryn was my right-hand woman in the café. I didn't *quite* have a head for business, just a talent for baking. Ten years ago there was a storm like this and they raced it back to the harbor. They were virtually home when they got a distress call and—I don't think I could've been this brave—they went back into the storm to answer it. They found the trawler and got the crew safely aboard but Jory was swept off the deck."

Locryn paused and took a deep gulp of brandy. "Petroc dived in after him, the poor blighter, but Jory was dead by the time they pulled him from the water. But the boat—the ocean—it was in Jory's blood. He lived on the waves and he loved his boat, Jake. Zoe and David just wanted to honor him and Petroc, who still goes out on nights like this. And still answers every call for help, even though he'd never admit it."

Jake didn't speak for a while. The wind howled down the chimney and the rain clattered against the windows like a handful of stones flung against the panes. But a clock ticked steadily, and Dorothy lay stretched full-length across the floor, purring like an engine.

Maybe Petroc was out there at this very moment? And all he could think was how glad he was to be indoors, and how he'd never be as brave as the sailors who went back out into the storm by choice.

"That's the saddest thing I've ever heard." Jake tugged at his hair, frustrated and embarrassed. Until he said, "I've got no right to make the wedding cake. It *has* to be you, Locryn."

Jake Brantham, relinquishing television space. Whatever next?

But Locryn shook his head.

"No. I don't want anybody else to think I'm trying to push myself into the spotlight." He picked up the sketches and tidied them like a newsreader at the end of a bulletin. "Merryn's been so strong for Zoe, but I saw how broken she was. Sometimes after closing she'd just sit down at a table and cry and — I've known Zoe and David all their lives, Jake, and their lives haven't been easy. It was never about the limelight. It was about doing one really special thing for a couple who deserve the best of everything, and you'll give them the best cake they could wish for."

"But the best cake is one made by *you*." Jake brushed his fingers over the back of Locryn's hand. Only for a moment. "It'll mean far more to them than whatever I come up with, and…I'm not much of a baker. I mean, I can do it. But it'll be average. Those cherry buns you made, that's seriously good cake. And your brownies. Loc, will you think about it? Please?"

Because this really matters. This is bigger than making good telly.

Locryn folded the arms of his spectacles and put them down atop the sketches, his expression thoughtful.

"I'm sorry about the kerfuffle at the meeting," he said. "We're really *not* unwelcoming, you know. And there are lots of people besides me who don't have beards. I can't speak for the *weird* side of things though."

"Fionn is…well…she's *telly*." Jake raised an eyebrow. "You know what I mean, don't you? Everything's *this'll make great telly*. Some sort of horrendous humanitarian disaster, or an orangutan in a rainforest going apeshit at the guy who's just chopped down his tree, not *crap, that's awful*, like a normal human being, she's…*fuck yes, great telly!* I'm really sorry about what she said. And I'm sorry about what I said on the boat. I mean, velvet curtains *are* a bit naff, but I can't walk into the *wreck* and say it's great.

And Captain Cod does look like he's Captain Birdseye's brother. But I concede. *Idiot brother* was a bit too far."

"He does the best fish and chips you've ever tasted. I'll buy you some tomorrow if you like." Locryn took another sip of brandy. "He knows every inch of your new galleon and every way to get a bargain when it comes to fitting out a kitchen. He's a useful fellow to know in this village."

"Okay. So. Captain — is that *really* his name?" Jake laughed as Dorothy leaped up from the floor onto his lap and settled there. "He's not really called Captain Pascoe or something?"

Locryn frowned as he considered the question, then admitted, "He's always been Captain Cod. And he's never looked any different, as far as I can remember!"

"Wow. Is he the Old Man of the Sea? Does he live in a cave and is he five thousand years old?"

"Maybe he's Neptune? Mrs. Cod always looks very pleased with her lot." Locryn laughed. "Almost as pleased as young Dorothy here."

Jake yawned. The wind howled long and low like a beast preparing to slay. "I should get going. But that storm hasn't given up, has it?"

He shook his head. "You're welcome to the spare room if you'd like. Freshly made croissants for breakfast, of course."

"Locryn, honestly, you've been too kind to me already. I can't kip in your spare room. Even if fresh croissants sound fucking amazing. After what I said…"

"I know, I'm a saint." The tone was deadpan, but Locryn's eyes danced with amusement. "Just…start again tomorrow. Maybe be a bit more *this* Jake and a bit less the other?"

Jake chuckled. "Yeah, but you know what the viewers want, Loc. *This croissant's fucking raw! You could've killed me!* Death by croissant. What a load of old crap."

"I've eaten in all three of your restaurants and each was as annoyingly good as the others. Even the boat thing didn't feel like a gimmick. I wasn't blown away by your ganache though, but I'm a hard man to please when it comes to satisfying my sweet tooth." He smiled, the mischief growing. "Maybe I can teach you a few of my secrets."

"All three? Fuck. That's — well, thanks for coming back!" Jake grinned. Locryn — in his restaurant, and his staff had never said a word. "And the ganache, I know, it's dry, isn't it? I've struggled with that bastard for too long and it's just come off the menu because I felt cross every time I saw it." Much like every time he saw Locryn, but because he was such a handsome sod, eminently more tempting than inept ganache. "Yeah. Maybe you could teach me some of your secrets. What was all that about your smugglers' tunnel?"

"It's right under your feet. Runs all the way down from the cottage to the beach. My grandparents lived here before me and generations of Trevorrows before them." Locryn drained his glass. "I bet you didn't know that I had smuggling blood!"

"Will the boat cake have a secret compartment full of contraband?" Jake laughed, until a yawn took him by surprise. "I think it's time for bed."

"I said I'd think about it, but it's up to the bride and groom." He put the lid back on the brownie tin. "Come on, Jake and Dorothy. Follow me to your dashing smugglers' quarters."

Chapter Six

When Jake arrived at the harbor the next morning he was surprised, and somewhat disappointed, to discover that the pirate ship hadn't sunk overnight. In fact, the village seemed to have survived mostly intact.

As had Jake, thanks only to Locryn's hospitality. If he'd had to wander much longer in the storm, Jake would've ended up in a sorry state, but as it was, he'd had a good sleep in Locryn's chintzy spare room.

And so had Dorothy, who Jake had left curled up on a chair by Locryn's Aga.

As Jake plunged into the noise and chaos of the ship, he wondered what the hell he was meant to do with the cat. And what the hell he could do about the crush he now had on Locryn. Because Jake couldn't ignore the appeal of a man with sparkling blue eyes, who looked so hot baking.

He'd last seen Locryn as he'd cycled away from the cottage with a merry wave, off to collect fresh milk from the neighboring farm. If Jake had seen it on television or read it in an interview, he would've laughed

Locryn's life off as fantasy, an elaborate storyline designed to sell his baking bibles. Yet it seemed as though it wasn't. There *were* hens in the back garden and goats in the front, two plump donkeys grazing in a lush paddock with well-appointed stable and a royal-blue bicycle with a wicker basket. Locryn's life was very real, and it was intimately bound up with the village where his ancestors had once been smugglers.

"Hey!" Bright-red fingernails clicked in front of his face as Fionn commanded, "Wake up! I've had an email this morning that you'll want to hear."

Fionn. Emails. A television crew. Clipboards.

Oh, the fucking tyranny of clipboards.

"Fionn, you *do* know that nice man in Nigeria doesn't really want to give you twenty million dollars?"

"Really? Thank fuck you told me before I signed the check!" She rolled her eyes. "There's a nice man in L.A. too, and he's looking for a British chef to launch a *major* new series. You're on the shortlist."

"L.A.? But I'm in Cornwall." And Cornwall was actually — did Jake dare admit? — rather nice. For the first time in ages, he'd woken up hearing the soft sigh of the wind in the trees and the waves crawling back and forth on the beach. He hadn't, for once, heard the *whoosh* of his pulse in his ears.

"There're two other names on the list but I don't know who they are." Then she gave a sly smile and whispered, "The only thing I've been able to get out of him are that none of them are bakers. But you'd know that, since you spent the night with one."

"News travels fucking fast around Porthavel." Jake combed his hand through his hair. He knew very well what Fionn was implying, and Jake couldn't help but be embarrassed by the fact that *staying the night with Locryn* sounded far more racy than it had been in reality. "You saw that bloody storm last night? I got lost in it, and Locryn, bless him, gave me a berth."

Fionn nodded. "I saw you leaving this morning." With a wink she added, "I won't tell. But don't go troppo, Jake. You'd go nuts stuck here with Locryn and his frilly doilies. Did he try to snog you into letting him make the cake?"

"There was no snogging, Fionn. Nothing like that. I was knackered and turned up looking like a drowned rat." *Complete with random stray cat.* But Jake didn't want to tell Fionn about Dorothy. "He…" *Nope, can't tell her about the dressing gown either.* "He gave me a brandy and sent me to bed. To sleep. Alone. And —"

An almighty crash followed by a cannonade of yells filled Jake's ears and he winced. A lighting rig had fallen sideways onto a table that one of the decorators had been using. Paint tins now rolled about the floor and Jake had to jump out of the way of a paint lid that was heading toward him at speed, hurling out Catherine wheels of fashionable, dull-gray matte all over the carpet.

"Fuck's fucking *sake!*" Jake shouted. "What the fuck is this? Why is this so fucking *hard?*"

But as he shouted, he realized something. He didn't feel the rage that he could hear in his voice.

"And as for the cake. Yeah, about the cake…"

Locryn hadn't exactly said he'd definitely make it, but Jake was sure he'd say yes.

Fionn folded her arms. When she spoke, her voice was cool. "What about the cake?"

Jake folded *his* arms. His *I'm in charge of the kitchen* pose. Because he knew that Fionn wouldn't be happy. "I've made a decision. Locryn's making the cake."

She laughed. "Bloody hell, he must've been good in bed!"

"Good at *what* in bed? Sleeping?" Jake shook his head. "I didn't shag Locryn!"

Jake glanced around. Everyone had fallen silent.

Fucking great.

"Sorry, did I say it was bloody break time?" Jake bellowed, and the buzz of work resumed around him. "Look, Fionn, this is to do with Zoe's family. It's personal, and it's so important for her wedding day that Locryn does the cake. For Merryn too. And David *and* Petroc."

"Let's go back up on deck, *Captain*." Fionn's expression had lost its strained mask of good humor. Now it was the face of the woman who struck terror into the hearts of commissioners across the media. "I want to know where all this is coming from, Jake. It's the least you can do if you're about to pull fucking rank!"

"Pull rank? I'm the executive producer on this show and it's my face the viewers see, not yours, so yeah, I have the final say. I'm not being pushed around by the genius who came up with *Celebrity Pancake Toss*." Jake headed onto deck, rubbing his forehead. He still had nightmares about *Celebrity Pancake Toss*.

From below he could hear the sound of sawing and hammering, and smell the paint rising through the salt air to assail him. It couldn't be further from the gentle aroma of baking that had welcomed him last night, and it was acrid despite the fresh sea breeze. Nobody would have guessed there had been a storm here last night, and he wondered if it had been like this the morning after Zoe's father died, leaving Merryn a widow, robbing a girl of her father and Petroc of his best friend.

It felt suddenly more important than ever to let Locryn make the cake. Not some cartoon of fondant and crispies, but something that would probably be closer to a work of art than a wedding cake.

Fionn put her hand on her hip and said, "So what's the story, Jake? What's changed?"

Jake leaned back against the handrail. It creaked under his weight. "Zoe's dad…"

Jake shook his head. He'd promised not to say anything, and he couldn't be sure that the story would have any effect on Fionn. But he didn't want people assuming that he and Locryn were lovers. After all, he'd stood in Locryn's kitchen wearing only shorts, and apart from some low-key flirting, nothing had happened. Fionn could have an edited version, because she didn't deserve to hear anything more.

"Zoe's dad died at sea, and Petroc tried to save him. And…Zoe's mum was working for Locryn at the time. The village pulled together, and Locryn didn't say as much, but you can bet he was there for Merryn and Zoe, above and beyond. Do you see, Fionn? If I bang on about the importance of local produce, and talent-spotting local chefs, I can't ignore a local story like that. Those fishermen are part of Porthavel's fabric, and it's a fucking dangerous job they do. I have to respect that, Fionn. If I make the cake, one, it'll be crap, and two, I'm an ignorant blow-in walking all over Porthavel, and it's not right."

He waited for the explosion, but it didn't come. Instead Fionn blinked, then tapped her lacquered nail thoughtfully against her chin. A few seconds passed before she said, "That's *brilliant*. Could we get them to talk about it on screen, do you think? We could maybe get shots of, I don't know, suitably big waves or whatever. Maybe we could show Zoe and David visiting the grave? Telling Dad about the wedding and all that?"

"*What?*" Jake stared at her in horror. "Are you high or something? We can't do that! It's private. I shouldn't have said anything, but seeing as you were intent on grilling me over the cake, then... You just need to know that the whole cake thing isn't just a whim and it isn't Locryn trying to steal the show. It feels like the right thing to do. Gut instinct."

"You're making a mistake. He'll be all over this show and if you hadn't noticed, his book's sitting above yours in the bestsellers as we speak. *Above.* And now you're giving him the starring role in your show? Jesus Christ!"

"I don't give a fuck about the bestseller chart!" Jake stared, wide-eyed. *Really?* But no, he wasn't. His books had been above Locryn's before, so why did it matter if Locryn's book was selling more than his now? "What I care about is this program, and at its core is a couple getting married, and fuck me if it's not going to be the happiest day of their lives. And it *won't* be if my ego and yours get in the way of a fucking cake!"

Fionn laughed, but it was a mirthless sound. "It's on you. If you're doing this, you need to know it's *all* on you."

"Yeah, that's fine. I'm executive producer, after all." *Doesn't hurt to remind her.* Jake glanced at his nails then back at Fionn. She was fucking scary but Jake wasn't going to stand down.

"On you." She jabbed her finger, then shook her head. "I've got a show to produce. I'll leave you to it."

Jake gave Fionn a sarcastic salute. "Aye, aye, Cap'n!"

"Someone's looking for you," was all she said. Then, with a sharp nod toward the dockside, she strode away across the deck of the ship.

Jake turned, smiling to himself. It would be Locryn, wouldn't it? Locryn, with Dorothy in the basket of his bicycle? He was bringing Dorothy round to Jake's later anyway. Maybe Locryn was taking her on a tour of the village first in case he could find her owners?

But instead, Jake saw Merryn, waving up at him from the quayside. Jake gripped the handrail. That poor woman. But she was smiling.

"You all right down there, Merryn?" Jake jogged toward the gangplank and ignored the worrying bounce under his feet as he crossed it to dry land.

Merryn shrugged and said, "I'm all right, not bad. Did you hear the storm last night? Bet you don't get that in London, do you?"

"I was outside in it!" Jake pulled a face. "No, not experienced weather like that before. Are you okay?" Jake glanced over at the row of fishing boats bobbing up and down in the harbor then smiled gently at Merryn.

"I need a word. Have you got two minutes?" She rubbed her gloved hands together. "It's too cold to stand around for long. Fancy a walk along the harbor?"

"Yeah, I'd love that." Jake shoved his hands into the pockets of his leather jacket. He'd need a proper raincoat if he was going to survive in Porthavel. "What's up?"

They began to walk as she told him, "I don't know if you're the person to talk to about this, but the lady on the boat, she's been asking Zoe and David all sorts of personal questions. *What's the gossip we should know, who's the village idiot,* that kind of thing. They're really worried about what you're going to make them look like."

Fuck me.

"Fionn, you mean? Gray hair, face like a halibut sucking a lemon?"

She nodded. "And she's been asking Petroc about losing his wife. Bev was my best friend, it broke his heart when she died — that didn't ought to be on the telly."

"No, no it's not going on telly, don't worry about that." Jake patted Merryn's arm. "I have final say and I want you guys to be happy with what goes on air." Jake sighed. "I'll speak to Fionn. Nope, nothing personal like that's going on the show. Is that okay?"

"Thanks." She smiled. "And Petroc, he's a lovely bloke, you know. He comes over all gruff and tough but he's soft as butter. She said to David, *your dad's a miserable old sod,* and he isn't really. He's just...shy."

"Petroc's a bloody hero!" Jake coughed, too late to hide his words. "Erm...look, I'd like to apologize on behalf of everyone on the crew for what may have been said by certain people. It's not on, and... Yeah. Sorry."

"Do you know? About Jory?"

Jake nodded. He looked down at his feet. "Locryn told me. I can't begin to imagine how painful it must've—still is. But it won't go out on telly, I promise."

"You're nicer than you seem on the telly," Merryn told him with a smile. "Petroc's a sweetheart really, you know. Last year, him and me were—well, it didn't work out, but he's a lovely man."

Jake grinned at Merryn. "Did you and Petroc go on a date? Afternoon tea at Locryn's café?"

"We went on a few," she admitted, blushing. "I've not had anyone since I lost Jory and it's been seven years since Bev passed away so we thought, *well why not*? But he was shy, and... Have you tried Locryn's afternoon tea?

"Haven't had time!" Jake chuckled. Merryn had made a good attempt at changing the subject, but he was curious. "Petroc was shy and...? You don't strike me as a shy sort of woman, Merryn! You're a go-getter!"

Merryn's blush deepened and she told him, "I was worried about him going out to sea, in case I lost him like I lost Jory. And when I told him that he told me he blamed himself for not getting Jory out of the water quicker. He's *wrong*, Jake, but he won't have it said. He needs some sense knocked into his thick, lovely head!"

"If the storm they were out in was anything like the one last night—it was bad enough being on land during that. Petroc deserves a medal. And so does Jory. Going back out there for the other crew." They were on the other side of the harbor now and Jake pointed across at the pirate ship, the sound of drilling and shouting in the distance. "How many of them over there would do that? Some might, but not many of them."

And certainly not Fionn.

Merryn looked out to the horizon, the waves calm and gray. "Locryn tried to talk to him. He's lovely, Locryn, but he's not a bloke's bloke, you know? Petroc thinks the world of him but he's not one to talk about his emotions and what have you. I just don't want Petroc to be lonely like he is. He's doesn't deserve it."

"How does he feel about the wedding, or hasn't he said?"

"Oh, he's happy as anything about that. He thinks the world of those two." She huddled into her coat. "She asked him to give her away but he said he didn't think it was his place."

"He's a very modest bloke, this Petroc, isn't he? And he won't listen to Locryn, and he won't listen to you." From where they were wandering on the quayside, Jake could see Locryn's café. He smiled, because he was fairly sure he could see Locryn in there, through the tangle of bunting. "What does David say?"

"That his dad's a daft old sod who needs a bit of company." She laughed. "And that Jory'd want him to give Zoe away *and* take me out too!"

"Petroc sounds like my dad—stubborn! But underneath, he feels a lot but isn't sure how to get it out?"

Merryn nodded eagerly. "That's it!"

"I don't know what to suggest!" Jake chuckled. "But I do have some news for you, and maybe Petroc'll want to hear it too. About the cake."

She waited, her eyes wide. And before Jake even spoke, he knew he'd made the right decision.

Jake grinned. "Locryn's going to make it."

With a cry of delight, Merryn threw her arms around Jake and embraced him. There were tears in her voice when she said, "Oh, you lovely, lovely man!"

It had been a very long time since anyone had called him '*lovely*' and Jake shook his head. "I'm not lovely, I just want to do the right thing."

"You *are* lovely." At the sound of a bicycle bell Merryn looked round. There was Locryn, heading off into the village, one hand raised to them. Merryn waved back, then told Jake, "You're both lovely. They should put you on the telly together. You can do the mains, he can do the puddings!"

Jake laughed. "That's a nice idea, but…"

But…

Why not?

Chapter Seven

Jake pottered happily in his farmhouse kitchen, experimenting with pasties and squab pies. He'd find the perfect recipe for Zoe and David, and seeing as Locryn would soon appear with Dorothy if her owners hadn't been found, he'd try out the recipes on *Cornwall's favorite TV baker*.

As the *Radio Times* had called him.

And wouldn't Locryn be impressed? There were pies and pasties cooling on wire racks across the kitchen table, all ready to be tested on the locals tomorrow. And they'd be filmed sighing and moaning over Jake's cookery for the show.

They always sighed and smacked their lips. There was never so much as a single voice of dissent.

That was the formula.

As he was surveying his imminent triumph, there came a knock at the door. The sort of knock that belonged to a baker and a stray cat.

Jake jogged through to the hallway. He went up on his tiptoes to see through the fanlight then, satisfied that it was Locryn and Dorothy, opened the door.

"Come on in! Can cats eat pasties?"

"Probably not, but I'm sure she will." Locryn held out the cat carrier he was holding. "No wicker cod, just a wicker basket! I've asked around the village and along the coast and it looks as though little Dorothy must've blown in with the storm. Have you got room for a cat in London?"

Jake took the carrier from Locryn. "I could make space? I've got a loft apartment."

Locryn frowned and asked, "Is that all right? Would she be better with me, perhaps?"

"Depends if you want a cat or not. You've already got all those goats and everything. And I found her. I kind of feel responsible for her." Jake lifted the carrier and peered inside. Dorothy blinked at him and started to purr. "My last pet was a goldfish when I was ten. She's not going to be as easy to look after, is she?"

As Locryn shook his head, the expression on his face was one of sympathy. He sighed and told Jake, "She's not. But everyone should have a pet, and I'm sure Dorothy would make herself at home if you'd like to keep her. If you don't think you can, I'll look after her for you and you can come to Cornwall and visit whenever you like."

"Would you mind?" Jake blinked. "She's a Cornish cat. I don't think she'd fancy a view of the Docklands Light Railway. She likes the sea."

"You never know, you might just fall in love with Porthavel and decide to move here instead." Locryn smiled gently. "But if not, I'll take care of her for you. You'll still be Dad, but I'll be...sort of Adoptive Dad.

I'll make sure Dorothy watches all your programs, don't worry."

"I'll let her watch your shows too. Sometimes!" Jake laughed. What the hell was he doing adopting a cat when he was on the shortlist for a US series? "Anyway, I've been cooking. Have a sniff. Can you guess what?"

Locryn lifted his chin and took a deep breath, savoring the aroma in the air. He closed his eyes and took another, then said as though it were the most wondrous thing he could imagine, "Pastry? Not *pasties*?"

Jake guided Locryn toward the kitchen, the cat shifting in her basket as he went. He didn't know what the landlady would make of a cat, but he was Jake Brantham, she wouldn't mind. "Oh yes, pasties! I've cooked loads of them. And you, Locryn, you get first go!"

"I need to talk to you about that producer chum of yours," Locryn said as he unbuttoned his coat and followed Jake. There beneath it was a shirt of bright blue this time, the same shade as his eyes. And Jake tried not to notice the three buttons that were unfastened, revealing a hint of the chest beneath, the chest he had equally tried not to notice last night. "But nothing comes before pasties. I'm a Cornishman, after all. I can't wait to see what a Michelin-starred legend does with our humble national dish!"

Jake stopped just inside the kitchen door. He put Dorothy down in her basket then set her free from it. She crept out, sniffing the air.

"Take your pick. Variations on a theme," Jake told him proudly. The pasties lay before them, row after tempting, savory row of golden pastry hillocks. Locryn threw his coat over the back of a dining chair and unknotted his scarf, though he left it hanging around his neck. He peered at the selection, inhaling the aroma again, then he reached out and took one from a rack.

Jake clasped his hands behind him. He felt the same nerves as when he'd applied for his first job in a kitchen and had made a none-too-shabby soufflé. The head chef then had been bowled over, and Jake smiled, confident in his skills. What was a pasty, at the end of the day? Pastry and a filling. Not hard at all, especially for a bloke with a Michelin star.

Locryn took a bite. He chewed it, his expression unreadable, then swallowed. After a second or so he took another bite, savoring it like a wine taster with a fine vintage. Only once he had swallowed did he ask, "That's lovely. What is that? Something they serve in the east end?"

"In the east end of Truro. It's a fucking Cornish pasty, Loc!" Jake laughed, slapping Locryn's shoulder. But Locryn wasn't laughing.

"It isn't. It's spicy, for starters."

"And? It's seasoning for the meat filling." Jake pointed to the tray that he'd set on the hob, fresh out of the oven with steam rising from the pasties. "*Those* have a dash of garlic!"

"Gar—" That little smile was nowhere to be seen now, replaced by a look of horror as he stared at the pasties as though they were laced with poison. "You put garlic in a Cornish pasty? What else are you going to surprise me with?"

Jake took a step back and a furious feline howl ripped through the kitchen. He snapped round to see Dorothy underfoot, urgently licking her tail. Then she hissed at him and wrapped herself around Locryn's legs.

Jake folded his arms. "Fresh coriander. Cornish-grown, before you ask."

"Coriander? It's a Cornish pasty!" Locryn picked Dorothy up and cradled her, no doubt keeping her from the horrors of the pasties. "Why would anybody in their right mind do this? What were you thinking, Jake? Are you ill?"

Wouldn't you like to know?

Jake swatted the table with a tea towel. The *whooshing* sound of his pulse had returned to his ears again and the rage he'd missed that morning was rushing back into his veins. "I'm a fucking chef! I'm testing recipes! Garlic, coriander, a bit of spice. Why not?"

"Then call it a *something else pasty* and I'll tell you it's beautiful, because it is, but—" He gestured toward the table. "Don't you dare call these Cornish pasties. Don't even think about it!"

"Oh, I'm sorry, I forgot the king of fucking Cornwall had graced me with his presence!" Jake shook his head. Just as he'd thought he'd been accepted by the Porthavelans, he'd transgressed and was the interloper again. *But the Cornish love their fish.* Jake picked up a plate bearing another pastry-shrouded offering and held it out to Locryn. "Don't suppose you want to try a salmon squab?"

And Locryn actually backed away, recoiling as though Jake had offered him a dead rat. He shook his head, his horrified gaze fixed on the pie.

Fucking king of fucking Cornwall. Burning a big wicker scone with a Cornish pasty perched on top.

"You can't put salmon in a squab pie, it's not civilized." Even Dorothy snuggled deeper against Locryn's chest, clearly Cornish to her very bones. "You cannot serve these to Porthavelans. They'll chase you off with pitchforks!"

Jake picked up one of his pasties and held it up at Locryn. He squeezed it so hard that the filling started to leak out of the end. "That's what *you* think, but I bet the Porthavelans won't! I bet they'll *love* them, and I bet they'll think you're a boring old stick-in-the-mud for shoving your nose in the air at my cooking!"

"Fine. Why don't you ask them?" He took another step away, backed up against the kitchen cupboards now, unable to escape the terror of the pasties. "We'll pack them up, pop them in Betsy's basket and take them to the pub right now! But don't say you weren't warned, Jake, because the supposed king of you-know-whating Cornwall did try to tell you."

"Where's your passion, Locryn? Why do you have to set everything in aspic?" Jake's voice was hoarse with frustration and he started to fling the pasties into plastic tubs. "I don't mean literally. I mean, you've got this fixed idea about what a pasty can be, and I don't understand. And neither will the folk down the pub!"

"My passion?" Even Locryn's voice was raised now. Still plummy, but raised. "Don't be absurd! Everything I do is with passion!"

"Is it *balls!*" Jake tried to tear a length of clingfilm, but it was too full of static and it stuck to his arm. "You're a fucking great baker, you really are, but...but... What are you holding back? Just—just take the fucking stick out of your arse and let go!"

And still he didn't. Still his jaw tightened, his chin lifting with an imperious tilt. What did it take to get a reaction out of the man? What would it take to break through the *'fiddlesticks'* and *'crumbs'*?

"Is this how you react to criticism?" Locryn's voice was clipped. "I have passion, I just don't feel the need to shout and carry on like you do. It makes people unhappy, and I don't want to make people unhappy."

"Loc, people watch my shows because it *makes* them happy! I dunno, maybe they can let go vicariously because I can shout *bollocks to non-stick!* and throw a frying pan into a river when they can't!" Jake gave up with the clingfilm and chucked it aside. He planted his hands on his hips. "You are *so* fucking good-looking too, they must be lining up for you, but what are you like with — with your partners? Horlicks, lights off and a hug?"

"You're frightening Dorothy." Locryn pressed a kiss to the cat's small head, his breathing short, filled with tightly controlled annoyance. But still there was no real reaction. Still he was clenched tighter than... Even Jake couldn't think what. "Horlicks, lights off and a hug is so me, however did you guess? And sensible flannel pajamas too, all topped off with single beds and no touching on Sundays."

Jake shoved his rolling pin into the washing-up bowl with a *splosh.* "No, you just get turned on by kneading dough. Because dough won't get upset when you complain that it's not fucking traditional enough. Except *your* dough would be, of course."

"Don't be vulgar." He looked away from Jake. "I don't get turned on by baking, why would you say — " Locryn settled Dorothy atop his coat and Jake sensed something change in the atmosphere, like it had last night just before the storm hit. But instead Locryn took another deep breath and told him quietly, "I don't think tradition is a dirty word. We're proud of our culinary heritage here. And kneading dough is an art form, far more than cooking a pork goujon will ever be!"

"Well, I'm sorry if my cooking's not good enough for you. Why didn't you join in pelting me with paper like everyone else in the village? Shall I just bugger off back to London? Would you be happy, then? Me and my shitty pasties?" Jake packed up the last few pasties, crushing them under the lid. *Not that it matters, no one'll like them anyway.* "I s'pose even your Cornish seagulls would clack their beaks if I threw them the ends of the pastry!"

"Why don't you?" Locryn asked. "Or better yet, why don't you just stop trying to be Mr. Shocking, cook a normal pasty and a normal squab pie and give Zoe and David the wedding they want, not the one your ego demands. And then yes, please *do* go back to London and have a good old laugh about us yokels. No Horlicks and lights off for Jake, you're too busy swinging off your Michelin stars, I expect, with your leather jacket and your showy London bus!"

"Is that what you bloody well think, is it?" Jake folded his arms and stared outside. How stupid of him to think that Porthavel wasn't so bad after all. And even more stupid to start feeling fond of the place. And of...

"Locryn, please, I'm trying my best. I want Zoe and David to have a wonderful wedding, I really do. I told Merryn that you'll—that you might do the cake, and she was over the moon." Jake stacked up the plastic tubs on the worktop. "And I'm experimenting with the pasties. And I know Fionn's rubbed people up the wrong way, and I'm fucking furious with her. This is all... Fuck me, it's all going to pot."

"I do have passion, it's just— Oh, what's the point?" was all Locryn said. Then he scooped up Dorothy and kissed her head again. "I'll say goodnight, young lady, and leave you and your daddy to it."

"Thanks for bringing her round," Jake said, subdued as he headed for the hallway. "And thanks for being a great host. I'll show you out."

"I'll do the cake," Locryn told him, pulling his coat on. "And the pasties were delicious, they just weren't Cornish pasties. That's all I was tryi— I'd be better off telling Dorothy, wouldn't I? What I have to say is of no interest to you whatsoever."

Jake closed his eyes. He regretted every word he'd said. He hadn't meant to sound angry, he just...

"I care, okay? That's all. I care about food. And you do too. We just care in different ways. I'm sorry. Okay? I'm glad you thought they were delicious, even if they were London pasties and not *arrrr me 'earties* Cornish ones. Sorry. Fuck me, off I go again." Jake opened the front door for Locryn. "You'd better go before I say anything else, which would only prove to you that I'm a massive prick."

"I'm sorry too." Locryn gave the hint of a smile and said, "I'd better get home and see how many chaps *aren't* lining up round the block to share my Horlicks! You'll do Zoe and David proud, I know that. Goodnight, Jake.'

"'Night. I'll see you around." Jake patted Locryn's arm as he passed him.

Chaps? Did he just say chaps*?*

As the door closed, the word '*chaps*' was the only one Jake heard. And it wasn't even a word he used. But...Locryn Trevorrow was gay? Bloody hell. No wonder he had a bike called *Betsy*.

And I stripped off in front of him.

Jake headed back to the kitchen, where his cat was sitting in the middle of the room, one leg aloft while she had a thorough clean.

Jake sighed. "I'm just glad you didn't do that in front my guest."

There was a knock on the front door.

Then another.

Maybe it was the Cornish pasty militia, summoned by Locryn to seize and destroy the culinary affront to their heritage.

Jake strode back to his front door and opened it.

"Oh, Locryn?" And as Locryn didn't look very happy, Jake steeled himself. "I won't say anything about the chaps, nonexistent or otherwise, don't worry. I'm not in the business of outing anyone."

The baker frowned. "I'm out, that's not— I just had a phone call. From Fionn."

Jake rolled his eyes. "Have I got to apologize for her again?"

This time the frown turned into a smile, and with a sigh Locryn said, "Maybe. She said you told her about Jory. Don't worry, I don't think you did it for any nefarious reason. I'm not going to tell you off. But she wanted to know if I could pop down to the pub and convince the locals to share their memories of the night he died. I don't think that's going to make Zoe very happy, or do *you* any favors."

"She *what?*" Jake's mouth fell open in alarm. "I'm sick to death of this. I told her it was off-limits. I only mentioned it, as vaguely as I could, so she'd understand why you should make the cake. I'm the executive producer. I'm her *boss!* What the holy hell is she playing at?"

He shrugged one shoulder. "I thought I'd better let you know, just in case she's asking other people too."

"We need to find her. Now. Before she speaks to anyone else. She's at the pub?"

"Grab that leather jacket that drives all the nice boys wild." Locryn smiled. "And follow me."

Is he flirting again?

No.

In seconds, Jake had settled Dorothy in the utility room with a bowl of water, leftover salmon and a newspaper on a tray, and was zipped into his leather jacket.

Jake glanced at the bike propped up against the wall. "Let's take my car."

"Where's that bus you drive around in on the telly?" Locryn winked. "I'm disappointed, but a car'll have to do."

"Dad's tarting her up over the winter. He's threatening to drive her down here if we're not careful!" Jake unlocked his gunmetal-gray Mercedes and climbed behind the wheel. Locryn took his place in the passenger seat, primly smoothing down his coat before he reached for the seatbelt. It was as much Jake as the bike was Locryn. Each had their brand, and Jake's was leather jackets and sports cars.

"See you later, Betsy," Locryn said, but Jake had an idea that he was teasing. As soon as Jake started the car, his stereo came on by itself and he pulled out of the farmyard to the strains of gentle rainfall and windchimes. He reached for the off switch.

"Shit. Sorry. Don't know how that got on there." But Locryn simply smiled, his serenity restored as he directed Jake through the narrow village streets toward the pub where Fionn was doing who knew what sort of damage.

Chapter Eight

Jake wondered if he'd get an award or a confetti cannon when he found a parking space on the narrow lane by the pub. He saw a people carrier right outside which he knew was one used by the production team.

"Looks like we've found the crew as well," he said as he got out of the car. "Maybe they all think it's *Fionn's From Wreck to Restaurant*? Bunch of bastards."

"Oh, don't take it out on the crew," Locryn told him. "They've already got some of the villagers in helping with the renovations and I've heard nothing but lovely things. They're very good for public relations, these chippies and camera people!"

"At least *they* are, while Fionn's busy bloody well undoing all their good." Jake shoved his hands into his pockets. "Let's *have a word*."

"A quiet one." Locryn pushed open the pub door, releasing a burst of noise and heat from within. Jake could see the taproom, and it was like looking back in time, dark wood and low lighting illuminating a small room filled with the same people who had pelted him with cake cases the previous evening. "Not a shouty one."

The pub fell silent as they walked in. It was like a Western. All Jake could hear were their footsteps across the wooden floor and his own heartbeat.

"Fionn! A word!" Jake shouted, but just so she'd hear. He wasn't *shouting* shouting. Not exactly. Fionn was perched at the bar, a glass of white wine in one hand and her mobile in the other, and if she heard Jake, she gave no indication.

Jake was vaguely aware that he was being greeted with the same air of suspicion that he thought he'd put paid to yesterday. *Bloody Fionn.* But Locryn was already giving the locals the full benefit of his charm, all smiles and gentle greetings even without buns to share.

Jake cupped his hands around his mouth. "Fionn! Hello, it's the executive producer here! A word, Fionn. *Now!*"

She put her phone into her pocket and looked at Jake. Then she grinned and said, "You didn't have to come all the way down here. I was handling it!"

"Handling it?" Jake shook his head. "I'm disgusted. What the hell are you doing, going round Porthavel asking people about...about... I told you it was *private!*"

Fionn lifted her glass and took a long drink, as though she had all the time in the world. It was almost insolent, like a teenager faced with an angry parent.

"I've set up a little stunt on Saturday down on the beach. Ten o'clock, you're going to be cooking pasties and serving them to locals," she told him. "Pip and Holly're going to use it for some advance goodwill and we'll be trailing it on *Saturday Breakfast*, obviously. There'll be all the equipment there waiting, just bring whatever ingredients you want to work with. This is what I do, Jake. Leave it to me and worry about the cooking."

"Worry about *cooking?* I'm worried you're going to turn the whole fucking village against me and my show!" He jabbed his thumb at Locryn. "And apparently you wanted Locryn to convince the locals to film their memories of the night Zoe's dad died. I'm in charge, Fionn. Don't you get that? If I say no, that's the end of it. *Especially* something like that. I'm bloody disgusted, I really am! It's gross. Even more gross than your *Celebrity Roadkill Restaurant.*"

"I called him"—she dropped her voice to a whisper—"because he's like the yokel whisperer. Look at him! They love him, Jake. He's got that benevolent lord of the manor act down pat, hasn't he? Probably find out he goes like a bloody train!"

Fionn nudged Jake and laughed her throaty bray of a laugh, the laugh of a woman who'd given up smoking a decade after her doctor had told her to.

"Don't you bloody well talk about him like that. Or the locals. You don't have any respect for the people who live here, do you?" Jake slapped his hand on the bar, underlining each word. "I. Can't. Work. With. Someone. Mocking. The. Locals! Fuck's sake!"

"Think of the good telly!" She seized his cheek between her thumb and forefinger, like an affectionate auntie with a toddler. "Now I've got to run, I've got a date in Locryn's café with the happy couple and their parents. A few talking heads in front of the fairy lights, then I'm off into Plymouth for sushi and mobile signal. Fancy it?"

"No, I bloody don't. And don't you bloody well trick them into talking about—about what happened. It's off limits. Got that, Fionn? It's off fu−" Jake's voice cracked. Locryn, so quiet, so calm, and yet so clearly furious in the face of the producer, robbed Jake of his ready box of swear words. He took a steadying breath, and as calmly as he could, said, "Got that?"

She released his cheek. "It's strictly twenty minutes on the subjects of wedding dresses, wedding cars and honeymoons. I'm not missing my sushi for anything. Don't worry, there'll be nothing controversial." Fionn drained her glass in a gulp. "So you were with Locryn again, were you? Holiday fling?"

"Get your mind out of the bloody gutter!" Jake rubbed his face. Her nails had scraped his skin. "Fine. Wedding dresses, cars and honeymoon only. I mean it, Fionn. I'm *serious*."

"Got it. And I've had some more intel on the US show. It's *brilliant*." She slipped down from her barstool. "Its working title's *Shock Chef* and it's a cooking contest, but every time the contestants make a mistake they get a little electric shock. I howled when I read the treatment! I've emailed it to you. It's *so* us. Imagine you bawling and swearing at the poor bastards and them getting shocked then getting all flustered so getting shocked again. And the money's off the chart. It's the big time. The dream."

So the world really has *gone insane.*

"It's the work of a fucking psychopath, more like." Jake stood aside. "I need a drink."

"See you on the beach." Fionn waved at Locryn as he approached the bar. "*Ciao*, Locryn, have a good night!"

Locryn answered with a smile as he joined Jake. He waited until Fionn had left to say, "No harm done.

We're used to it. You should hear some of the people we get in the summer. Can I get you a drink?"

"Yeah, I'd like that," Jake said. He folded his arms against the bar and looked along the line of taps. "A pint of your local ale, I think."

"You'll have to leave the car because I'm such a Dudley Do-Right," Locryn pointed out. "But it's worth it. And we don't have a local ale, but we do have a *stunning* cider. You'll never have tasted anything so wonderful, I guarantee it."

"Cider and a taxi it is!" Then Jake paused. "Do you *have* taxis around here?"

"They're horse-drawn, of course." Locryn laughed, signaling to the landlord with a nod that it was a yes on the pints. He glanced toward the opening pub door, then frowned. "Did I hear wrong, or is Petroc supposed to be in my café being interviewed for the show? Because he isn't."

Jake turned to see Petroc heading for the bar. "Don't tell me Fionn pissed you off before she even got to the café!"

"I know, I know." Petroc was addressing the two men in his rich Cornish drawl before he even reached them. "But I need a quick nip of Dutch courage before I go along for my interview. I get nervous when they turn the camera on. What've I got to say that anyone wants to hear? Ask me to talk fishing and I'll be here until tomorrow, but weddings? That's for the ladies, that is."

Jake chuckled and made a space for Petroc at the bar. "Bet you could talk about wedding cars, though. Could hire a nice old Daimler, eh?"

"Frock first, cars in ten minutes." The landlord lined up three pints of cider on the bar. "I don't know how you boys do it, performing for the cameras like you do. You're brave lads!"

"You're the one who's brave!" Jake picked up his glass and saluted Petroc. "Were you out in the storm last night? I was walking about in it and it was bad enough. I couldn't go out on the sea in that!"

He nodded and took a drink of cider. "I was and I didn't want to be! I'll tell you this, if my boy's getting wed then I'm thinking I might be a grandad one day. I'm wondering if it's time I dropped anchor and retired."

Locryn glanced at the landlord, as though this was something they never thought they'd hear. He lifted his glass and said, "We'll drink to that, eh, Jake?"

Merryn will be pleased!

Jake raised his glass to him again. "Too right. You deserve it! Time to have some fun. *And* be a grandad." Jake took a sip and let the mellow taste of the cider run through him. Then he winked at Petroc and asked, "Am I going to be doing a wedding special for you too? Any ladies waiting in the wings?"

"Oh, no." Petroc laughed a throaty laugh. "Who'd have me but my Bev? I wouldn't get that sort of luck twice in one lifetime. The ladies'd run a mile!"

"Come off it, Petroc! Ruggedly handsome bloke like you!" Jake had a swig of his cider, then asked, "Anyone in the village you'd take on a date? Afternoon tea at Locryn's café?"

"Certain lady with a love of lippy and lacquer?" Locryn prompted. "She's still waiting for your next date!"

But Petroc shook his head. "I've no claim to Merryn, not after what happened to her man. She's a fine woman, she wouldn't want me hanging around reminding her of what she lost."

Locryn gaze met Jake's. After a moment he said simply, "You're wrong, you know."

Jake nodded. "You're a hero, Petroc. That's got to count for something, right? I get the impression that if you asked Merryn on a date again, she might say *yes*."

"She deserves a bloke like you. Handsome, go-getting, not an old sea salt!" Petroc said. Jake wasn't sure that a man like him was quite what Merryn would want in a boyfriend. The whole gay part might be a problem for starters. "Or like our Locryn, but Locryn if he liked ladies. She's classy, is Merryn. Very put-together."

"Well, I'm not into ladies either," Jake admitted. "But yeah, Merryn *is* very glamorous. Single life, though, eh? Free and easy? You don't want to give it up?"

But Petroc's wistful look was all the answer Jake needed. The trawlerman might try to hide it as he lifted his glass and drained the contents, but Jake had already seen the reflection of Merryn's longing in his face. And when he met Locryn's gaze, he knew that he'd seen it too.

"That's me off to be on the bloody telly then!" Petroc stifled a burp. "Pardon me, gents, but my public awaits."

Locryn patted him on his broad back as he stood. "Help yourself to a slice of whatever you fancy." He smiled. "Bit more power to your elbow."

"I hear Locryn does an excellent cream horn!" Jake caught Locryn's gaze and winked. The Cornishman held the look, his eyes sparkling even in the low light of the taproom.

"Do you fancy one?" Locryn asked Jake as Petroc departed. "Made with passion, in case you were wondering."

"I wouldn't mind having a nibble on your cream horn." Then he lowered his voice and said, "Wouldn't mind having a lick, either."

Locryn's mouth fell open. He blinked then leaned closer and asked quietly, "How do you take your Horlicks?"

Oh, Locryn, you delicious, saucy bastard.

"Naked," Jake replied. "And you?"

"Hot," he whispered. "And not nearly as often as I'd like."

"We should do something about that, shouldn't we?" Jake edged up the bar until he was shoulder to shoulder with Locryn. "Name the day, Loc."

Locryn glanced around the bar as though looking for a hidden camera, returning his gaze to Jake before he asked, "Are you teasing me or—?"

"I'm not, no." Jake brushed the back of his hand against Locryn's. "I'm flirting with you because I fancy you, Locryn. Do...do you like me, or are you pulling my leg with all this flirting?"

"You're gorgeous." He moved his hand a little, letting his fingers accidentally-on-purpose rest against Jake's. "And you've got such passion for what you do. That's always a bit of a turn-on."

"Even if I put coriander in a pasty?" Jake teased. "So when you come back to mine to collect Betsy...? Although I don't have Horlicks, I'm afraid."

"I was going to say I don't have a stick up my arse." Locryn raised his eyebrow. "But that sounds like a filthy joke."

Jake rubbed his forehead in embarrassment. "Yeah, sorry about that. Not the thing to say, was it?"

"I know I can be a bit prim." He smiled. "I just — We're protective of our pasties. But you never know, you might hand out your London pasties to the village tomorrow and prove me wrong!"

"You could be right, though, and Fionn will take great pleasure in filming it for posterity as it's *great telly*." Jake rolled his eyes. "*Please* tell me your producer isn't massive pain in the — doesn't make you want to scream as well?"

"I'm my own producer. It was the only way to stay sane." Locryn emptied his glass. "Shall we have a wander along to the café and see how it's all going?"

"I think you made a wise choice, Locryn." Jake finished his drink and hopped down from the barstool. "Let's check and make sure Fionn's behaving."

Chapter Nine

As they left the pub together, Jake had the distinct impression that something in the evening air had changed. A subtle shift, almost a sense of settling. He wasn't sure what would happen as the night wore on, but for the first time since he'd arrived in Porthavel, he felt relaxed. Maybe it was Locryn's influence, when he wasn't ranting about pasties at least.

They didn't hold hands as they wandered to the café but they walked close together. Closer than they had before.

The weather was surprisingly uneventful compared to the wildness of the night before, the village quiet. All except for Locryn's café, whose lights were spilling out onto the quayside from its illuminated windows.

"Cream horn?" Locryn asked innocently as they reached the door. "On the house for the chap in the leather jacket."

"Can't say no to that!" Jake patted Locryn's arm as they went inside. At first all seemed calm. Zoe and David were sitting together on one side of a table bearing a cloth of pale blue gingham and opposite them were Petroc and Merryn. In the middle of the table was a china teapot and in front of each, a cup and saucer. A plate containing tempting pastries was beside the teapot and to all intents and purpose, it was a scene of village perfection. An afternoon tea by moonlight.

Until Jake looked at their faces. To a one, the four wore thunderous expressions, and Merryn's arms were folded tightly across her chest. He need only see Fionn, her mobile clamped to her ear behind the counter, to know that she was the source of the trouble.

What is it now?

Jake strode in, rubbing his hands together. He did his best to smile. "Evening, everyone. You must all be tired, having to shoot so late? Fionn, can these lovely people be allowed home now?"

It was David who spoke, one of the few occasions Jake had heard him speak. "Mr. Brantham, we thought we'd be dealing with you, but —"

Zoe looked at Merryn, then at Jake, and said angrily, "This isn't the sort of program we want. I want to get out of this contract. She's upset Mum with all her talk!"

Merryn heaved a sob. "I said it wasn't to be talked of, I *said*, then *she* told me there wouldn't be a wedding if we didn't, and when she said *reconstruction in a water tank* — !"

Jake's newfound calm collided with a rapidly advancing wave of rage. He shoved his fingers into his mouth and emitted a shrill whistle that could've been heard in Taunton. "That's *it*. Fionn, get over here now!"

"*Sympathetic mood-building reconstruction,*" Fionn corrected. Petroc said nothing, but patted Merryn's shoulder, the gesture as gentle as he was hulking. Fionn pocketed her phone and looked at Jake. Then she clicked her fingers, but she remained where she stood. "This is the Christmas special. Think Noel in a children's ward with a sled full of presents!"

"Yes, Christmas special. What's supposed to be festive about forcing a family to revisit something as painful as—as—?" Jake threw up his hands in frustration. "Fuck me, Fionn, do you not have an ounce of cocking compassion? And I told you, it's not to go in the program in the first fucking place!"

Merryn started to cry in earnest now, and Jake shook his head as he offered her his hanky. Petroc put his arm round her shoulders too, hushing her gently as Zoe rose to her feet and addressed Jake.

"She's horrible! I wouldn't have anything to do with her if I was you." She jabbed a finger toward Fionn and dashed away her own tears with the back of her hand. "Because she's a cow! And if I knew a cow like her, I wouldn't want anybody to think she was a mate of mine!"

Fionn emerged from behind the counter, shaking her head as though this was all too much. She told them, "It's reality telly, love. You don't get the wedding of your dreams without a few tears."

"They're meant to cry over my crap attempt at Cornish pasties," Jake said, "or because the cake topper gets trodden on and someone replaces it with Barbie and Ken! Not because you're forcing everyone to relive trauma! It's not happening on my show, Fionn, and you know that because I've already said no!"

"Jake, have an eclair and calm down." Fionn plucked up an eclair from the counter and threw it. It landed short, splattering on the polished wooden floor.

And as Locryn's voice suddenly thundered across the café, Jake knew once and for all that even the king of Cornwall could be pushed too far.

"That's enough!" Everyone looked at him and he blinked, apparently as surprised as they were. When he spoke again, his usual calm was restored. "Consider yourself barred, Fionn. You've upset my friends, shown no respect to my café *or* my eclair and— Please leave. And before you ask, no, I won't sign a release so you can put this on air."

Jake clapped his hand on Locryn's shoulder. "Nice one," he whispered. Then he looked up at Fionn. "Go on, sling your hook. We're having a meeting tomorrow, us two. And to borrow one of your favorite telly phrases, *you won't want to miss it!*"

Fionn shrugged and said, "I'll have to check my schedule. I've got a full day tomorrow." Then she put her handbag over her shoulder and strode across the café toward them. When she reached Locryn she told him, "I think they'd go a bundle over you in the States. If you fancy it—"

"Goodnight," he replied. "I won't ask you to clean up the mess you've made."

With a cheeky wink, Fionn turned away. She was a picture of composure until her spike of a heel came down in the splattered eclair then, with a shriek of, "Fuck me, you fu—" Fionn flew up into the air and landed with a *smack* against the floorboards.

"Ooof! You want a good pair of stout wellies for Cornwall, Fionn! Not those spiky things!" Jake started to laugh, but as he did, he noticed that Fionn's leg was stuck out at an angle that no human limb had any right to be at.

Oh fuck it.

"My sushi!" she wailed. "Bloody hell!"

"Someone ring an ambulance!" Jake had done his first-aid training and knew a broken leg when he saw one. "Petroc, you take Merryn and the happy couple to the pub, okay? Locryn and me'll see to this."

"Should I?" Petroc asked Merryn, "Fancy a drink, Merryn? Oh, and the youngsters, of course."

"I'd love a drink." Merryn shook out her hair, and with that one gesture was the sassiest woman in Porthavel. She looked over at Fionn and rolled her eyes. "Shame you weren't filming *that*," she said as she got up from her seat.

"Weren't we?" Fionn asked the cameraman, who shook his head in response. "Call it a night, boys. And, Jake, pass me my phone. I can't walk but I can still Skype."

Jake shook his head as he passed the phone to her. "Try not to move, okay?"

He took out his own phone and rang nine-nine-nine. The remaining crew began to pack away for the evening, taking down the lights and folding down the reflectors, but not one of them approached Fionn to see how she was.

"Tell them I need the air ambulance, and some gorgeous guys in uniform," Fionn instructed with a saucy wink.

A quarter of an hour later, the beat of helicopter blades heralded the arrival of the air ambulance.

Jake whispered to Locryn, "Surprised she's not being taken away on a broomstick, the old witch!"

Fionn hadn't wasted a moment though, and was instead making phone calls to one high-powered executive after the other, discussing filming schedules and money, transport and star names. Only when the café door opened and the *'gorgeous guys in uniform'* appeared did she put her phone away.

"Knights in armor," she called. "Thank God!"

As Fionn was assessed, all the time asking the medics if they'd considered reality TV, Locryn was tidying the café. He looked so domestic, so at home, Jake thought. But still gorgeous. Jake waited with a mop to clear up the squashed eclair. He didn't want Locryn to have to do it, especially not when the sight of wasted baked goods were upsetting to him.

"I'm going to Plymouth," Fionn advised Jake. "Not for sushi, sadly. Can you manage without me for a day?"

"It might be a little bit longer than a day," one of the paramedics told him. "Your wife's leg looks pretty bad."

"She's not my wife, she's my producer," Jake said coldly. "Don't hurry back, Fionn. You take your time and get that leg nice and better."

It couldn't have happened to a nicer person.

Locryn handed the helicopter crew a large box of delicacies and, with Fionn still barking into her mobile, they stretchered her from the café. Before the door closed one of the men darted back inside and asked Jake, "Can I get your autograph for my wife? And can you write *fucking scallop* on it?"

Jake grabbed a napkin with Locryn's carefully printed italicized name on it. He scribbled *sod off with your fucking rancid scallop!* and signed underneath.

"There you go, now fuck off!" Jake laughed. With a cheery slap to Jake's shoulder the man departed, leaving Jake and Locryn alone.

Jake puffed out his chest. "Well, that spares me the job of sacking her from the series."

"I've never barred anyone before." Locryn sighed, surveying the café. "How on earth did you end up saddled with her?"

"She seemed okay when I started working for her, but the more successful she's become, the more terrifying she's got. She's a fucking media monster, and she'll probably do well for herself and exploit every last fucker in her path." Jake put the last finishing touches to his mopping job and admired the clean floor. "You'd never know the creator of *My Haunted Dildo* had broken her leg on the floor just there, would you?"

"*My Haunted*— That can't be real?"

"The dildo or the program?" Jake asked. "She really did produce that show, and, yeah, it made me question a lot of things. Such as, *what the fuck is wrong with people who watch this fucking twaddle?*"

Locryn turned off the main lights, bathing the café in the gentle glow of the soft bulbs behind the counter. Then he said, "And kneading dough can actually be very sensuous, I'll have you know. More sensuous than a haunted dildo, that's for sure!"

"Sensuous? So that's why you do it in your dressing gown?" Jake smiled at Locryn. "I don't think I've ever got the knack of kneading, sensuous or otherwise."

"I couldn't sleep the other night on account of this infuriating, bad-tempered, gorgeous, leather jacket-wearing Londoner who'd swaggered into the village and kicked up a stink." Locryn pursed his lips, then smiled. "Kneading took my mind off him until he turned up at my cottage and took his clothes off."

Jake laughed awkwardly. "Timed that well, didn't I? Did the kneading help a bit?"

"It *did*. Right up until you wet T-shirted your way into my kitchen." Locryn ruffled his hand through his hair and told Jake, "And if you don't have the knack of kneading, I'll be happy to teach you."

"Will you?" Jake waggled his fingers at him. "Have I got the right tools?"

Locryn took off his coat and was already unfastening his cufflinks when he assured Jake, "It's all a question of what you do with them."

Jake peeled off his leather jacket, revealing his fitted T-shirt beneath. "It's not wet this evening. Is that okay?"

"I'm sure you'll do." Locryn rolled up his sleeves then crossed to the sink. As he washed his hands he glanced over his shoulder and asked Jake, "What about the Merryn and Petroc conundrum, then? You know about them?"

Jake went over to the worktop and leaned against it. "Yeah. Merryn told me they'd been dating but Petroc just won't… He's lost his friend, he's lost his wife, and I suppose he got scared when he realized he was getting close to Merryn. Maybe he thought he'd lose her too?"

As Locryn spoke he moved around the kitchen, adding ingredients to a large mixing bowl. What surprised Jake wasn't that, but that he made no effort to measure them. In went flour and salt, and more, as though on instinct. An instinct that Jake had never seen quite as well-honed in anyone except himself.

"Wouldn't it be wonderful if Petroc and Merryn could be at the wedding as the couple they both really want to be?" He was at the fridge now, scooping butter into the mixture. "Does matchmaking ever really work? What do you think? You're the worldly city chap, I'm just a baker from Cornwall."

"Matchmaking? Do people still do that? They use apps now!" Jake laughed. "But I like what you're saying. And now I don't have a producer on the show. Shall we have some nice scenes with Merryn and Petroc together, showing the viewers around Porthavel, that sort of thing? Write some dates for them into the show, without them *thinking* they're dates?"

Locryn grinned. "Yes! They could have afternoon tea here and talk about the progress that's being made on the boat." He held up his hand and added, "That's not me trying to get in on the gig, don't worry. It's your show, but it's a chance to bring two good people together. Since Zoe works here and Merryn did before her, it seems like a good place, don't you think?"

"It's a fucking brilliant idea, Loc! Let's do it!" Jake clapped his hands. "Are you licensed? We can sneak in a cheeky champers afternoon tea too!"

"Am I licensed? Bubbly afternoon teas are my summer staple!" He returned to the worktop where Jake was leaning and began to mix the ingredients. "Petroc's camera shy but Merryn's a natural. If anyone can put him at his ease, it's her. People are going to love her, aren't they? The West Country's answer to Liz Taylor!"

"Just a bit! I'm glad you were the one to say it though. Lovely woman. And the last thing we need is to see her in tears on screen." Jake bobbed his head. "You know, I think we make better producers than Fionn. We get a romantic wedding, *and* we get a romance!"

"I never would've had you down as a romantic." He glanced across at Jake, a little too casual when he asked, "And there's no handsome fellow waiting for you in London?"

"Nope." Jake shook his head. "I'm—I've been too busy. I've had the odd bloke here and there, obviously, but I don't have a boyfriend or anything like that."

Locryn said nothing, but the look on his face left Jake in no doubt that he was happy with the answer. For a little while they fell silent, Jake watching Locryn work, the enjoyment of watching someone so accomplished something that had never left him. Nowadays it was usually Jake who was the expert, but this was Locryn's world, bunting and all.

Eventually Locryn scattered a handful of flour across the worktop. Then he looked up and asked, "Ready?"

Jake rubbed his hands together. "Yeah! Where do you want me?"

"Watch me for a couple of minutes, then we'll swap places." Locryn tipped the bowl and the dough landed on the worktop with considerably more grace than Fionn had employed when she had hit the floor. Then he put his hands on the dough and began to knead.

And all Jake could do was watch.

Locryn's hands were large but elegant and they kneaded the dough with all the care of a caress. There was more tenderness in the way Locryn handled his culinary creations than there had been in some of the lovers Jake had known. He looked like an artist, dusted with flour rather than paint, and it was mesmerizing. Gone was the prim, buttoned-up man who had recoiled from Jake's efforts at Cornish pasties and in his place was an artist entirely at ease and at one with his work.

There was plenty of passion in Locryn Trevorrow, Jake realized.

Jake leaned his head on his arm, watching, observing not just Locryn's hands and the dough he was kneading, but the movement of the muscles in his arms and the smile in his eyes as he worked.

This'd make great telly.

They needed more close-ups on Locryn's face though. Far, far more. Then Jake could watch at his leisure and enjoy the love in Locryn's expression when he was doing what every baker does naturally.

After a few minutes had passed, Locryn looked toward Jake and smiled. Then he took a step away from the worktop and brushed the palms of his hands against each other.

"Your turn, Chef. Show me how the man with the Michelin stars does it."

"Erm…badly?" Jake laughed as he took up position. He pressed his fingertips into the dough and it was warm from Locryn's hands, then he started to knead it but… "Am I more *pummeling* than *kneading*?"

Locryn leaned his elbow on the worktop beside Jake and watched, hovering there like a fretful parent. Now and again Jake had the impression that he was about to speak, but he remained silent until Jake spoke to him. Then he said, "Don't be angry at it. Think of it as though you're giving a very special massage. Savor it. *Experience* it."

"Feel the dough?" Jake asked, remembering his demand to Locryn live on television. *'Feel the meat.'* But then, he hadn't thought Locryn capable of comparing kneading bread to a massage of all things. "I reckon I can manage a special massage." Jake ran his hand over the curve of the dough and whispered, "Look at how round it is, like a buttock. If I pretend that a saucy baker is lying on his bed in his storybook cottage, his bottom on view, all warm from the sun coming through the opened curtains, and I stroke it just like this, then I…"

And with both hands, Jake grasped the dough, then folded it over on itself before pulling and stretching. Then he rolled it into a ball over the floury surface and pressed his knuckles in, rocking against it.

Fucking hell.

Locryn was watching his hands, his fretful expression replaced by something rather different. His lips were slightly parted, his blue eyes dancing as he lifted them to meet Jake's gaze. Another moment passed, the air crackling between them. Then Locryn cleared his throat and asked, "Do you know many saucy bakers?"

"No, just this one guy. He mentioned something about his cream horn." Jake quirked his eyebrow at him. "He's so fucking hot. He's got these strong arms…"

"Strong arms help with the kneading…amongst other things," Locryn replied, his voice husky. Then he moved to stand behind Jake, so close that the electricity in the air seemed more fizzy than ever. Those strong arms reached around Jake and Locryn entwined their fingers together atop the dough. He was so close to Jake that they were almost touching, almost embracing, Locryn's cologne filling the space, his hands sure. "Not too rough, not too gentle. Just think of your saucy baker."

Then, as if they were one, he guided Jake's hands into the dough.

"I'm thinking of him. I'm struggling to think of anything else." Jake half-closed his eyes, breathing in Locryn's cologne and the scent of the dough. "Locryn, you bastard, you've made baking sexy!"

"I told you," Locryn whispered, his lips close to Jake's ear, "I have plenty of passion. I just don't always know how to let it out."

"I can help you with that," Jake promised. "I hope."

"Tell me more about this naked baker of yours?"

"He's got big blue eyes, the sort of blue I imagine the sea is here in the summer. And they sparkle. You know when the sunlight's on the waves and it's so bright you should look away but you can't?" Jake chuckled. "And I forget to swear my head off when I'm around him."

Locryn laughed gently and Jake felt the slightest brush of his dark-blond hair against his cheek. It must be an accident, he told himself, even as Locryn placed a kiss against the side of his neck, as tentative as it was soft.

"Oh, God, Locryn, do that again." Jake moaned. "Please."

Jake wasn't used to such slow teasing. Men and women flung themselves at him, even if Jake wasn't interested. And now, that slight touch of Locryn's hair sent desire singing through Jake's blood.

The second kiss was as tender as the first, as filled with promise and heat. Their hands were unmoving now, fingers still linked.

Jake slowly, slowly turned his head, whispering, "I want to kiss you, Locryn..."

"Be my guest," was the gentle reply as Locryn's lips brushed against his.

Jake's lips tingled at the touch of Locryn's soft mouth and he only danced his lips against Locryn's. He could have clasped Locryn with his dough-covered hands, he could have pressed him with the weight of his body to the wall and kissed him with all the fierceness of his passion. But instead, their kiss was as gentle as a murmur.

And when it ended, Locryn's smile was gentler still.

"You're not nearly so terrifying as I thought you might be," was his conclusion.

"Terrifying, me? I'm a cute little lamb, really." Jake rubbed the tip of his nose against Locryn's. "Well, I am when I'm holding back. And I *will* hold back, if you want me to."

"What I *want* is another kiss, Chef."

"And you will have one!" Jake ghosted his lips over Locryn's then, with a little more fire than before, kissed him. What would Locryn make of it? Jake didn't want to send him reeling away in horror. There was something almost delicate about him, a gentleness that Jake had mistaken for that same prim quality that Locryn had accused himself of. In a world filled with Fionns, he was like a breath of fresh coastal air.

But he didn't seem shocked at all. Instead he met the heat in Jake's kiss with his own, his arms tightening around his waist.

Jake cupped Locryn's face, dough stuck to his fingers, kissing Locryn with increasing fire. This was Locryn Trevorrow, for heaven's sake, the quiet, meek, *sugar* and *fiddlesticks* baker.

It's always the quiet ones.

And that definitely wasn't a rolling pin that Jake could feel pressed against him. The image of Locryn naked on the bed returned, but naked anywhere would be just as wonderful. Even naked on a flour-scattered worktop in a cozy café by the sea.

Jake slid his hand down to Locryn's buttocks and squeezed the firm flesh. A special massage? Jake would happily give it, and —

"Ahem, sorry."

Jake looked up and found himself eye to eye with one of the show's runners, a keen young man in a track suit. "What the fuck?"

Locryn stepped back then scooped up the well-kneaded dough, bustling away across the kitchen as though nothing irregular had happened at all. Nothing irregular that had left a clear and doughy handprint on his tempting bottom.

"I thought I'd left my clipboard in here." The runner nodded over to the serving hatch. "Ah, there it is!"

Jake laughed. "Grab it and sod off, and I'll see you tomorrow!"

Locryn called breezily, "I would've looked after it. Goodnight!"

"'Night!" The runner grabbed the clipboard, then his eyes widened in surprise. "Mr. Trevorrow, you've got a—on your—erm…"

Jake willed Locryn to take the hint but instead he looked at the young man, his brow furrowed in confusion. Then he glanced over his shoulder and blushed a deep red.

"Clipboard," Locryn told the runner with a bashful smile. "And grab a bun if you like."

Terrible choice of words.

The runner glanced at Jake and Jake furiously rubbed a cloth over his hand. "Thanks, Mr. Trevorrow!"

And as the runner hurried off, Jake saw him pick up a cream horn.

It would be.

The door closed with a tinkle from the bell and the two men were alone again. Locryn drew in a deep breath then said with just a hint of mischief, "Oops!"

"Well, I wonder what they'll be talking about in the guest house tonight?" Jake said as he picked the last bits of dough off his fingers.

"I'll deliver the loaf there once it's baked." Locryn laughed. "It's the least I can do to go with the gossip."

"The sensual loaf? It's a baguette, right?"

"I'm afraid it's a standard white farmhouse. They're perfect for teaching technique," Locryn told him, tidying the worktop. "But a standard white farmhouse has plenty to recommend it too. Shall we have a wander up to your place? I'll bring the saucy loaf along and bake it tonight."

Jake zipped himself back into his leather jacket. "I won't get lost in the dark with my very own local guide. I wonder what stray I'll find on the way tonight? I'm hoping for a donkey!"

"I'll introduce you to mine. They love making friends."

Locryn put the dough carefully back into its bowl and covered it over with a tea towel, its jaunty sunflower print exactly what Jake had already learned to expect of him. He put on his coat and picked up the bowl, then balanced a small box on top of it and said, "Ready, Chef?"

"Ready, Baker!"

"Chef and Baker." Locryn opened the café door onto the moonlit village. Jake could hear the soft lapping of the waves down on the beach, somewhere in the darkness. "That sounds like it deserves a Michelin star or two."

"Oh, at least three!" Jake grinned. He was surprised to see Locryn offer his arm, ever the gentleman. Even Locryn looked surprised as he looked down at his own arm.

"Go on," he teased. "Nobody's going to see. Your fearsome reputation's safe with me."

"Well, if you insist!" Jake looped his arm through Locryn's. He wasn't used to wandering about arm in arm in public, he was more of a stride-along-hands-in-pockets sort of man. "Are you sure you're not seducing me, Mr. Trevorrow?"

Locryn chuckled and admitted, "I wouldn't know where to start. But I do have a little something for you in this mysterious cake box, which I hope might do the seductive job for me."

"It's not your haunted dildo, is it? No, hopefully you don't have one of those!"

"I don't need one!" Locryn's laughter left Jake in no doubt that he was very much in on that particular joke. He nodded toward the box that rested atop the tea towel. "Go on, have a look."

Jake unhooked their arms and opened the box. There inside it, innocent until it became an innuendo, was a cream horn.

"What's the best way to tackle your cream horn, Loc? Shove it all in at once or do you suggest a gentle nibble?"

"*My* cream horn specifically? Never take a bite and try to suck out the cream—it won't end well." Locryn blinked, all innocence as he considered the question. "I suggest a gentle nibble to start with. Take your time. Savor it, let your lips caress it, taste it. And when you're feeling confident, you can really settle down and enjoy it as enthusiastically as you like!"

Jake swallowed. His own cream horn had returned to his trousers. Locryn, in bed, stretched naked across a chintz quilt. *What a picture that is.*

"Well, you know me, I'm enthusiastic when it comes to food!"

"I imagine you have a healthy appetite." Locryn glanced down, casual as anything. "I do do a rather good baguette, if I say so myself."

"I know, one of your baguettes was pressing against me earlier!" Jake closed the box and linked his arm with Locryn's again. They strolled along the harbor front, the only living souls as far as the eye could see, though Jake could hear seagulls crying overhead. "I was really fucking impressed by how fast your dough could rise."

The Cornishman gave a laugh and admitted, "You had exactly the right kneading technique. How could it do anything *but* rise? We should practice together again, don't you think?"

"Yeah, there's more I need to learn. *Much* more."

"And maybe we'll share a Horlicks as well as a cream horn," Locryn suggested, as saucy now as he had been prim earlier. It suited him though, Jake liked it. "I've been thinking about those pasties of yours. We need a neutral tasting panel, don't we?"

"We do. What do you suggest?" Jake remembered the stacks of plastic boxes containing his hopeless prototypes. They paused and looked out through the bristling masts and fluttering pennants toward the open ocean, where stars were reflected on its surface like twinkling Christmas lights.

"I'll put them out in the café tomorrow, free of charge." The café? The place where Locryn supposedly created the most exquisite Cornish cream teas known to man? "And I'll label them as *tasty pasties,* because if I put *Cornish pasties*, you won't have a fair hearing. We can leave a little comment box and people can give their opinions. What do you think?"

Jake ran his hand back through his hair. *Is this wise?* "Oh, why not? But you have to read the comments first, and edit out the ones that might make me want to throw things."

"I behaved badly earlier. But I *am* the king of Cornwall. And you *are* Captain Jake, they tell me."

"Yeah, I am! Watch out or I'll make you walk the plank on my pirate ship!"

Locryn chanced a kiss to Jake's cheek and they strolled on, turning away from the harbor and into the narrow streets. They walked in contented silence between brightly painted cottages where soft lights glowed, catching the occasional snatch of a television program or the sound of laughter from within. It felt as though Porthavel was theirs and theirs alone, as though the pirate ship wedding might not turn into a catastrophe after all.

What would you call this feeling?

With a glance toward Locryn, Jake realized that it was contentment. There was no stress, no sense that it could all go wrong, just a peaceful sensation, as comforting as floating in a warm ocean. Was he finally relaxing?

Kneading dough *was* magic.

"Tell me about Jake," Locryn said. "How on earth did you end up with boats as your gimmick when you drive round in a London bus on your programs?"

"Quite simple, really. The cheapest place I could find when I decided to set up my own restaurant was a retired canal boat café! The guys from the last kitchen I'd worked in took the piss and called me *Captain Jake*." Jake laughed, thinking back to the faithful *Lucy May* on Regent's Canal. To her traditional paintwork and the geraniums in salvaged buckets, to the small kitchen where he'd somehow managed to cook for thousands of people and made his name. "And after that, as you know, I ended up with an old party boat on the Thames. And I was set."

Locryn laughed and said, "I wasn't expecting that at all. How marvelous! I can't imagine the sheer hard work that must've gone into a success like yours. No wonder you ended up being such a sweary so-and-so."

"Hard work *and* luck!" Jake said. "*Lucy May* got a hole in her bottom — *don't* laugh! And I would've lost her, I would've lost *everything,* if my canal boat family hadn't leapt on board and bailed out!"

"Do you still have her?"

"She's back to being a café again now. I let one of my staff have her. They're doing quite well. Great coffee!"

"And leaf tea, I hope." As they reached a bend in the road, Locryn paused. He turned and Jake turned with him, realizing as he did that they were now above Porthavel. Below them the village was laid out like a miniature, clustered around the harbor that gave it life and had, in the eye of the storm, taken it away. Locryn sighed softly and told Jake, "This is my family. My publisher and the TV people think I'm mad because I haven't turned what I have into an empire, but then it wouldn't be me, would it? Your restaurants are all *you.* That's not luck, it's passion."

"Passion and being a tenacious bastard." Jake put his arm around Locryn's shoulder. "It's a lovely place, Porthavel. I won't lie, I cursed being sent here to start with. Well, okay, as you know, I passed out! But it's grown on me, day by day, even if the weather did its best to get rid of me."

"God, that was awful, I was worried sick." Locryn tipped his head and let it rest on Jake's shoulder. "I rang

Fionn to ask how you were and she said you'd picked up food poisoning from a rival's restaurant. She didn't tell me who, but…not a very good advert for them!"

Jake could've clung to the lie, could've pretended that he was an indomitable male who never had a day off sick. But that wouldn't have been true.

"Look, you should probably know, that wasn't food poisoning."

He felt the soft sweep of Locryn's hair as the baker lifted his head and told him, "If it was the goujons, it's okay to tell me. I won't bolt."

"No, it wasn't that." Jake took a deep breath. Precious few people knew what was really wrong with him, and even Jake wasn't that sure. "To cut a long story short, it's stress. Boring old stress. At least, my doctor says so. My blood pressure's a bit too high and…well, she reckoned that spending a couple of months in Cornwall was one of the best things I could do, but she didn't factor in a pirate ship, a storm or my producer pissing everyone off and breaking her leg!"

"Stress?" Locryn pronounced the word as though it were the most extreme obscenity he could think of. Maybe it wasn't a word he was familiar with, living here in this storybook village, living a charmed life. "Then you're talking to the right man. And you're in the right place to give it the heave-ho."

"Seems like it," Jake replied, cautious. He didn't want to jinx anything. "Maybe I should take up breadmaking? It takes so long to do, and I'm thinking, maybe that's good. Nice and slow. None of this — " Jake clicked his fingers, "*Come on, come on, hurry up, out the way, get on with it* nonsense which is all I ever hear in London."

"But I'll bet you're putting plenty of pressure on yourself too, aren't you? You're the very best at what you do, that's not an accident."

Jake shrugged. He didn't want to admit it, but Locryn was right. "I don't know how to stop, that's my problem. But I wouldn't have come as far as I have if I'd just sat on my arse and picked my nose."

"The thing with being the best—and I know, because I've got one of *the best* for a father—is that it's addiction." He put his arm around Jake's waist, his hand resting on Jake's hip. "You have to keep on surpassing yourself. Or rather, you *think* you do."

Jake wondered what on earth Locryn meant. "But aren't I meant to? I can't go *backwards,* Loc! I can't close everything down and go back to the *Lucy May.* Or to jobbing in other people's kitchens."

"No, but you can take a bit of time off and actually enjoy what you've struggled to create, can't you?"

Can I?

The idea had never occurred to Jake before and he stood there in stunned surprise. Vague notions drifted in his mind but he couldn't grasp any of them long enough to turn them into words. Instead, his mouth moved as if he was trying to speak, but no sound came out.

Until he managed to say, "I'd never thought of that before."

"You could always think about it now," Locryn suggested. His head settled against Jake's shoulder once more. "There's a lot to be said for looking at the ocean when you want to put things into perspective."

The edge of the sea was illuminated by the harbor lights, and beyond the ocean was dark, nothing that Jake could see but he could feel it, somehow. And when he closed his eyes, he could hear it—the roll and splash of the waves drawing back and forth on the sand, the chuckle of water against barnacled hulls, the distant rippling cry of night birds somewhere in the dark.

The sea didn't care how many restaurants Jake ran, how many Michelin stars he'd accumulated, how many top reviews or television shows he had to his name. But it didn't leave Jake feeling bleak. Instead, something else stirred inside him, a connection to something infinite, something that was inside him as much as it was out there in the sea. An echo in his genes, perhaps, of a time before people, when his ancestors had lived under the waves.

They stood there in silence together, nothing pushing Jake to move, nobody clamoring at him for an answer, for a signature, for a moment in the limelight. Looking out over the edge of the land, as so many had before him over the centuries, he didn't feel like '*TV's Jake Brantham*' anymore. He felt like the young man who had dreamed of glory, who had lain awake planning elaborate menus and whiled away his weekends experimenting in his mum and dad's tiny kitchen with its old gas stove and the grill that never lit on the first try.

And it felt wonderful.

All the tension had gone from Jake's body and his shoulders sagged. Not in a defeated way, but now Jake realized that it was his stress that had kept him going, had kept every muscle in his body taut.

And he didn't need it. He didn't need to be on point and raring to go when he should be raring to get to sleep. There wouldn't *be* any restaurants if he kept blanking out.

"Yeah, maybe I do feel relaxed. A bit," Jake said.

"And Dorothy's waiting for a cuddle from her dad," Locryn reminded him. "Let's get you safely home to your little girl, and I can pick up those London pasties of yours ready for our unfocused focus group tomorrow."

As his house came into view, the stones white with moonlight, Jake wondered how he could possibly have ended up lost the previous evening. It seemed like such a straightforward walk out of the village, but the ferocity of the storm had changed the very landscape itself. And he was glad it had, because he wasn't sure he would be arm in arm with Locryn right now if it hadn't. It felt oddly like coming home.

When he opened the front door, Dorothy trotted into the hallway then flopped down on the floor and rolled about.

"That's quite a welcome!" Jake crouched down to stroke her, then she rubbed herself against Locryn's legs. "It's good to know she likes both of us!"

"She's a lovely little thing. I wonder where she came from." Locryn stooped so he could scratch behind Dorothy's velvety ears. "I've had a wonderful night, in spite of the broken leg. Thank you, Jake, for not thinking I was an insufferable snob."

Jake gently touched Locryn's cheek before settling a soft kiss on his lips.

"I don't suppose—" Jake shook his head. No, he couldn't ask Locryn to stay. It was far too soon. In London he could start and finish a relationship within a week, but not in Porthavel. "I'll help you load up Betsy."

With the box containing the cream horn safely on the kitchen table under Dorothy's, Locryn and Jake piled Betsy's basket with the pasties, and nestled among the stacked containers was the bowl of dough, still covered with its bright tea towel. As Locryn stood at the door, holding the bike and its precious cargo steady, Jake knew that this was the right thing to do. Locryn was right too. Some things were better savored.

"I think that's that." Locryn smiled, chancing a cheeky ring of the bicycle bell. "Give my love to Fionn when you hear from her, and I'll make sure everyone that comes in gets a pasty or a squab."

"Don't tell them I made them. I want them to be honest." Although they probably would be honest, especially if they knew they were Jake Brantham creations. Jake gave Locryn one last hug. "I'll see you around tomorrow then?"

He nodded. "Definitely. Why don't I pop along to your galleon once the café's closed? I can see how things are going and we can look at the feedback together."

"I'd like that. And maybe I can cook dinner?"

"I'll never say no to that. But don't forget that cream horn, because Dorothy won't!" Locryn leaned closer and kissed Jake softly on the lips. "Sweet dreams, Captain Jake."

"Night-night!" Jake waved Locryn off, and once he'd rattled off across the uneven farmyard courtyard, Jake stood in the quiet for a while, enjoying the calm.

Then he went inside and was just in time to see Dorothy, claws extended, trying to take the lid off the cream horn's box.

"That's how we'll fall out, young lady!"

Jake settled her for the night, then he headed upstairs with a cup of cocoa and the cream horn. It might not've been cocktails in a West End nightclub, but it seemed a much better way to end the day.

Chapter Ten

Jake passed a busy day on the pirate ship, but although they were one person down, they seemed to progress far better without Fionn around. And that was even after Jake had dispatched a runner to the nearest supermarket to stock up on whatever Dorothy might need.

He'd put the word around the Porthavelans who were helping on the ship about his mystery cat, and none of them knew where Dorothy could have come from either. Perhaps she was one of life's unsolvable enigmas, and now that Jake was oddly chilled, he decided it didn't matter that much.

It was just after lunchtime when his mobile rang and there on the screen he saw Fionn's name. Only then did it occur to him that he hadn't been in touch to find out how she was.

Jake went out on the deck, where it was quiet and no television cameras were ready to swoop into his face. "Fionn? Hey, got your feet up while we're all working our arses off?"

"You don't know the half of it, sweetie." She laughed, though, so perhaps it wasn't all bad. "It turns out that I've made a total balls of my leg and the medicine here is a little too Cornish for my tastes so I'm off home tomorrow, laid out across the backseat of a limo, to see my little chap on Harley Street. So you really need to get your bum over here before I go, because we have serious business to discuss, hon."

Do I or do I not bring her a chocolate eclair?

Yes. Of course I should.

Jake looked at his watch. He could fit everything in, he didn't need to run about. "I'll be over when I can. I could pop by this evening when we've finished up here?"

But what about Locryn's plans to visit the ship? What about dinner?

I can do it.

"Whatever you like. I'm about to have a pedi then I'm doing nothing except taking phone calls about a certain *shocking* chef show." Fionn laughed again, a laugh honed by a hundred cigarettes. "And tell lovely Loc that he can relax. I won't be calling my lawyers. In fact, I've just closed a deal with Sky for *When Bakeries Go Bad*, so I owe him a thanks for the inspo! People falling on their faces and getting a jam doughnut in the eye, that kind of rubbish. They've got a cute footballer who's desperate to break into telly so he's going to present it. It'll soak up the pissed dad audience on Boxing Day."

Jake rolled his eyes. "So you didn't pitch *When TV Producers Throw Baked Goods About Like a Toddler Having a Tantrum?* Maybe the title needs some work, but still."

"Working on it. Got it jotted on the iPad as *Telly Tantrum Traumas*. Look, Jakey, I'm going to have to fly, the pedi girl's loitering about like a spare prick at a wedding." From somewhere in the hospital, Jake heard the sound of nervous laughter. "I'll see you tonight, cap'n, if you can tear yourself away from the hot baker!"

"Yeah, see you. Bye."

Jake ended the call. Just think, Fionn off to London in search of opioids and weeks, if not the entire shoot, in peace. With a smile, Jake trotted back inside the ship and got on with his work.

* * * *

The sky was growing dark outside when Jake heard footsteps descending into the galleon. Then a plummy voice called, "Permission to come aboard?"

"Come on in!" Jake bounded up to Locryn and put his arm around his shoulder. He couldn't wait to show Locryn what they'd been up to. "What do you think? Looks a bit different, doesn't? No more scary 1970s bistro curtains. I do like a slatted shutter."

"Good heavens!" Locryn blinked and looked around. It was still a building site of course, and lights and cameras were positioned between dust sheets and paint pots to capture every moment of the renovations, but there was no denying that the garish pirate ship was well on its way to becoming something Jake could put his name to. "You and the Porthavelans have really been working hard. Look at this place!"

"Are you a little bit impressed, Locryn?" Jake chuckled. "It's still a ship, but it's...well, it's getting there. How'd you get on today?"

"Well, I delivered the loaf to your crew." He put his arm around Jake's waist and peered around the ship again. They were alone now, work having finished for the day, and Locryn chanced a kiss to Jake's cheek. "And I gave away all the pasties. Any word on Fionn's leg?"

"Pop a cork, because Fionn is buggering off back to London tomorrow!" Jake hopped from foot to foot. His glee made him immune to his concerns about how well the pasties had gone down with the locals. "I'll have to go and see her in Plymouth in a bit, but if you don't mind the drive, we can grab something there if you like? Or I can knock up a quick something when I get back."

Locryn's eyes widened and he said, "She's leaving? Oh, that's wonderful news. People're going to be *very* happy to hear that." He seemed to realize what he'd said then and quickly composed a look of sympathy. "Obviously, I hope she's not in any pain, but... Well, she's not an easy lady to get along with."

"It's all right," Jake said. "You can be glad about her misfortune because if it had happened to anyone else, that steel-hearted cow would've exploited it."

"I've got an idea." Locryn clapped his hands. "If you're dead set on it we can have something spiffy in Plymouth, but I don't want you to have to cook after that drive so how about when we get back, we call in on Captain Cod and get a good old chippy tea? My treat. Then we can look through the feedback forms and stuff our faces all in one go?"

"That's brilliant! I won't be in Plymouth long, besides, I don't want to leave little Dot on her own. Ready to go?"

He nodded. "Unless you'd rather I stay here and cat-sit? Up to you, I wouldn't mind if you're worried about leaving her. I'll give her some supper and we can have a bit of a play."

"Stay, Loc, it's fine. I'm sure you'd rather not see Fionn ever again! And especially not cranky with a broken leg." Jake laughed. "To be honest, I'd rather not either, but there's some stuff to sort out with her, then I can draw a line under it."

Locryn smiled and his cheeks colored a little. He'd been caught out, and he knew it. "Can I borrow your keys? And I'll make sure the table's all set, ready for our fish and chip supper when you get home, if you don't mind picking it up in the chefmobile?"

Jake fished the keys out of his pocket and passed them to Locryn. The fob, presumably from a local souvenir shop, was of a large enamel crab holding a flag that said *Porthavel* on it. "Thanks, Loc. I'll bring you a sausage with your chippy tea too as a thank you!"

"How can I say no to an offer like that?" He put the keys into his coat pocket. "Let me know when you're on your way home. I'll make sure everything's ready."

Jake slipped his arms around Locryn. "You know I'd rather stay with you instead of go off to see the Telly Gorgon?"

"I sort of hoped you would." He kissed the tip of Jake's nose. "But don't we want to be absolutely sure that she's really gone?"

"We do. Short of shoving her off a cliff!" Jake hugged Locryn tightly, then did what he'd been thinking about all day. He brought his lips to Locryn's and kissed him. It was the sort of kiss that he knew would give him the fortitude he needed to tell Fionn that her services were no longer required, which she had probably guessed. Even better, he had an excuse now too. She could hardly focus on producing the show when she was facing rehabilitation for a broken leg, after all. It just wouldn't be fair.

"Don't be too long." Locryn smiled and escorted him up onto the deck. "We'll be missing you."

Reluctantly, Jake got behind the wheel of his car and waved to Locryn as he set off. It was getting dark so he saw little of the beautiful coastline, but he focused on the relaxation music playing in his car. He used to have rock and rap blaring out at top volume, but he was now getting into his forest sounds playlist, although the ear-splitting whoop of a monkey that came on halfway through nearly scared him witless.

But it made him laugh. Because it was a monkey, and imagine taking a monkey into a hospital to see Fionn, and imagine how shocked she'd be, then imagine how quickly she'd try to turn it into a pitch. Then imagine the monkey running riot, throwing the patients' grapes around and swinging from a curtain track.

Jake was still laughing when he arrived at the hospital.

He found Fionn in a private room off the ward. She was propped up against a pile of pillows like an empress, resplendent in pajamas of dark purple silk, her leg encased in a heavy cast from the bottom of her toes to above her knee. Her toenails, Jake noted, were immaculate.

"Didn't bring flowers," Jake said. "Didn't you say you've got hay fever?"

Fionn was tapping at the screen of her tablet as she replied, "No sense of smell anyway. Thirty years of fags does that to a girl." She threw the tablet down onto the bed. "Come and sit down, we've got some telly business to discuss."

Jake pulled the chair into position by the bed. He tried not to look at her plaster cast, nor the bare toes poking out the end. Her skin was bruised but her nails were fabulous.

"You know that I *love* working with you and all my telly chefs, Jake, don't you? But even I've only got so many hours in the day and the fact is, whoever Mr. L.A. chooses for *Shock Chef*, he wants me to produce." And Jake realized what was about to happen. *She* was dumping *him*. "So if it's you out there buzzing the dumbnuts who are willing to sign up to be juiced for cutting a tomato in the wrong way, that's going to be fucking grand for me but...fact is, lovey, it might *not* be you. And if it isn't, I'll still be heading off to Hollywood. I've signed on the dotted line."

Jake folded his arms. He thought the entire concept was laughable and cruel, but never having had a Hollywood call before, Jake wondered how it all worked. "If I signed up to it, would I get executive producer? And a big glittery star on my dressing room door?"

"The studio has to *want* you, and you know you're on that shortlist and you know I'm going to be pushing hard to get you the gig. I can't imagine anyone better suited for firing a couple of hundred volts into the knackers of a bunch of losers like that." Fionn hooted with laughter, glancing at her tablet screen again. "I'm just picturing it. You screaming and shouting, them quaking and blubbing. It'll be the making of whoever lands it. And the money's going to be sky-high. There's a real appetite for this kind of thing right now and you could be right at the front of the line if you play your cards right. But you *can't* turn into Locryn, Jake. He's sweet as a button but they'd chew him up and spit him out in the States. What is it they say? Cute for a taste, but not for a swallow."

Jake's mind drifted back to Locryn's cream horn that he'd devoured in bed the night before. He shook away the image. As he glanced at the bowl of grapes by Fionn's bed, Jake remembered the monkey.

And felt rather mischievous.

"Can I have a monkey? You know, just sort of hangs around my neck, gurning at the contestants. Badass monkey with big scary teeth."

"What's the health and safety like over there?" She frowned, toying with one of her chandelier-like earrings. "But you know what, I'm going to mention that when I talk to them. That's going to wedge you in their minds good and proper."

Jake hid his smile behind his hand and coughed loudly as laughter rose up inside him. *Captain Jake and his badass monkey in…Monkey Kitchen.*

What a load of old crap.

"I was going to say, don't worry about *From Wreck to Restaurant*. You get that leg of yours better, Fionn, okay? We'll soldier on."

"I know I'm letting you down, but would it be a massive ball ache if I bowed out of this one? Give me the credit and the cash if you insist—I *know* you'll insist—but creatively, I'm going to have to let you take the reins." Fionn pouted her blood-red lips but for Jake, the sun had just burst out through the cloud. "Let me focus on getting you the States gig, yeah? I don't need a leg to sell you to Hollywood. All I need is my gob and my phone."

"That's a shame." *Bollocks, it's not.* And Jake had already decided he'd see if he could change Fionn's credit from *producer* to the more humble *production assistant.* "Yeah, see if they'll take Captain Jake and his monkey."

And then we'll know for sure that popular culture is doomed.

"So you know what I'm going to say, don't you?" She lifted a biro to her lips, as though taking a drag on a cigarette. "You can't get attached to Cornwall and you *can't* get attached to the blue-eyed baker, yeah? Think of him like a weekend home? You can head down here now and then for a bit of fun then back to the real world. Maybe back to L.A. if they like what they see on the showreel."

In the past, even a week or two ago, Jake would have exploded and raged at Fionn for being so crass. He'd never use someone like that, even if his past relationships had only been casual.

Instead, he shrugged. "It's a nice place. You know I had my reservations, but it's really not too bad."

Fionn took another drag on her biro, leaving red lipstick on the barrel as she took it from her lips. She looked thoughtful then said, "Got to wonder about him though, don't you think? You know he had investors wanting to finance a chain right across the country, no questions asked. There'd have been a Locryn's in every town, churning out scones and whatever else he does. Think Gregg's but with posher fonts. But he says no, he's happy with his little café! He still makes everything himself with half a dozen villagers to help. What's that all about?"

She shuddered as though a cold draught had passed over them but Jake pictured the garden bakehouse that Locryn had shown on his television specials, cozy and homely as he crafted his bakes. "What's the point of the telly shows and the cookbooks if you're not going to seriously monetize? He's well-off, that one, but he could be *raking* it in. He's probably a bit nice but dim in that way rich boys are."

"Maybe he's…I dunno…happy? And isn't his brand handcrafted bakes? That eclair you chucked about yesterday was artisanal. Not easy scaling that up across the entire country. He'd wreck his brand if he did that. Imagine if there was a Brantham's on every waterway in Britain?" Jake knew that Fionn probably could. "Nope. Not happening."

Fionn's bed creaked as she hoisted herself back against the pillows and lowered her voice to say, "Do you know what my L.A. contact told me just now? Locryn was offered a *permanent* slot on *Good Morning America* after one of the anchors came to Porthavel just to taste his macarons — catering the pudding table at a royal wedding does things to Americans — and he turned it down. He'd have had to appear once a week, chuck on a Union Jack apron, cook something picturesque and make millions. And he said *no*. That's not someone who's right in the head."

And Jake would've turned it down too. "What would Locryn do with millions anyway? Cover his bike in gold leaf and put rubies on the spokes?"

"Oh, yeah, I forgot that bit. They wanted him to ride into the studio on the bike too, with all the ingredients in the basket." Fionn laughed. "You'd have bit their hands off for that, wouldn't you?"

"So they wouldn't even have had him beamed in by satellite from Cornwall?" Jake was now even less surprised that Locryn had turned it down than he had been before. "No, I wouldn't have signed up for that. I'd have been a laughingstock."

She shook her head. "You'd have been making it big in America. People don't laugh so loud when you're making the serious money."

"Well, we'll soon find out when me and my monkey are electrocuting people for making leathery omelets, won't we?" Jake looked at his watch and pictured Locryn lounging with Dorothy on his lap. Had he been here long enough to escape? Would it look rude?

As he was formulating his exit strategy, a blast of heavy metal music tore through the room and Fionn looked down at her tablet, then swept her finger across the screen to silence the noise.

"I've got a Skype in five with a bloke about the *Going Tits-Up in a Bakery* special. Cheers for coming, sweetie, but do you mind slinging your hook?"

Halle-fucking-lujah!

"Yeah, of course, I'll be off, then." Jake got back to his feet. "Get well soon!"

But not that *soon.*

"I'll keep you in the loop. Say hello to the baker for me!" she said with a wink.

"Will do!" Jake waved as he left the room, then once he was out of sight he jogged his way to the exit, signing a few autographs as he went.

Chapter Eleven

Jake made straight for Captain Cod's fish and chip shop. The premises were small and neat, with *Captain Cod* written in huge letters on the stripy awning. He went in and behind the counter stood the white-haired man who Jake remembered from the village meeting.

"Captain Cod?" Jake asked. "Or are you Captain Haddock?"

"Captain Cod the last time I looked!" He rubbed his hands together and laughed, his accent a rich Cornish burr. "I heard word as you were knocking about. I thought you'd come in for some proper grub. A Captain Cod Blackbeard's Bonanza should fill up a beefy lad like you!"

Beefy?

Jake patted his stomach. It was *almost* still flat.

"Dare I ask what's in your Blackbeard's Bonanza? Is it that massive cod off your old ship? Hope you take the hat off first!"

"That's about the size of it." The old man laughed. He seemed a little less hostile now, Jake thought. "I miss that big bugger."

The anthropomorphic cods had been put into storage, earmarked for hijinks at the wrap party. Jake drummed his fingers on the counter.

"Got space for them in here?" Jake glanced around at the pristine, white-tiled interior with its posters of cartoon fish and adverts for deep-sea fishing trips. Captain Cod looked around too, as though considering it.

"I have for the little ones, if you're sure you don't want them. I didn't know how much space I'd have when I opened, but there's room for those lads." Captain Cod shook his head, suddenly rueful. "It's my big cod I really miss. That one that's taller than what I am. You keeping him on deck, are you? He's like my son, that cod, but I've nowhere to put him in here."

Like his son? Fuck me.

"What about on your roof? Or would it need planning permission?"

"On the roof, you say?" He tapped his bearded chin. "That's a thought to think about. I don't know how I'd get him here though, or up there. What about your telly program, would they want to film that? Be a nice bit to warm the cockles, don't you think?"

"Could do. Just needs a crane!" Jake stroked his chin. It wasn't a bad idea and now that he was producer... "Yeah, let's do it! Oh, and make it two Blackbeard's Bonanzas, will you? And chuck in a sausage."

"Two Bonanzas coming up," Cod told him. *Cod. Does he have another name? Maybe he had been baptized Captain Cod, his destiny set from birth.* "I was sorry to close the old girl down but I've got a touch of hearing trouble as I've got older, you see, and choppy weather played a bugger with my sea legs. I'd be listing port to starboard and chucking curry sauce over the customers! Better here on dry land and a youngster like you making something of the pirate ship, giving her a second go at the booty!"

"Nothing I can't handle!" Jake assured him. "Do you want to have a look around, see what we've done?"

Captain Cod sucked in air through his teeth, not that Jake could see them thanks to the beard, but he knew the sound well enough. It was the sound made before a plumber doubled his estimate or a mechanic stuck another zero on the bill.

"Would there be cameras?"

"No, not filming," Jake replied. "Just you and me, having a look round your old ship."

"This fish was swimming in the sea this morning. Fresh, local, simple!" Cod beamed, slamming his fist into his palm with every word. "I'd love to see my old girl. You let me know when I can have a gander and I'll be there."

"Whenever you're free," Jake said. "Just pop by."

"There we are now. Batter bits an' all!" Cod rolled up first one huge parcel, then the second. He spooned mushy peas from a silver vat into two Styrofoam cups and put the lids on tight. He passed the parcels over the counter toward Jake. "And while you're here, you can settle something Mrs. Cod and I have been hearing about London. Is it right you can't get mushy peas in a chippy there? Mr. Locryn said as he asked for mushy peas and they tried to sell him a tin! What's all that then?"

The thought of Locryn wandering wide-eyed around London was an endearing one. "Tried to sell him a tin? Well, that's London for you!"

Cod nodded, his expression serious at the very idea of it. Then he smiled again, his eyes crinkling. "On the house, young man. I hear my old boat's looking a picture. I'll come by tomorrow morning and see what I can see."

"On the house? No, I—hang on, look, I've come prepared!" Jake took a crisp new twenty-pound note from his pocket and passed it over the counter. "I don't expect to be fed for free, Captain Cod."

"You'll need your money for that there crane." Cod chuckled. "It's a way to say sorry for chucking a bit of paper at you. From one captain to another."

"I should've been kinder," Jake said. He folded the bank note and slipped it into the lifeboat-shaped collecting tin by the till. "And that's for *another* captain!"

And with the hot parcels of food safe in his custody, Jake left the chip shop. There was a spring in his step as he climbed into the Mercedes too, because he knew that in the house that overlooked Porthavel, Locryn Trevorrow was waiting for him.

* * * *

Jake knocked on his rented front door. "Two Blackbeard's Bonanzas coming up!"

A few seconds passed before the door opened and there was Locryn. Dorothy was cradled in his arms and on his cheek there was a dusting of flour. He couldn't have been baking though, because there weren't any ingredients in the kitchen. In fact, apart from food for

Dorothy, the kitchen was shamefully empty for a renowned chef.

Over the smell of the fish and chips, Jake detected something else. Not just Locryn's cologne or Dorothy's warm fur, but...

Jake kissed the Locryn's floury cheek, then said, "Hello, darling. Can I smell flowers?"

"Flowers and a speedily put-together apple pie to welcome you home, using Porthavel's own crop." Locryn held up Dorothy for a kiss. "I hope you don't mind, but the cupboards were empty so I've stocked up for you. And I've got a lovely fire going in the sitting room. You need it on a night like this."

Jake kissed the top of Dorothy's head, then kissed Locryn's cheek again. "I'm so bloody glad to be home! And *especially* glad you're here." Jake closed the door behind him. "What's all this about cupboards and fires and flowers? I don't deserve all this, Locryn!"

"Autumn flowers," Locryn told him, taking the wrapped dinners. "And Dorothy was only alone for twenty minutes while I dashed around the village stocking up. Glass of white?"

"I'd love a glass, thanks, and I'm sure Dorothy didn't mind too much!" Jake took off his jacket and hung it on a peg then peered around the door into the sitting room. A fire was roaring in the grate, instantly making the rented house feel like a home. "Didn't think to light the fire, but then I wouldn't know how! I don't have a fireplace in my flat."

"No fireplace!" Locryn gave a theatrical shiver as he strolled into the kitchen. There was the apple pie on the table, its latticed top dusted with sugar, the pastry a perfect, golden hue. *Speedily put-together? Bloody hell.*

"I'll pour the booze, you dish up the feast? And tell me all about Medusa with the broken leg."

Jake got out the plates and started to unpack their dinner.

"Do you want the paper or do you go straight off the plate?" he asked as he crumbled the end of his fish onto a saucer for Dorothy.

"Paper," Locryn assured him as he took a bottle of wine from the fridge. "Doesn't everyone?"

"I'd like to think so, but some people." Jake held up one of the pots of peas. "Captain Cod told me about your adventure in London when they tried to sell you peas a tin! The poor man was shocked."

His companion laughed, pouring the wine as he nodded. He held one of the glasses out to Jake and told him, "So was I, darling."

Jake took the glass. The wine was even chilled. He took a mouthful, then said, "So, Fionn. She's been busy. She's keen for me to do that show where people are electrocuted for fun, I suggested I have a monkey sidekick—"

Jake stopped. "Sorry, it's ridiculous—there was a fucking monkey or a baboon on my relaxation CD, and…"

"Electrocuted for fun? Not much fun for them." Locryn handed him a set of cutlery. "Shall we snuggle in front of the fire? I hope you don't mind me invading your house like this, it just seemed a bit… I don't know. *Austere.*"

"Invade all you like!" Jake took the cutlery and slipped it into the back pocket of his jeans. He admired the worktops, which teamed with produce. "It looks like someone actually lives here now."

Together they pottered into the sitting room and settled on the sofa. Fresh flowers weren't something Jake had ever thought of buying, but as he inhaled the fresh scent of the blooms, he wondered why it had never crossed his mind. Locryn wasn't made for New York. He definitely wouldn't get any mushy peas there.

"Is the leg all right?" Locryn asked carefully. "Am I looking at a big lawsuit?"

"She'd never get anywhere even if she tried. Six of us saw her throw the eclair, then she fell on it, the silly twat." Jake shook his head. "Nope, she's not suing. In fact, she was so inspired by the experience that she's got a Boxing Day special on Sky about *Bakeries Going Bad* or something."

With a bark of hearty laughter, Locryn unwrapped the mountain of food that Captain Cod had parceled up. Jake wasn't sure he'd ever been quite so domestic as this for a long time, but life moved more slowly here. Unless you were renovating a pirate ship to a wedding deadline.

Feedback. How had he forgotten the ever-approaching moment of truth?

Jake started to carve into his enormous battered cod and casually asked, "So, pasty feedback? I didn't see a crowd wielding pitchforks, so not too bad, then?"

And Locryn paused for just a fraction of a second too long. A fraction of a second that threatened to undo all the relaxation Jake had been feeling.

They hated them.

"Not bad at all," Locryn assured him. "People had lots to say. The general consensus was that the mystery pasty maker had a talent for flavor."

There is a but.

The fish on Jake's fork, which had stopped halfway to his mouth, began to flake off, and an interested Dorothy padded into the room. "Lots to say about what?"

"About lots of things." Locryn gave him a sideways glance. "Promise not to start swearing?"

"I haven't so far." Jake put his dinner down on the side table and fed more fish to Dorothy as he nursed his wine glass. "Hit me with it, Loc. I need to know. Pasties are serious business."

Locryn nodded. "Everybody loved the taste and I didn't say who'd made them, just that it was a local cook who wanted an honest opinion. But even though everyone loved them, I lost count of how many people said, *but I'd rather have a Cornish pasty.*" He winced, as though awaiting a clap of thunder. "I've got the feedback postcards in the kitchen."

Jake dived into his wine glass and swallowed. Then, fortified, he said, "Shite."

"Eat up, don't let it get cold." Locryn smiled, a hint of Mary Poppins about him all of a sudden.

Jake put aside his glass and got stuck into the chips. "Now these are fucking *magnificent!*" After devouring his way for a while, Jake said, "How would *you* define a Cornish pasty, Locryn? And yes, I might get you on the show giving your definition to camera! Proper Cornish baker talking about the local dish."

"I'd define them like any right-minded Cornishman. A lovely minced beef with potato, turnip and onion. And we can supply all of that in Porthavel. Then just the right amount of seasoning, a lovely sprinkling of salt and pepper." His eyes sparkled as they settled on Jake. "Personally, the Trevorrow recipe is a shortcrust one, but every family has its own. And you already know about the crimp, because you crimped your own!"

"Was the crimping okay at least?" *Potato. Turnip. Onion. Beef. Potato. Turnip. Onion. Beef.* No coriander. No lamb mince. No chicken. Just those four simple things and that was it.

"It was perfect, a work of art," he replied. "You could've been born a Cornishman."

"It's a start, isn't it? And it's got to be a Porthavel-style one. After all, we're in Porthavel!" Jake speared another chip. "This is a fucking amazing chippy tea. Might be the best one I've ever had. No wonder that geezer's called Captain Cod! Although he could be called Captain Golden Batter instead."

"And if you *had* been a local baking hopeful, you'd have had a repeat customer." Locryn dipped his fork into the peas. "Ted from the pub kept on coming back for more. He said he'd stock the lot of them as *unCornish pasties* and asked me to tell the mystery cook that he was a fan!"

"*UnCornish* pasties? The cheeky fucker!" Jake laughed. "Once I've got the Porthavel pasty down pat, we can let Ted in on the secret."

Locryn handed Dorothy a little bit of fish. "So you're the sole producer now? How does it feel to be captain of your ship again?"

"Well, having made Fionn walk the plank." Jake spluttered with laughter. "I've told her, and she's agreed — well, she was sort of volunteering — to leave the show. And I can't tell you how fucking relieved I am. Wouldn't have surprised me if she'd tried to bring electrocution into *this* show as well. But she's gone now, and *I* call the shots. And if you'd like a production credit, too, Loc?"

"*Me*? For telling you the contents of a pasty? That's very kind, but…" Locryn reached out and patted Jake's knee. "If you need any help with the show or even if you just need an endless supply of cream horns, I'm all yours. But I don't need my name on anything, darling. This is your baby."

Jake playfully prodded Locryn's shoulder. "What about your cake? You should have a credit for that at least!"

But he shook his head. "As long as Zoe and David like it, that's my credit. Speaking of which, Petroc let us down last night, darling. He left the pub after one drink and Zoe and David had to escort Merryn home. We need to up our efforts."

Jake slapped the arm of the sofa. "Buggeration! We're going to get the pair of them together even if we have to babysit them!"

"What about us?" The question was casual, as casual as Locryn's gentle glance. "Are we together, do you think? Can I call you my boyfriend, even if I only tell Dorothy?"

"I'd say we are. Wouldn't you?" *But what happens at the end of the shoot?* Jake didn't want to think about that yet. "And I don't care if the whole of Porthavel knows."

Locryn beamed, as happy as a child on Christmas morning. He was so far from the sort of man that Jake would usually go for, but Locryn was the sort of man that he wasn't sure he'd ever met before. And maybe that's why they went together so well, and there was still a lot of the shoot left.

And it's not like I'll get the job in L.A.

"This shoot's going to be fun now, isn't it?" Jake rubbed his hands together with glee. "We're dating, we've got a wedding to sort, we're matchmaking, oh, and shit, I've got a new restaurant!" Dorothy climbed onto the arm of the sofa and rubbed her face against his arm, as if reminding him that he'd forgotten something. "*And* I've got a cat, who needs to see the vet. Oh, fuck it, you know what, I'm busy but in a good way."

"And on top of all of that good stuff, we've got an apple pie!"

Jake licked his lips. "Do you always spoil your boyfriends like this, Loc? I don't understand how you were still single."

"I just haven't met the right fellow, you know how it is." Locryn looked bashful. "I like spoiling you. I want to take care of you even though I'm sure you don't need me to."

Jake ran his fingertips back and forth down the back of Locryn's hand. "I think you do, actually. I've been butt-kicking, sweary git *Jake Brantham* for so long that I'd forgotten sometimes I do actually need a hand."

He lifted Jake's hand to his lips and kissed it. "Time for pud?"

Chapter Twelve

Dorothy had stretched herself out full-length in front of the fire, clearly happy with her lot. Jake watched her for a while then realized the time.

"Loc, you've got cakes to bake and a café to run. Will you be okay getting home on your bike?" Jake wasn't sure if they were quite at the *invite to stay over* stage, in case his offer seemed too much like a crap come-on.

"Betsy will see me safely home," Locryn assured him lazily. Then he gave Jake a mischievous look and asked, "Should I let it ring three times when I get back?"

"Yes, or I'll worry!" Jake hopped up from the sofa and held his hand out to Locryn to pull him to his feet. "Heave-ho, Mr. Trevorrow! And I would say *blow the man down*, but that's just rude."

Locryn took Jake's hand and let him pull him to his feet. There was a touch of mutual choreography involved that sent Locryn neatly into Jake's arms and they shared a lingering kiss. Not for the first time Jake wondered if he should invite Locryn upstairs, but he'd never had a courtship quite like this one. He didn't want to get it wrong so early on, when life was so right.

The kiss went on, and Jake pulled Locryn closer to him. Jake couldn't help his moan of pleasure as he realized that Locryn was aroused, and he ran his hand up into Locryn's hair, combing his fingers through Locryn's dark-blond locks.

This is one hell of a goodnight kiss.

Locryn's hands, the hands that had been so elegant and accomplished as they kneaded the dough last night, slid over Jake's back, caressing and exploring. He sighed into the kiss, a soft expression of pleasure.

"This is going to make cycling an interesting experience," Locryn told him with a glimmer of mischief as they broke for air, their bodies still tight together. "I've had the most lovely evening."

I can ask, can't I? And he'll probably say no, but...

"Why don't you stay here until it's died down?" Jake cupped Locryn's firm buttock and pressed him closer. Cream horn, baguette, whatever euphemism worked, Locryn's erection was very tempting indeed. "What I'm basically saying is...stay the night?"

"I want to, but..." Locryn studied Jake's face, that soft smile playing on his lips. "I have an early start in the bakehouse tomorrow. It's not fair to you."

"The joys of dating a baker!" Jake gazed at Locryn, stroking the pad of his thumb over Locryn's lips. "I don't mind, really."

Locryn kissed Jake's thumb, then said, "You might think you don't mind. But eventually you will." And in that, Locryn filled in every question Jake might have had about why his gorgeous, generous new boyfriend was single.

Because he has to get up early.

"But we'll see each other tomorrow, won't we?" Locryn asked. "And I don't have to get up early *every* day."

"I don't mind an early start," Jake told him. "I fancy a jog along the coast. I've got lots to think about now I don't have a producer."

But Locryn was shaking his head. It was a no. And Jake knew that it was a no because some other fucker had made his life hell for those early starts. *Bastard.*

"I'll pop into the café," Jake promised. He tried not to sound disappointed. "Dorothy, Uncle Locryn's heading off now!"

She seemed to understand and approached with a questioning *miaow.* Locryn scooped her up and kissed her on the tip of her tiny nose, then he handed her to Jake. Without a word, Locryn reached out and stroked his fingertips gently down Jake's cheek. Then he said, "Sweet dreams, darling."

"May your dough rise and may your oven be warm." Jake gave him a gentle kiss, then they headed for the hallway. Dorothy wriggled free and darted off, leaving Jake to open the door. Locryn stepped out into the cold night, buttoning his coat as he went. He knotted his scarf then, with one more kiss for Jake, took Betsy from where she was leaning against the wall.

"May your pirate ship be ever…" He paused, then grinned. "*Strong-masted.* Cheerio for now, boyfriend."

"Night-night, you sexy bastard." Jake winked at him then, with a pang, closed the front door. It wasn't forever, of course, just for tonight, but the irony of it was that Jake had a feeling he'd be wide-awake early anyway. After all, if Locryn was in the café tomorrow, then where else would Jake drop in for a coffee after his run but there?

And it had been a lovely night, so he had nothing to complain about.

Jake leaned back against the wall, smiling like a giddy teenager. Maybe he'd stand there for an hour or two, just thinking about Locryn and remembering his kiss.

Or maybe he'd answer that light, melodic knock at the door, unless he'd imagined it? But as the knock sounded again Jake knew that he hadn't, even as he told himself not to get his hopes up.

Jake yanked the door open with such enthusiasm that the handle nearly came off.

His voice was hoarse with desire when he said, "Locryn?"

"I'm very light on my feet when it comes to my early starts." Locryn's smile was small, teasing. "You won't even hear me leave."

"Oh, come here!" Jake pulled him into his arms and pressed his lips to Locryn's smile. Locryn's arms encircled him as their kiss grew deeper, slower now they knew that they had all night to enjoy each other. Jake dragged Locryn into the house and toed the door closed without breaking from their kiss.

Then they stood in the hallway, tight in each other's arms, their kiss slow and deep and lingering. The fabric of Locryn's coat was cold from his jaunt into the night but his lips were warm, hot even, and his hands settled on Jake's back, one sliding down to caress his bottom.

Jake moaned into their kiss. He slipped one hand under the collar of Locryn's coat and began to encourage him out of it.

"Come upstairs?" Jake whispered, before kissing him again. There was a soft swish as Locryn's coat slipped down his arms and landed on the floor then

Locryn's hands were on him again, sliding beneath Jake's T-shirt and across his naked back. This time it was Locryn who gasped, the sound sending a jolt of fresh desire through Jake.

He'd happily hear that sound over and over and over again and would never get bored of it.

Jake gripped the hem of his T-shirt then pulled it off over his head and let it fall. Then he ran his hand through Locryn's hair. Should he have stripped off? Locryn had seen his chest before and Jake suspected he'd be perfectly happy seeing it again. And from the look of anticipation on Locryn's face as he swept his gaze over Jake's body, he knew that he was right.

"Upstairs?" Locryn suggested, his voice an excited whisper. He was already unknotting the scarf he wore, the house as warm as the night had been cold. Jake joined his hands to Locryn's and helped him to unknot it.

"Upstairs," Jake replied. It was easier said than done when neither could keep his hands off the other. They kissed their way up the flight of stairs that led to the landing and there were more of those heated gasps from Locryn, his kisses filled with the enthusiasm that Jake would never have expected of him.

Jake pulled Locryn through the door to his bedroom and they nearly lost their footing. Jake laughed as he righted himself and drew Locryn inside.

They collapsed onto the bed, the duvet like a crisp cream meringue. Jake spent a moment wondering what Locryn would think of the room's plain decor with its muted nautical theme, but that vanished as quickly as it had arrived in his mind. Instead, he wondered what Locryn would make of *him* as the evening wore on. It wasn't quite as nerve-wracking as worrying about what the locals would think of his pasties though. Few things were.

Locryn turned his head on the pillow and met Jake's gaze. He blinked, then said playfully, "You're a very difficult man to pedal away from."

Jake toyed with the button on Locryn's shirt. As he went around with the first three unbuttoned anyway, Jake didn't have far to go until the shirt was gone.

"What changed your mind?"

"I don't do anything without thinking about it first. And sometimes I spend so long thinking about it that the moment's gone." Locryn drew his fingertip down Jake's chest. "I didn't want to lose this moment."

Jake shivered with pleasure at Locryn's touch. "I'm glad. And you haven't." Then Jake untwisted Locryn's next shirt button and his view of firm, haired chest increased. Locryn looked down at Jake's hands almost shyly, the intensity of his breathing increasing with every passing moment. Then he kissed Jake again, one hand moving to rest tenderly against his face.

Jake kept going until all the buttons were undone, then he gently parted the fabric and bared Locryn's chest in all its glory.

"You should do a topless segment on your shows, Loc, really." Jake smiled. "*Wow.*"

"I'll leave that to you and all those *time to change into my whites* segments," Locryn told him, bashful again. "I don't know if the world's ready for shirtless baking just yet."

But Jake suspected differently. The world would *definitely* be ready for this, but he was more than happy not to have to share.

"Off?" Jake whispered, taking the edge of Locryn's shirt. In reply, Locryn sat up just enough to allow Jake the slip the shirt from his shoulders. He threw it aside and took Jake in his arms again, crushing a hungry kiss to his lips.

Jake almost let go of Locryn in surprise. This was passion, and it was coming from Locryn. And Jake could only respond in kind, his kiss fiery and urgent. Jake pressed his bare chest to Locryn's and tangled his legs with his. He hadn't expected his evening to end like this.

Locryn's hands, so elegant and accomplished, so thoughtful in their every movement, now reached for Jake's belt. He was already tugging it free of the buckle when he seemed to remember exactly who he was, though there was no timidity in his voice when he asked, "Can I?"

Jake's hips bucked toward Locryn. He wanted him so much. "Fucking hell, yes!"

With a delighted laugh Locryn unfastened Jake's belt, his fingers falling to the button of his jeans without wasting a moment. He nudged it from the buttonhole then teased down the zip as he admitted, "I haven't stopped thinking about you since you stripped off in my kitchen. Things like that don't happen in Porthavel."

"Even with all the rain you keep getting?" Jake laughed. He shifted his hips to bring down his jeans and kicked them off. All he was left with was a lewd pair of shorts.

"Even then." Locryn settled down against the pillows, drawing Jake back into his arms for another kiss. This time is was slower, sensuous, and Locryn pressed his body to Jake's, circling his hips to tease him with the hardness of his erection.

"Trousers off?" Jake whispered. He ran his hand over the tempting shape that he'd felt press against him while they'd attempted to knead bread — and had only managed to end up kissing. Locryn gazed up him, his large eyes filled with excitement and affection.

He nodded and whispered with just a hint of devilment, "Aye-aye, Captain."

Jake saluted him, then began to unbuckle his belt. He went as slowly as he could bear to, all the while his hands trembling with desire. He'd been wrong to question Locryn's passion, he knew, especially as Locryn's lips skimmed over his jaw and throat to his shoulder. Every kiss was as gentle and heated as the last, that soft mouth tracing the contours of the muscles that he was savoring.

With Locryn's trousers undone, Jake helped him to wriggle out of them, and he was treated to the sight of Cornwall's best baker wearing nothing but a pair of jolly tartan shorts. They were more cheerful by far than Jake's plain, no-nonsense black ones and Jake couldn't help but chuckle.

"You're wearing the happiest shorts in the universe!"

And not only happy, but very much aroused, too.

"Not very Cornish, I know." Locryn lifted his head from Jake's shoulder and smiled. "But I couldn't find any with a pasty and scone pattern. And I did look."

Jake slipped his thumb inside the waistband of Locryn's shorts. "Would you like to go first, or should I?"

But Jake suspected he already knew the answer to that. This was Locryn, after all, bashful, considered, careful. The man who thought things through. He wasn't going to be the first one to lose his shorts tonight.

"I will." That was another surprise, not the first of the evening. With a shrug he added, "So long as you don't object?"

"Why would I?" As Jake pulled Locryn's shorts down, he felt as if he were about to indulge in a delicious, forbidden pudding. And finally, Locryn was naked, and Jake kneeled up beside him, gazing down and taking in the decadent view.

"Fucking hell. That's quite a sight."

"A nice one, I hope?" Locryn reached over and drew his fingertips over the shape of Jake's erection. "You're not about to shout at me, are you?"

"The only thing I'd shout is *I've got the fittest boyfriend in Cornwall! And he's got an amazing cock!*" Jake closed his hand around Locryn's very impressive erection and gently began to stroke. As Locryn sank back into the pillows Jake roamed his gaze over his lover's body, watching the tell-tale quickening of the rise and fall of his chest as he surrendered to Jake's touch. Those enchanting blue eyes slipped shut and Locryn gave a soft murmur of pleasure, his hips shifting instinctively.

"What would you like, Locryn?" Jake asked, his voice soft as butter. He didn't want to ask how long it had been since Locryn had been with a man, but he had a feeling it had been a while and Jake didn't want him to look back on their evening together as a damp squib of an encounter.

Locryn opened his eyes, his gaze languid as he watched Jake. For a few moments there was nothing but silence, then he said, "Lots of kisses to start with. I just really want to spend the night in your arms."

Jake lay down next to him, one arm loosely around Locryn as he went on caressing him.

"Like this?" Jake asked, as he returned his lips to Locryn's. He answered with a nod, his palms sweeping over Jake's chest. With every extra moment that went into the kiss, Locryn's touch found a new confidence, and Jake heard his breath catch as he teased his fingers beneath the waistband of Jake's shorts.

Jake groaned with desire. He usually got straight to the point, his no-nonsense approach extending to the bedroom. But not with Locryn. Jake had discovered a whole new pleasure, that of patience.

"Can we take these off?" Locryn whispered. "Is that all right?"

"Yes, please, before I burst through a seam," Jake said. Together they stripped the last scrap of clothing from him and he basked in the appreciation of Locryn's gaze, which roved over his body. He could hear Locryn's breath grow hoarse with desire as he closed his fingers around Jake's erection and began to stroke him. All the time he was pressing kisses to his jaw and lips, his touch no longer tentative.

Jake tangled his legs around Locryn's, keeping him close, admiring the strength in his limbs. Who could've imagined this? Apart from Jake, in bed with a cream horn. And in that bed now there was no room for innuendo at all.

"You're not scary at all," Locryn murmured. "You're lovely. But I won't tell anyone."

"I am *now*, at least. You're rubbing off on me." *So much for no innuendo.* Jake started to laugh. Locryn laughed too, burying his face against Jake's shoulder, and snuggled Jake even closer, holding him tight.

The strength of him and the scent of him were a heady mix, and Jake's laughter faded as he kissed Locryn with passion. "I want you," he whispered between kisses. Locryn's hand still caressed his erection, and he groaned softly into their kiss in response, the need in that simple sound intoxicating. He was all instinct and sensation, his heart pounding beneath Locryn's palm as he stroked Jake's chest, teasing his nipple between his fingertips.

"I want you," Jake whispered again. He cupped Locryn's buttock and gave a squeeze, a none-too-subtle hint.

"I'm all yours," Locryn murmured dreamily. It wasn't until his hand skimmed round to rest on Jake's bottom that it occurred to Jake that they might both be thinking along rather *too* similar lines.

Oh sod it. "Loc, do you normally…erm…how can I put this? Loc, are you a top?"

"Usually," he replied, his tone light enough to suggest that the thought that they might *both* be hadn't yet occurred to him. Until now. "Why — *Oh.*"

And it had all been going so well.

"Yeah…*oh.*" Jake tapped Locryn's buttock. "I don't. I mean, I *have*, but…" *But this is Locryn. Sexy Locryn with the muscled arms and no manscaping whatsoever.* And Jake fancied him and wanted him and desired him, cared about him and could only think of some sort of delicious blending of their bodies, and would it matter, would it truly, what went where?

"You *have*, but you'd rather not?" Locryn's tone wasn't accusing, but all Jake could see was the possibility of the sculpted limbs and broad chest slipping away. It wasn't that he had never bottomed, just that he would prefer not to. But did that mean that he and Locryn had to end here? Wouldn't that be ridiculous?

"I haven't done it for a while. I wouldn't—I wouldn't want to be a disappointing shag, if I'm honest. Sorry, that's not very romantic, is it!" And Jake laughed awkwardly.

But Locryn didn't laugh, he simply smiled and shook his head. Then he said, "Oh, I don't mind! I'm what you might call *versatile.* A versatile baker."

"You've just become even more perfect." Jake linked his fingers with Locryn's and brought them to his mouth to kiss them. Locryn stroked his hair as he did, his hand gentle in its caresses.

"Apart from pasty filling," Locryn added as an afterthought. "I'm not versatile when it comes to that."

"I noticed!" Jake kissed Locryn's full, tempting mouth, then drew his lips lower, kissing down his neck and onto his chest. He looked up at Locryn and asked, "Should I go lower?"

"You can go anywhere you like," was Locryn's spirited reply. "I'm a tiny bit out of practice but it's all coming happily back to me!"

"It seems to be!"

Jake kissed and nibbled Locryn's nipples, tasting the salt on his skin. Beneath him Locryn sighed, something close to a purr slipping from his lips as his back arched up toward Jake's mouth, chasing the touch of his kisses. With a hint of laughter he murmured, "Sorry!"

Jake kept going, no longer teasing but enjoying, then he began to move lower and kissed a circle around Locryn's navel before dipping the tip of his tongue inside.

There was another soft purr of pleasure, the muscles in his stomach tensing and releasing on instinct. He whispered Jake's name, caressing him more slowly as he surrendered to their shared pleasure.

Jake couldn't ignore Locryn's insistent erection a moment longer. With one long sweep of his tongue, Jake traveled from his stomach to his erection and delicately took it in his mouth.

The effect was electric. Locryn's hips bucked up from the bed toward him and he gave a cry of sheer delight. And even *that* was plummy. Jake smiled, despite his lips being around Locryn's erection, and he rose and fell on him, caressing with his tongue.

Locryn wasn't such a quiet man after all, it seemed, judging from the gasps and whimpers of pleasure. He clutched at the bedsheet with his free hand, his body writhing beneath Jake's touch. Locryn's obvious joy was a spur to Jake and he was even more enthusiastic now, gripping one arm around Locryn's waist and the other about his thigh as he sucked and licked.

And those thighs. Cycling everywhere paid off, that was for sure.

When Locryn's orgasm claimed him it was with a cry of Jake's name, but it didn't sound quite like the no-nonsense *Jake*. Instead it had transformed into a sound of decadence and joy, and it was wonderful to hear.

Jake brought Locryn into his arms then, and planted soft kisses along his shoulder, catching the shivers that ran through Locryn's body. He clung to Jake, his eyes closed, a gentle smile on his face. In fact, he was probably the most content man that Jake had ever seen.

"I suppose I should make a quip about *enjoying your cream horn*?" Jake grinned. Locryn's eyes sprang open, his brow quirking into an arch.

"I think you probably should!"

Jake rubbed the tip of his nose against Locryn's and said, "That was the biggest, creamiest horn I've ever had the pleasure of tasting, and I hope you'll let me enjoy more in future!"

"Whenever you like," Locryn told him with keen enthusiasm. "How am I doing in the passion stakes? Not quite as prim as you feared!"

"You're a firecracker!" Jake tickled Locryn's stomach. "You're a Cornish pasty with a spicy middle!"

"I've had a couple of years to simmer." He smiled, pulling the duvet over them. "There's no wonder I was getting a bit pent-up! Sorry I took out my frustrations on your pasties, darling. Gosh, that sounds so wrong, doesn't it?"

"You raged at my meat!" Jake snuggled under the duvet, his arm around Locryn. "A couple of *years?*"

How could someone like Locryn be single for that long?

"We were only together for six months." He shrugged and said, "It was the early starts that did for him in the end, they're not for everyone. You'll be used to it, being in the business? Don't you chaps head off to the market at the crack of dawn?"

"Oh, definitely. I'll be down on the harbor, jumping from trawler to trawler as they come in, snapping up the fish!" Jake pictured himself doing just that, until a round, white-haired old fellow came into mind. "And I'll help Captain Cod get from boat to boat, too. I won't take all the best catch for me."

Locryn turned onto his side, studying Jake's face. "You should see the village on summer mornings before the tourists arrive. The market's full of fresh fruit and veg, all picked along the coast. You'd love it."

Jake's eyes were wide. "*Really?* You have time to go to it sometimes, don't you? You're not always in the bakehouse first thing in the morning?"

"I used to be, but I have a little team in the village who share the load now," Locryn replied. "And that's as far as I go. I don't need an empire, I just want what I have."

Jake remembered Fionn's confusion earlier, her complete bewilderment as to why Locryn wouldn't want a bakery in every town, all churning out fast food, mass-produced versions of his beloved bakes. But Jake understood, because Jake finally understood Locryn, and he was as different to Fionn as it was possible to be.

"A little team," Jake mused. "I like the sound of a little team. All hand-picked artisans, all excellent bakers?"

He nodded. "Just the five of us. No qualifications needed, just a love of baking. A little bakehouse family."

"Five, as small as that?" Jake had lost count of how many people worked in his restaurants. "And if anyone dangled a carrot and said, *Locryn, here's a bank vault full of fifty-pound notes, they're all yours if you open a chain*?"

"It's happened a few times," Locryn admitted, lazily drawing his fingers down Jake's side. "I thought about it. I pictured the mansions and the tropical hols and all of that. And I thought about what makes my bakery special, how my café's a one-off, not a chain that arrives prefabbed on a lorry. Then I said very politely, *no thank you*. The telly and the books are fun, but none of it comes before Porthavel and the bakery."

A very polite no thank you from Locryn was, Jake knew, the equivalent of a ranty *fuck right off and keep fucking off till you can fuck off no more* from him.

"Told them to stick it. Good for you!" And as Jake kissed Locryn again, he knew that Locryn would never leave Porthavel. He'd never be happy in Jake's warehouse apartment. Like a selkie, he would always long for the sea. But the thought didn't stop Jake, because they both wanted this. And Jake had no idea what would happen.

"I didn't quite say *stick it*, but it was along those lines." Locryn smiled. He looped his arms around Jake's neck and whispered, "So at the risk of inviting more cream horn jokes, I've never been to bed with however many Michelin stars it is that you've got."

"Seven," Jake replied. He didn't want to come off as Mr. Billy Braggart, but… "York and London each have two, and Whitstable, God love it, has three. But I have to say that the team at Whitstable are bloody good."

"Seven's certainly very impressive." Locryn composed his face into a look of utmost seriousness. "But you don't make cream horns, do you?"

Jake chuckled. "Well, that must be why only one of them's got three stars!"

"I'm sure they'll all be bristling with stars before too long. They're exquisite." His fingers brushed over Jake's hip and stroked along the length of his erection. "Just like you."

Jake shivered in anticipation. "Is my versatile baker ready?"

"Ready, Captain." He gave a louche salute. "I've never been to bed with a pirate before."

"Shiver my timber!" Jake grinned. "Sorry."

But Locryn just kissed his hair and told him, "Hopefully we'll do more than shiver it!"

"Hold tight, Loc." Jake rolled over and rummaged in his drawer. He was always prepared. Then he turned back to Locryn, armed with a condom and lubricant. "I don't have ones with bumps or ridges, and I certainly don't have any glow-in-the-dark ones. Simple is fine, don't you think?"

"Simple is everything." Locryn plucked the condom from Jake's fingers and tore open the wrapper. Jake wasn't as surprised as he might have been, given the unexpected heat that Locryn had already demonstrated. In fact, as his lover's accomplished hand rolled the condom over his erection, he was already looking forward to discovering more of those hidden passions.

Once Jake was ready, he kissed Locryn onto his back. "How do you like it, darling? Like this, or...?"

"This is probably my favorite," he admitted. "And it seems right for this evening, don't you think?"

"Yes, then I can put my arms around and keep them there all night." Jake kissed Locryn, and just as he'd promised, held him as he brought their bodies together. Locryn's arms were around his neck again and he lifted his legs around Jake's waist, the tilt of his hips bringing them closer than ever.

"You feel wonderful," he sighed, his eyelids heavy. "Jake..."

Jake slowly sank into him. Locryn was a man of such contrasts. The firm, strapping legs around Jake were such a surprise paired with Locryn's dancing blue eyes. No wonder Jake couldn't resist him. He was the most attractive man he'd ever seen. And Jake was so glad he'd chucked aside his reservations, because Locryn's gentleness was his strength. And besides, Locryn wasn't all that he had first seemed.

However they did it, however they made this work, Jake knew that it had to. He didn't want this to be an affair for a season, finished with autumn. In Locryn's arms he didn't feel anything but happy, and they had so much to learn about each other.

Jake found the rhythm that Locryn seem to enjoy most and he moved slow and deep, catching Locryn's moans and sighs in kisses. The encounter was so sweet, yet so intense, too, and Jake was aware of emotions stirring in him which he'd never known before. A deep, caring affection that made Jake solicitous of Locryn, concerned that his every movement would bring him pleasure and joy.

And it *was* joyous, from the sensation of being held by those firm thighs to the touch of his hands as they caressed his back, every kiss deep and lingering. Locryn's hips moved in unison with Jake's, a soft glow of perspiration settling across his broad chest.

Jake paused, resting his forehead against Locryn's. "I'm so fucking glad you came back," he breathed. Then he continued, thrusting faster, his passion getting the better of him.

"You're terribly sweary." Locryn gasped, catching Jake's lips with his own. His eyes flashed with mischievous excitement. "I love it."

Jake rested his head on Locryn's shoulder, kissing the side of his neck. So many sensations ran through him, his perspiring skin tingling wherever his body met Locryn's. "You gorgeous fucker, you!"

Locryn arched his neck against Jake's kiss and reached down, closing his hands on Jake's bottom. Then, as Jake sensed his own orgasm approaching, Locryn slipped one elegant finger between his buttocks.

Jake exploded with a stream of expletives, panting out each filthy syllable as a blaze of pure joy burst through him. He held Locryn as tight as he could but as he trembled, his grip was not as sure.

Locryn's arms were embracing him again, cradling Jake against his chest. He kissed Jake's hair, murmuring, "You're wonderful, you know."

"And sweaty. And sweary," Jake whispered, exhausted with effort, and very, very happy. "Loc, that was...*you* are really, really special."

He shook his head. "We work well together, don't you think? Much better than Horlicks."

"*Much* better than Horlicks." *Working together?* There was the germ of an idea there, but Jake was too wrung-out to grab it. All he really wanted to do was lie here in his lover's arms, and as he listened to Locryn's steady heartbeat, he realized that was all he *had* to do. Life was slower in Porthavel, and the beds seemed more comfortable too.

Chapter Thirteen

Jake had wrapped one of Locryn's scarves around his neck. It was a fresh autumn day and because it made *'good telly'*, Jake was standing on the beach, within sight of a rockpool, making pasties.

He'd done this sort of outside cookery shoot before, which he called *Extreme Fucking Street Food*. The ingredients were in glass bowls on a folding table, and a miniature portable oven was set up as well.

A few days had gone by since he and Locryn had shared his bed, and there hadn't been much time for perfecting his pasty recipe. There'd been producing tasks to perform on top of filming the odd segment, a decision to be made about tablecloths, and emails to deal with from his other restaurants. And, most importantly of all, there had been Locryn.

Today Locryn was part of the impromptu audience of villagers that had gathered on the beach to watch. The crowd was large and Jake recognized plenty of faces from the galleon or the village, including the bride and groom and Merryn, but of Petroc there was no sign.

He and Locryn would work something out, he had no doubt about that.

Without breaking his narration to the camera, Jake met Locryn's gaze across the beach. He was wearing his glasses and his hair was ruffled by the wind and as Jake looked at him he was pitched back to the previous evening, wrapped in Locryn's embrace on the sofa as the fire burned in the grate. Dorothy had been curled up there with them too, a plate of freshly made jam tarts piled high on the table just within reach.

Am I actually enjoying domesticity?

Bloody hell.

"So I'm just crimping the pastry on my unCornish pasties" — Jake laughed, pre-empting the audience — "No, I lie, this *is* a Cornish pasty. I'm stood here freezing my fucking arse off on a Cornish beach and I'm half-sunk in the fucking sand, so Cornish fucking pasty, so there!"

And with that, Jake clanged the oven door shut on the pasty and brushed his hands together.

"Are you quite sure about that crimp, Jake?" called Locryn, apparently nothing more than an innocent, slightly concerned baker. "It looked a little wobbly from over here."

"I'm a little wobbly, I'm half under-fucking-water!"

In a classic *here's one I made earlier move,* Jake produced the pasties he'd made earlier that day, all ready to be sliced and eaten in bite-sized pieces. The camera rolled again and Jake came out from behind the table, his shoes protesting against the slurping sand as he headed for the crowd.

"Pasties! Come on, you lot! Try them out!"

The Porthavelans gathered round for a taste of the pasties and Locryn joined them, though he'd already tried more than his fair share during Jake's practice runs. Jake had attempted to use the feedback forms, had done his best to absorb their comments, but this was the moment of truth. If they still complained, there was a serious chance of pasties being thrown.

It'd make good telly, after all.

As one by one the crowd tucked in, Jake heard a susurration of *mmmmm* around the audience. This pleased him, until he realized that the sound was more polite than ecstatic.

Oh, fucking balls! Fuck me!

He looked at Locryn again, hoping that his desperation wasn't evident on his face. His lover was chewing thoughtfully then, unaware of Jake's eyes on him, he looked down at the pasty in his hand.

And frowned.

Jake flung the remaining slice of pasty across the beach. A seagull flew down to it, pecked at it, then threw it aside in apparent disgust, and with a few easy beats of its wings, vanished into the heavens once more.

"Bugger," said Jake.

The first person to speak up was a little boy who had spent the entire demonstration poking a withered stick into a rockpool. He sniffed the scrap of pasty he held and said, "The filling's all right but the pastry's gross!"

Don't sugarcoat it, will you? Say what you really think.

"I wouldn't say *gross*," Locryn told him. "Maybe not as light as it could be but—"

"No," piped up an elderly woman with the curliest lavender perm Jake had ever seen. "No, he's right, Locryn. This pastry's not as good as yours. Yours is perfect, and compared to that, this is soggy at the bottom! I'd chuck the pastry and have the filling with a lovely fresh cobbler and some taters."

Seven Michelin stars and I can't make fucking pastry!

A murmur of agreement went up among Jake's audience. *Cobbler* seemed to be the only word for it. Yet amid the complaints and the frequent repetition of the words *'soggy bottoms'*, there was a light shining.

"That filling though," an old man with a nostalgic gleam in his eye was saying to his younger neighbor, her head bobbing in enthusiastic agreement. "Just like my old lady used to do. Brings back some memories."

And gradually the gripes and moaning gave way to a new consensus, one of appreciation and approval.

"Perfect if not for the pastry," said Captain Cod's equally round wife to her nodding husband. The camera turned on her and she beamed into the lens. "You want to ask Locryn for his recipe, Captain Jake!"

Jake folded his arms.

But Mrs. Cod wasn't finished. She and the camera now looked toward Locryn and she told him, "And you want to ask Jake for his filling. Your pasties are nice enough, but this...this is like a pasty filling that floated down from heaven!"

High praise indeed.

Jake beckoned affectionately to Locryn. "Come over here, pastry whisperer!"

He could almost hear what Fionn would've been saying at this moment. *Give him a hard time, really bollock him, get in his face. Who does he think he is? Give the public a bit of that Jake hairdryer treatment.*

But how could he do that to Locryn? Locryn in his dark-blue overcoat and rainbow scarf, Locryn with the twinkling eyes and occasional spectacles? Locryn whose chest felt so good to snuggle up against?

With a look of exaggerated apprehension, Locryn picked his way over the beach toward Jake. He still held a small piece of pasty in his hand and even from here, Jake could see that they were right. The pastry was soggy.

"Hello, chef," Locryn said. "That's a cozy scarf you're wearing."

"Watch out, Locryn," David called, teasing. "I've seen his shows! It's never good news if he's smiling like that!"

"Cover your ears, kids!" Merryn called, and everyone laughed.

"I think it's time Locryn showed us how he makes his not-soggy-at-all pasties!" Jake arched his eyebrow. "Loc, you up to the challenge?"

Locryn looked like a rabbit in the headlights. He pressed his hand to his chest and said, "Me? I wouldn't dare go against a man of your talents!"

"Go on, Loc!" Merryn shouted. "Go on, you do lovely pastry!"

Jake went behind the table and held up a glass bowl. "Come on, Loc, I'll even do the washing up!"

"Come on, boss!" Zoe joined in the cheers of encouragement. "I bet you can teach Jake a thing or two about how we do things in Porthavel."

And when she and her mother exchanged a glance, it carried more than the promise of Cornish pasties. *They're matchmaking us*, Jake realized. *A bit late for that!*

Locryn was beside Jake now, taking his time as he folded the arms of his spectacles and slid them into his pocket. He surveyed the ingredients on the makeshift bench, enough for a couple of extra takes should they be needed, and took a deep breath, considering the challenge. Then he shook his head.

"No, the pork goujons were a fluke. I *know* Jake's filling is the best I've ever had."

Jake blinked at him. Then he realized.

"Oh, the *pasty* filling!" Jake recovered himself and patted Locryn's shoulder. "Just give it a go!"

Merryn wagged one of her perfectly painted nails at them. "Jake, you do the filling, and Locryn, you do the pastry. There you are!"

Jake glanced at Locryn. "Not a bad idea. Two-person pasties. Loc?"

"Oh, go on then." He nodded, already taking off his coat as a runner approached with a radio microphone. As Zoe stepped forward to take his coat and Locryn rolled his sleeves, he said, "Let's see what magic happens when London and Cornwall collide."

Jake gave Locryn a discreet tap on his bottom. "Excellent! Off you go, Loc. And I'll crack on with the filling."

"Can you tell us a bit about pasty history?" the director urged Locryn. "And, Jake, maybe give us a bit more about Dave and Zoe's wedding dinner. And have a yell at Locryn if you like. Fionn said to remind you it's good for box office to hear a bit of a roasting."

"I'm only going to yell at Locryn if drops that rolling pin on my foot!" Jake tried to sound light, but his intent was serious. And he'd have a word with the director later. *No more fucking shouting.* Then he put his ingredients together and started to talk. "David and Zoe have asked for a Cornish wedding so we're working on the perfect Cornish pasty. I'm using local, fresh ingredients. And, Locryn, you're on the pastry. How do you get it so light?"

"This is shortcrust," Locryn said, for the benefit of the audience. "There're two golden rules that my grandmother taught me. Be gentle, be quick, and you won't go far wrong."

Jake didn't often cook alongside other chefs for entertainment. He was more used to roasting them on television as they fumbled and panicked. In his restaurant kitchens it was different, of course, but nurturing and training didn't make good telly. This was more like those celebrated kitchens where people learned from each other, driven not by the terror of another sweary outburst, but the shared aim of producing fantastic, fresh food.

"You don't like to linger when it comes to pastry, Loc?" Jake sprinkled a pinch of pepper over the contents of his bowl, then stirred.

"Pastry's an instinct," Locryn replied. "It's like walking — better if you don't stop to think about how it works whilst you're doing it!"

Jake chopped an onion at lightning speed and while he did, he went on talking. "So, Loc, did you train as a pastry chef? How does that all work?"

"I trained as a barrister—" Locryn faltered, then asked, "Actually, do you mind if that bit doesn't go in? I'd rather it didn't if it's not a terrible trouble."

The director looked to Jake for a reply, telling him, "We can snip it if you like. Jake?"

"Yeah, that's fine, we'll edit that bit." *A barrister?* Jake'd had no idea. "So you were born with the knack?"

Serenity restored after his unexpected if rather less than scandalous revelation, Locryn replied, "When I was a little boy, my grandparents lived in an old smugglers' cottage, and for a lad like me, it was like going back in time. I played in the tunnels and built dens in the caves under the cottage, cozy by my campfire with a pasty fresh out of Gran's oven. To me, she was magical, conjuring the tastiest things from the simplest ingredients, and she taught me too. Almost everything I know about baking, I know because of her, and she gave me a passion for it that's never gone away."

"That's great! Now, I've been in Locryn's kitchen" — *and I stripped off to my shorts* — "and you've got a lovely Aga. Is that your grandma's original oven, then?"

"It is." He nodded, rolling out the pastry. "And the bakehouse where I work has a mixture of modern and traditional equipment, because I love having the choice. Baking's really such a huge part of my life, it's one thing that's been constant for as long as I can remember, and there a comfort in it."

"Therapeutic, right?" Not something that shouty, sweary Jake would ever have said, but still. *Balls to Fionn!* "So, kneading bread, you can get a lot of rage out doing that?"

Locryn paused, thoughtful again. "I think you could possibly avoid the rage in the first place by having a good old knead. There's a lot to be said for it, kneading away your cares."

"Does pastry have the same effect?" Jake leaned against the table, admiring Locryn's light touch as he worked. There was a dusting of flour on his forearms and hands, an expression of contentment on his face. It was quintessentially *him*.

"I just love baking." He smiled. "I love making bread and pastry and cakes and I love the care that goes into a mille-feuille or the rustic finish of a gorgeous loaf. And to see people enjoy it is the cherry on top really."

"Yes! I love cooking for same reasons. Creating something from — what's this? An onion, bit of potato." Jake beamed at Locryn. "When someone enjoys something I've cooked, it's great."

And when they all think my pastry's crap, it's not so fucking great.

"And cooking is collaboration in a lot of ways, isn't it?" Locryn stood aside to allow Jake to spoon the mixture onto the pastry. "I learned to cook from my gran and I've been able to teach other people what she taught me, but I'm always learning, there's always something new to discover."

Jake tried not to press himself against Locryn, but they were standing so near to each other that it was inevitable. And very pleasant. And in front of a crowd, but surely people would only assume that they were used to dashing about in busy bakehouses and kitchens where everyone always fell over one another.

"There we are, your pastry's stuffed!" Jake had to stop himself from kissing the patch of flour on Locryn's cheek. "Do you want to crimp, Loc?"

"I think that honor should be yours," Locryn suggested. "Or we could finish it together?"

"Go on, then!"

The crowd craned their necks, moving just a little nearer as Jake's and Locryn's hands met on the pastry. Zoe looked to her mother and said a little too loudly, "Awww," her face set in an affectionate smile. Jake was acutely aware of how close Locryn was now, how their fingers were working so nimbly together and how this was going to be the pasty that would knock the socks off the Porthavelans. Together he and Locryn could do anything.

One camera had come in close, pointing straight at their hands, the other was a little farther back, on their faces. And finally. The folding and crimping was done.

"Into the oven it goes!"

"Forty-five minutes until the moment of truth," Locryn said as he put the pasty onto a baking sheet and passed it to Jake to go into the oven alongside his earlier effort, which he could already see was far from golden brown and perfect.

He put the sheet in and closed the door as the director called, "Cut! That's going to make a lovely bit. Twitter's going to love it."

"Great!" Jake slipped his arm around Locryn's waist. It was only when he heard another *awwww* from the audience that he realized what he'd done in front of the crowd. But he didn't flinch. Nor did Locryn, who put his arm around Jake's waist in turn, earning them a third *awwww* that turned into something like a whoop from some of the crowd when Locryn planted a soft peck on Jake's cheek.

Jake grinned at him.

You really did just do that!

So Jake touched his fingertip to Locryn's jaw and brushed his lips over Locryn's.

"Come to the café later?" Locryn suggested. "We can have a cuppa and look over the wedding menu with Zoe?"

"Yeah, okay! On camera?"

"Come to the café!" Zoe agreed as she approached over the sand, David's hand held in hers. She glanced back over her shoulder to where Merryn was chatting to a group of women and dropped her voice to ask, "Can I have a quick word? I don't want Mum to hear."

Locryn peered toward Merryn and said with a smile, "What's up?"

"Since you two look like you don't any help getting together," she whispered, "what're we going to do to get them together?"

"Merryn and Petroc?" Jake glanced at Locryn. Thank goodness they weren't the only people who thought they should be together. "Well, we had some thoughts."

"So did we." She tugged at David's hand, bringing him forward. "We've tried everything, but Petroc's too shy!"

"He changes the subject every time we drop a hint. It's obvious Merryn likes him, and he likes her, but — " David shrugged. "Don't know what to do now."

Locryn brushed his hands together, dusting the flour from his palms as he promised, "You leave it with us. I've got a pasty plan hatching." Then he turned to the milling audience and told them, "To celebrate kissing a chef on Porthavel beach and since we're waiting for the pasties to cook, I'm giving away gingerbread mermaids at the café for the next twenty minutes, but *only* if you put a donation in the lifeboat fund. Merryn, would you mind shepherding people in an orderly fashion?"

"Of course!" Merryn, stepping over the sand in her silver trainers, guided everyone back toward the path. "This way, everyone, for Locryn's gingerbread!"

"See you back here for the big pasty moment!" Locryn called, waving them off. Then he turned his attention back to his companions and said, "I think I have a plan and I'm not sure if it'll work, but it's one that Petroc won't be able to run out on."

"Are you going to train Merryn up as a mechanic so she can help Dad fiddle with his car?" David laughed. "She might break a nail!"

"I hope *fiddle with his car* isn't a euphemism, young man," Jake joked. "But it *should* be!"

But Locryn shook his head. "No. Jake and me are going to do some tasting menus and serve them in the café after closing. We'll invite you two, of course, and Petroc and Merryn, and we'll have some nice wines as well that we think might go well on the wedding day." He took Jake's hand and squeezed it. "The cameras will roll, we'll all sit around eating and chatting until you and the crew get called away to do some bits to another camera and Jake and I have to pop into the kitchen to get the next selection ready. I know it's not exactly romantic, but it'll mean that Petroc and Merryn have to actually stay in one place, alone, and talk. It's a start, isn't it?"

David nodded keenly. "Yes! I like that, Dad won't shift, and if there's wine about, nor will Merryn!"

"Obviously this'll only work if my new boyfriend's willing to spend the next couple of days chained to the kitchen." He turned his gaze on Jake. "What do you say?"

"There's few places I'd rather be," Jake replied, and kissed him.

"We'll leave you to it," Zoe told them with a wink, ushering her fiancé back. Only when they were a good few feet away and heading for the café did Locryn break the kiss.

"Fancy a walk along the beach?"

"Go on, then. I haven't had the chance for a stroll down here yet. Other than when I wandered down in the storm!" Jake took Locryn's hand. "Can I see your house from here?"

Locryn nodded, extending his arm to point along the beach. "Just before the headland, sheltered by the cliffs. Do you see it? The goats are all on the lawn."

And so they were, tiny white pinpricks against the bright green slope of grass. The cottage was idyllic and needed only a curl of smoke to rise from one of its chimneys to perfect the view.

"You have such a lovely home," Jake said.

"What about that view? The cliffs, the ocean." He sighed as they strolled on. "What's Jake's view? Do you look out over the Thames?"

"Almost," Jake replied. "I've lived there for ages. I could afford somewhere in a much nicer spot now but I never have the time to get round to moving."

"Do you love it though?" Locryn's voice was enthusiastic, but Jake already knew that it wasn't the place for a man like Locryn. "It must be exciting to be in the thick of it."

"Can't say I notice, really. I seem to spend most of my time trying to block it out!" Jake swung their joined hands back and forth. "It's handy to have loads of stuff on my doorstep, but you've got the *sea* on yours."

"And goats." Locryn smiled, kicking his feet in the sand. "And two fat donkeys."

Jake laughed, his eye on the cottage as if he half-wondered it would disappear like a daydream. "It's a perfect place for a baker like you, but I can't see a barrister living there. How did—I had no idea." Then Jake's words halted in his throat. Would Locryn want to talk about something he'd never mentioned before and wanted to have edited from the show?

"There's no great story, no skeletons in the cupboard," Locryn assured him. "Dad's a barrister, his dad was a barrister, blah, blah, blah. It wasn't...it wasn't *me*. I ran away back to the Aga, left a trail of unfinished exams in my wake. Tell me about you instead. I want to know what amazing place you trained at, which stellar culinary school turned you out!"

Jake scrubbed his hand back through his hair. Locryn had clearly been at some fancy university somewhere and Jake's experience had been very different. "Erm...it was a technical college! And before that, my parents' kitchen. After college, I got a pot-washer job at a restaurant and the head chef said I had potential, and that's it really."

"So where did the Routemaster come into it?"

"Dad was a bus driver, and his dad before him. It's how I ended up in the burger van outside the bus station. Dad put in a good word for me." Jake sniffed the air, and for a moment the tang of salt and the vegetable scent of the seaweed vanished under the remembered smell of greasy fare. "All day Saturday, I used to work there. And I haven't eaten a burger since!"

Locryn turned to face him as he asked, "I bet you were happy though? You must've been to buy a bus!"

"Dad used to take me out on the bus when I was little." Jake grinned as he remembered being *Little Jake*, wearing a bus driver's hat that was too big for him. "Mum worked at the hairdresser's and they were busy on Saturdays, so he'd buy me a packet of sweets and a comic, and I'd sit there going round and round London on his route. I loved it!"

"That's the sort of memory a chap should have!" Locryn put his arm around Jake's waist as it occurred to Jake that Locryn's parents didn't seem to figure much in his memories. Life with his grandparents was all romance and intrigue. His parents were *blah*. "Will you take me for a sightseeing trip on the Routemaster? A proper London bus with a proper Londoner."

"Yes! And I'll even get you a Dip Dab and a *Beano*. How's that sound?" Jake laughed. "Neither of us have ended up as our parents thought we would, eh? Dad thought I should be a bus driver too but when he found me putting mashed potato in one of Mum's icing bags, he said, *You want to be a chef!*"

"And I bet they're proud as anything, aren't they?"

"Yeah! Dad can't wait until the bus is ready to bring down! And your—" Jake stopped himself. Something had happened in Locryn's family and he wasn't sure if he should ask him about it. It was better, surely, if Locryn volunteered it. He could already picture a blustery, ambitious barrister father spluttering at the thought of his son having more fun in a kitchen than a courtroom.

Above them a flock of seagulls squawked and circled, waiting for the next round of pasties, but Locryn's attention was all on Jake. "When he brings the bus, I'd love to do him an afternoon tea. Your mum too, if she'd be tempted?"

"They'd love it! And Mum says she's coming down on the train. She never got into buses!"

"I hope they'll think I'm suitable for their son," he teased. "I'll polish my shoes and fasten a couple more buttons."

"They're going to *love* you!" Jake said. "I'm hoping the bus'll be on the road in time for the wedding, but I don't think we'll be able to drive it down to the harbor!"

Locryn cocked his head to one side, a breeze ruffling his hair again. "The wedding's only a week or so before Christmas. It'll be magical." He lifted Jake's hand and kissed it. "Is Porthavel working its magic on you? Have you felt better since you arrived?"

Jake paused and, swinging Locryn's hand, gazed out to sea. He closed his eyes and breathed in a lungful of briny air, then he opened his eyes again and nodded.

"Yeah. Porthavel's working its magic. And you are, too."

"And Cornwall's not so far from London." Locryn kissed Jake's hand again. "I really like you a lot, Jake. You're like a breath of gorgeous fresh air."

"Sweary fresh air?" Jake joked, trying to distract himself from dwelling on Locryn's words. Because Jake would have to go back to London, and— "No, it's not far at all. *At. All.*" He gave Locryn's hand a reassuring squeeze.

"Five minutes!" The director's voice rang across the sands toward them, sending the seagulls into a circle again. "Then we're back!"

Jake called up at the seagulls who were circling overhead. "You better love *this* version, you noisy bastards!"

"Darling, if our joint pasties are better that your solo effort, I don't mind if you cut me altogether and just say that you made them. It's your show, after all."

"I'm not going to lie to the viewers and claim responsibility for *your* amazing pastry!" Jake bounced up and down, the wet sand squelching under his trainers. "Come on, I can't wait to taste it!"

As they headed back, the crowd was gathering once more. Word had clearly spread around the village because the audience was even bigger now, and a good number of them were still munching on the gingerbread Locryn had so generously made a gift of. It might be off season but it was still Saturday and whether it was the pasties or gossip about the kiss, the moment of culinary truth was suddenly the hottest ticket in Cornwall.

A runner intercepted them to check their radio microphones, then Jake and Locryn were behind the fold-up table again. It had apparently sunk an inch or two since Jake had last seen it. But he didn't care. The smell coming from the oven was divine.

"Let's hope it tastes as good as it smells!" Jake said.

"Are we doing your solo first or cutting straight to the one you did with Locryn?" the director asked. "Yours aren't looking great!"

"Yeah, thanks a fucking lot, I know mine are shit." Jake picked up a tea towel and prepared to open the oven. "Let's cut straight to the Brantham-Trevorrow co-production."

"Not exactly shit," was the verdict of the smiling director as he strode away toward the camera. "Just a bit sad!"

To Locryn, Jake whispered, "Knowing you've got nice, firm buttocks, there shouldn't be a soggy bottom on these!"

The cameraman, whose headphones were connected to the radio microphones, looked rather surprised to hear that, and Jake chuckled.

"Well, you *are* the expert in—" Locryn glanced toward the cameraman, then bashfully mouthed the word *bottoms.*

"Especially *yours!*" Jake gave Locryn's bottom an appreciative squeeze. His reward was a kiss to his cheek as the assembled audience gave a saucy cheer and the runners did their best to make the table look halfway decent as the coastal winds blew across the beach.

"Ready when you are, Jake," called the director. "Action!"

"It smells bloody good," Jake said, his hand ready on the oven door. "Join me in a countdown, Loc? Starting from three."

Together they counted down to the moment of truth. And even before Jake opened the door, he knew that it was going to be a triumph. It had the scent of one, that was for sure.

"Wahey!" Jake cheered as he opened the oven and steam curled from the door. The pasty, perfect and golden, was waiting inside like a piece of treasure. He took out the tray and put it down on the table. "Now that's one handsome fucking pasty!"

"Perfect!" Locryn announced as the crowd gave a hearty cheer. And it certainly looked it, there was no denying that. "Do you think we should invite the bride and groom to sample our efforts before the seagulls swoop and carry them away?"

"Yes!" Jake gestured Zoe and David to come forward. "Over here, bride and groom."

David had his arm around Zoe's waist and drew her to the table. "It looks great!" David said. Forks were handed over and the pastry broken, sending a fresh plume of steam swirling upward into the clear blue of the autumn sky. And when the moment came, of course Zoe and David fed each other. They were well versed in the rules of the almost-wed by now.

Jake stroked his chin, watching for their reactions. Their eyes were wide, either in disgust or a transport of delight.

Please don't hate it.

"Oh!" Zoe exclaimed, the sound causing David's eyes to grow wide for a telling second. "That is — I've never tasted anything like this. Dave?"

David had snuck a second a mouthful and was nodding with energy while wafting his hand in front of his mouth as if he were trying to cool it. So he gave a thumbs-up. Then another, with such enthusiasm that Jake suspected he'd have tried to give thumbs-up with his big toes if he hadn't been wearing shoes.

"David, Zoe" — Jake looked from one to the other — "is *this* the pasty you want to have at your wedding reception?"

"I want to have it for every dinner until then as well!" Zoe scooped up another forkful and paused with it halfway to her lips. "You two — this is the most gorgeous pasty I've ever had!"

Jake put his arm around Locryn's shoulder. "That is fucking brilliant. Thank you!"

"That's marvelous! Splendid!" Locryn beamed, which was as close to '*fucking brilliant*' as he was ever going to get, Jake guessed. And he wouldn't have it any other way.

Chapter Fourteen

Jake pulled up outside the cottage with Dorothy in her carrier.

"We're going to see Uncle Locryn. And you must behave and not riot with his donkeys, got that?"

Dorothy had turned her back on him.

Jake waved through the window as he walked up to the front door, Dorothy in his other hand. She was on her feet now and the carrier lurched as she moved inside it. The door opened before he had even reached the end of the path and there was Locryn, his smile warm and welcoming.

"Hello! Dorothy, you missed the goats." He kissed Jake's cheek. "They've gone off to bed, but I have a lovely fresh fillet of haddock ready and waiting for our girl."

"You've just made her day. And now you've made *mine.*" Jake kissed Locryn's cheek and stepped inside his cottage.

Locryn closed the door and Jake was greeted afresh by the scent of baking bread and flowers, just as he had been at his own house when Locryn was on cat-sitting duties. After a few more seconds spent cooing and fussing over Dorothy, Locryn said, "And because I suspect we'll be doing lots of tasting tonight, I thought a simple supper? I've baked that baguette you wanted and there're some lovely Cornish cheeses and my own pickles and chutney. Which isn't a euphemism, it's just chutney."

"Fruity, is it, like you?"

"Fruity?" Locryn's eyebrow shot up. "I like that, it suits me."

"Fruitier than a Porthavel orchard!" Jake put down the cat carrier and pulled Locryn into his arms, one hand stroking through Locryn's hair. "Kiss me, my fruity baker."

And of course Locryn obliged, with all the heat and passion that he hid beneath his gingham veneer of 'fiddlesticks'. He slipped his arms around Jake's waist, his hands sliding into the back pockets of Jake's jeans, then kissed him right back into the closed door.

How Jake loved Locryn's bursts of lust, and he let Locryn push him against the door, giving himself over to all the strength in his boyfriend's toned body. In her carrier Dorothy voiced her loud complaints at the delay in her supper, but Locryn wasn't about to be deterred. He squeezed Jake's bottom through the denim as they kissed, massaging with the tips of his fingers.

All that experience kneading bread came in handy, it seemed. Jake slid his hand up inside Locryn's shirt, stroking his smooth back and feeling the gentle pull of his muscles.

"We have to plan a wedding and a romance," Locryn murmured even as he roamed his lips over Jake's jaw. "But all I want to do is go to bed with you."

"Don't tempt me." Jake groaned as he drew his hand out from Locryn's shirt. "The sooner we get this sorted, the sooner we can test out your mattress springs."

"Yes, Captain." Locryn smiled as he took a step back. "Come and try my baguette? It'll help you muse on menus and matchmaking."

"If it's as good as all your other baking, then this is going to be a bloody brilliant baguette!"

Jake crouched down and opened the cat carrier's door. Dorothy ran out and headed straight for Locryn's kitchen. With his hand in Locryn's, Jake followed, and there on the table was a simple feast, just as Locryn had promised.

"Dorothy first, of course," Locryn told Jake as he escorted him to the fridge. "Help yourself to wine then grab a seat while I flake madam's fish!"

Jake took a bottle of white wine from Locryn's well-stocked, neat fridge and he filled the two glasses that were waiting for them on the table. As he sipped, he looked over a packet of cheese that Locryn had put out for them. "Is that goat's cheese? From your goats?"

"The Trevorrow goats have to earn their keep!" Locryn looked down at Dorothy, who was winding around his legs, purring loudly. As soon as her china plate of fish was on the tiles she plunged into it, leaving Locryn to join Jake at the table. With a flourish he pulled back a blue gingham tea towel, and there beneath it was the fabled baguette. "Baked especially for my sweary chef."

Jake leaned down and paused a couple of inches above the perfect loaf. He sniffed and was transported to France, to a simple village bakery he'd visited once, where they'd let him loose on their baked goods. It hadn't done much for Anglo-French relations, perhaps, but Jake could smell an authentic baguette when one crossed his path, and Locryn's was perfect.

"*Parfait, mon* dear Locryn!" Jake said, without a trace of a French accent. In reply Locryn handed him a gleaming bread knife.

"Do the honors, darling, then let's get plotting."

Jake sawed into the loaf, carving each of them thick hunks of bread. Then he drew back his chair and ate a piece bare, savoring the taste. "That's amazing. I can tell it's one of yours, but it's still like a proper baguette. Fucking hell."

And Locryn beamed so broadly Jake could positively feel the warmth from his smile. "Not very Cornish, but it never hurts to broaden one's horizons!"

Jake began to load a slice with cheese and chutney. He was in his element, surrounded by tastes and textures.

"Good Lord, this is fucking amazing! Do you make this cheese? And is there any spare for my restaurant?" Jake smacked his lips. "Would make a great special!"

"There's a little cheese producer a couple of miles inland and I learned the ropes from them but now I fly solo," Locryn replied. "Quite a few of the farms around here make cheeses, so every cheese we've got tonight is fresh, local and simple. Because that's the Captain Jake way!"

"Too bloody right!" Jake raised his glass. "So that's local cheese well and truly on the menu in my restaurant. Hmmm...goat's cheese tart or mini soufflé on the wedding menu as the vegetarian option? Would the Porthavelans go for that, Loc?"

"Soufflé feels more of an event but it's still Porthavel-friendly." Locryn carved off a small piece of cheese. "Aren't they an adorable couple? Jory would've been so happy to see what a remarkable young lady Zoe's become."

"Mini soufflé it is!" Jake took another bite of bread. "They are a lovely pair. Do you think Zoe will go off and have her own café one day?"

Locryn opened one of the pots of chutney and Jake caught its rich tang, conjuring up a world of village greens and afternoon tea. Locryn's world.

"I think she should, but she says she doesn't want to leave the café. She really grew up there with Merryn after she lost her dad." Locryn dug a spoon into the jar. "But I've been wondering about the café myself. It's the baking that I love. Running the café day to day takes me away from that so...don't you think it's time I appointed a new manager? Someone who knows and loves the place as much as I do? Someone whose mum helped me get it off the ground in the first place?"

Jake slathered butter on another piece of bread. It had to be local butter, and it was creamy and delicious. "Someone called Zoe, by any chance? That'd be a lovely wedding present for her!"

"I get more time to bake and Zoe gets more in her pay packet. I *hope* she'll say yes but if she doesn't, she'll know the offer's open and we'll just keep on as we are." He put the jar down and emptied the contents of the spoon onto his plate. "Listen to me, talking about business to a man who probably employs hundreds of people! I keep forgetting the ship's for a TV show. In my head you're just a chap who wandered into the village and bought a pirate ship!"

"I *have* bought it. Well, it was bought with my money, at least, for the program. Then at the end of the series, the restaurant is given to the community, and — " *And I go home.* Jake swallowed. "But it's really good that you care about your staff. I try to but there's a lot them. And when I'm off filming, it's all at a remove. My managers are great, though, I wouldn't hire anyone who treats the others badly. I dunno, it was nice when I was on the *Lucy May*. There was me and a few staff, and..." Jake put down his piece of bread and rubbed his forehead. "You know, sometimes it all seems a bit too much."

"And when do you take time for yourself?"

After a sheepish pause, Jake replied, "When I'm asleep."

Locryn tutted and spooned out another teaspoon of chutney. "What can we do about that? You need to actually enjoy the fruits of all this work."

Jake pouted. "When I retire? I don't know, maybe it's no surprise I was passing out. I thought I didn't want to slow down, but now I have – a *bit* – it's not too crap."

"I thought you'd hate the pace of village life," Locryn admitted. "But there's a lot to be said for it."

"Yeah, it's not all that bad. And it improved when they stopped throwing things at me!"

With a soft laugh that betrayed just a touch of remorse, Locryn began to spread butter on his slice of baguette. "So, a wedding dinner. Three courses of locally sourced goodness?"

"*Yes*. Has to be. Cheese, pasties, fish." Jake pounded his hand with each word. "I want local vegetables and some Trevorrow bread, too, if you wouldn't mind?"

"I'd love to. Nobody in this village can prepare fish like Captain Cod." He held up his hand, clearly expecting Jake to protest. "I'm not suggesting cod and chips twice, but you have to see that man fillet. It's like watching an artist at work."

Jake tapped his chin in thought. "Sounds promising, and I hate to sound like bloody Fionn but getting that old sea salt filleting on screen would make great telly!"

"He'd steal the limelight wonderfully, you know." Locryn picked up another jar and began spooning the pickle inside onto his plate. "So, do you think my plan to get our older couple together might work? Even a little bit?"

Jake topped up their glasses. "We've got to try, and it's a good idea. Make it romantic and stop Petroc running off!"

"Right! Let me grab a pencil and paper and we'll start plotting our tasting menu for two!"

They started off well but soon the piece of paper was covered in asterisks and crossings-out. Jake watched in fascination as Locryn wrote. His handwriting was so neat and tidy, but with the occasional, and very Locryn, swirl. There were puddings to try, which were Locryn's area, and Jake was curious. Ice creams and tarts and little trifles all made it onto the list, and Jake's stomach rumbled loudly as he pictured the puddings all lined up.

"I'm keen!" Jake said, and patted his stomach.

"I brought a little selection back from the café for you to try." Locryn rose to his feet and began gathering up plates and cutlery. "If there's anything you fancy that we don't have, I don't mind making some extra bits and bobs."

"Go on, I'd love to try one of your puddings!"

But because this was Locryn, the table was cleared and everything tidied before he began producing desserts and cakes from seemingly nowhere. There were choux buns and fruit cake, creamy meringues topped with autumn fruit and biscuits with chocolate or ginger, as well as golden-crusted jam tarts and delicate, artistic examples of patisserie that reminded Jake of summers in Paris.

It was the most decadent spread he had seen in his life.

Jake tried to pace himself, only taking a taste here and there, but he returned to each dish, surprised all over again by each pudding, cake and biscuit. Finally beaten, he sat back in his chair and patted his stomach.

"I don't know where to start. And if you give Merryn and Petroc a spread like this, they might fall in love with your cooking instead of each other!"

"So long as they don't fall in love with *me*. That's a complication none of us need!"

Dorothy had appeared from the chair by the Aga and climbed into Jake's lap. As he fussed her, he gazed happily at Locryn.

"Nope, we don't need complications like that!"

"Try an eclair," Locryn told him. "There's a little twist to this one. Pistachio cream."

Jake took a deep breath and reached for the eclair. And when he bit into it, he felt as if he'd lifted up into the air.

"What the—Loc, I don't even know how you... That's *incredible!*"

There was that smile again, as bright as the Porthavel sun must be in summer. "I tried it in the doughnuts first, but its natural home is an eclair. Don't you think? I want the dessert course to look like a Cornish Versailles at its most outrageous."

"It really, really works!" Jake licked the cream and chocolate from his fingers. "What about a mountainous *croquembouche?* I bet yours are a work of art!"

Locryn's eyes grew wide, envisioning the masterpiece. "A dozen different fillings or more. Just imagine."

"*This* high!" Jake held his hand out above the table. "And chocolate shellfish and seashells, or sugar, studded over it!"

Locryn seized Jake's hand in his excitement and exclaimed, "All wrapped in spun sugar— No. *Orange* spun sugar, to give it a nice bit of zing!"

"That's it! Yes!" Jake flung his arm around Locryn. "Won't it be the best fucking wedding dessert Porthavel's ever seen?"

Chapter Fifteen

Full of food and wine, Jake and Locryn each took an eclair up to bed and lounged for a while. After kissing away the crumbs, they both fell asleep.

At some point in the night, Jake awoke. He heard the waves sighing against the beach and it took a moment for him to realize there was a sound missing from the room. He couldn't hear Locryn.

Jake reached across the bed and discovered that the sheets were empty. He blinked, then saw a line of light under the bedroom door.

Locryn must've gotten up.

Jake pulled on his shorts from the scattered clothes on the floor and wandered out onto the landing and saw that the light was coming from downstairs. He heard footsteps but they were only the light pattering feet of Dorothy, who seemed to be guiding him toward Locryn.

Where else would Locryn be but the kitchen? The door was open and Jake followed Dorothy in. And there, apparently wearing nothing more than his glasses and a dressing gown, was Locryn. Kneading dough.

He looked up as Jake and Dorothy entered, greeting them with a smile. Without pausing in his kneading he asked, "Did I wake you? I was too full of thoughts of wedding menus to sleep and I thought we might enjoy some sourdough with our breakfast eggs."

"No, I just woke up. Don't know why…" Jake yawned and went over to the table where Locryn was working. He kissed his cheek. "Sourdough and eggs for breakfast? Sounds good!"

"Would you like to lend a hand?" Locryn turned his head and caught Jake's mouth with his own, kissing him softly. "A late-night knead?"

Jake kissed the side of Locryn's neck, just above his dressing gown's collar. "I would be more than happy to help." He stretched his fingers then circled Locryn's wrists with them. "I like your wrists. Nice, solid wrists for kneading."

"I'm glad you approve," Locryn purred. "You have the most…*appealing* hands."

Jake stroked down from Locryn's wrists, settling his hands over Locryn's. "Hands you know rather well now," he said, and kissed Locryn's neck again. In reply Locryn tilted his head back, meeting Jake's touch with a sigh as together, they joined their fingers in the dough.

Jake began to knead with Locryn, his arms around him and his body pressed behind him. He went on kissing Locryn's neck, then slipped one hand from the dough and softly touched the bare triangle of Locryn's chest at the collar of his dressing gown. Locryn's answering gasp sent a thrill of excitement through Jake, propelling a dart of heat into his veins. He pressed back against Jake just a little, the dressing gown soft against his bare skin. Jake swept his hand lower and pulled at Locryn's belt so that the dressing gown fell open. It was then that Jake realized that Locryn had nothing on underneath at all, and was gloriously erect.

As was Jake.

"And no Horlicks to be seen," Locryn whispered, a note of mischief in his voice. "I want you, darling, in case it isn't obvious."

Jake curled his hand around Locryn's erection and began to caress him. His voice low with desire, he asked, "Here, in the kitchen, all floury?"

"Would that be too naughty?" Locryn's hands still kneaded the dough for a few seconds more, a perfect cocktail of the domestic and the sensual. Then he gave a low moan and turned his head to seek out Jake's lips.

Jake kissed him, still stroking, his other hand now caressing Locryn's nipple. Then he broke from the kiss and, half-breathless, said, "It would be *very* naughty. Naughty like a chocolate torte served with extra cream."

"That's very, *very* naughty." He caught Jake's mouth again.

Jake responded, their kiss deep and passionate. He took a moment to catch his breath and growled, "I want you, now."

"Have me," was the gasped reply. "Please..."

Jake dropped his shorts then returned to stroking Locryn with one hand, the other tugging Locryn's dressing gown off. And Locryn, because he was Locryn, took a moment to throw the dough into its bowl and push it aside. He was ever the dedicated baker, it seemed, which was just one of the many things Jake found so irresistible about him. With Locryn naked in his arms, Jake groaned in pleasure. "I don't suppose you've got any johnnies kicking about down here?"

"Try the pocket in my dressing gown," Locryn instructed. "I put some in there before our shower yesterday."

Jake smiled to himself as he remembered their shower together. He picked up the dressing gown from the floor and took out one of the condoms. "And —" Jake glanced around the kitchen, wondering what they could use. Locryn clearly hadn't quite grasped the delay. He followed Jake's gaze around the kitchen.

"Don't worry, darling," he said. "I don't think Dorothy's going to watch."

"I hope not!" Jake chuckled, then he kissed Locryn's neck again. "I mean...we can't use butter, can we? What else have you got?"

Without so much as a moment of delay Locryn replied, "There's aloe next to the Aga. I *believe* we could use that."

"Oh, of course! Perfect for a burn in the kitchen, and perfect for a —" Jake went off to the Aga to fetch it. *A bum in the kitchen.* What a puerile thing to say. Locryn watched him, utterly and gloriously at ease, little white blooms of flour here and there on his skin.

"You *can* say bum," he said with a fond smile. "Because we're both thinking it!"

Jake laughed. "All right, a *bum* in the kitchen. And you do have a fucking fantastic arse, lovely and firm." Jake returned with the aloe vera and gave Locryn's bottom a tap. Locryn rewarded him with a playful wiggle, then flattened his palms on the tabletop, letting the soft kitchen lights bathe the contours of his sculpted back. When he glanced back over his shoulder, there was fire in his gaze.

Jake prepared himself, as relaxed as if he were always naked with lovers in the kitchen. Then he embraced Locryn around his waist and pressed inside him. Locryn's head rolled back until his hair brushed Jake's cheek and a low groan of desire slipped from his parted lips. With a soft murmur of Jake's name he circled his hips, their bodies as deeply joined as they could be.

Jake rasped his lips across Locryn's shoulders and returned his hand to Locryn's erection, stroking in time with his forceful thrusts. He ran his other hand over Locryn's stomach and chest, enthralled by the touch of his toned body. Locryn's lips sought his again, their kisses charged with a new heat as their bodies moved as one. They caught each other's moans and sighs, reveled in them, utterly lost in each other.

Clouds of flour rose up from the table as it rocked back and forth, creaking with each of Jake's thrusts. As he roamed his hand over Locryn's torso, a trail of flour and butter from who knew where followed in its wake.

And who would have thought the nicest baker on telly could be such a saucy raunchpot?

Nobody would've put the nicest baker and the scariest chef together in a million years. Yet here they were, bent over the kitchen table where just a few hours earlier they'd discussed the filling in Locryn Trevorrow's eclairs. Now they were surrounded by the delicate aroma of aloe and with the decadent feeling of butter under Jake's fingers as he stroked his lover's chest.

"I want you on the table," Jake whispered. "I want to look at you."

"Anything for Captain Jake," Locryn purred. He met Jake's gaze and told him innocently, "Anyone would think you liked to see me covered in flour."

"Like a manly goujon?" Jake kissed him while he carefully withdrew. Then he patted Locryn's thigh. "On the table, Mr. Trevorrow."

Once he had turned, Locryn slipped his arms around Jake's waist and kissed him. For a few seconds he let it linger, then he lay back on the kitchen table, one arm pillowed behind his head.

"Can you pop my dough somewhere out of harm's way?" He blinked at Jake through dreamy eyes then asked, "How's this?"

Jake set the bowl on the worktop, then he climbed onto the table and lay on his side next to Locryn, kissing him, caressing his body again.

Jake admired Locryn, his very own floury Adonis. "Fucking gorgeous!" he declared. With a bright laugh, Locryn cuddled Jake into his arms and dotted kisses across his face, liberally covering him in flour too.

Jake kissed him back and soon their kisses deepened, and now lying face to face, their bodies were once more joined. Jake smoothed his fingers through Locryn's hair, enjoying him, wanting to touch and feel every part of him. Locryn's hands were running over Jake's back and moving lower, gripping his bottom again as his legs wrapped around Jake's, one foot stroking his calf.

Jake was hungry for Locryn, ravenous with passion. He moved with deep thrusts, bringing their bodies as close together as he could. Every thrust earned one of those unbridled moans from Locryn and he teased his fingertips between Jake's buttocks again.

Reaching between their bodies, Jake took Locryn's erection and stroked it, swift and sure, faster now as he sensed their climaxes nearing. Jake nibbled Locryn's ear as little clouds of flour puffed into the air around them. His lover arched his neck, his gasps getting faster, more urgent, and he lifted one leg around Jake's waist, those muscles that Jake would never tire of taut and strong. That was all it took to push Jake *almost* over the edge, but he moaned, trying to hold back. "Oh, Loc, fucking hell, you sexy fucking bastard!"

"Don't *ever* stop being you," Locryn gasped, a fresh fire in his kisses. He let his fingers push a little deeper, his free hand tangled in Jake's hair. "You're *perfect*."

"Bloody hell, no, *you* are!" Jake half-closed his eyes, gazing down on the most wonderful sight in Cornwall—a debauched Locryn Trevorrow with flour in his tousled hair and lust in his sparkling eyes. Tomorrow Locryn would be prim and proper again, serving up delicate pastries in his chintzy café, and nobody but Jake would know what really lay beneath the neatly pressed shirts and gentlemanly nature. And here was Locryn, naked, moaning with lust and looking utterly delicious on the kitchen table where he'd probably be mixing a boozy fruitcake for his next Christmas special.

The thought of the contrast between the private and public incarnations of Locryn excited Jake and made his thrusts and his caresses ever wilder. He wanted to draw out the naughty version of Locryn.

"I love it when—" Locryn lost the thought in a moan, a second finger joining the first. He arched his back and gasped, "Just…be sweary!"

"All right then." Jake nibbled and licked Locryn's earlobe and whispered, "I love fucking you, you hot, hot fucker!"

"Oh *yes*!" Locryn cried, his fingers thrusting to match Jake's pace. "Don't stop!"

"I want to fuck you hard. I want to fuck you slow." Jake matched his words to his thrusts, then, almost breathless, he whispered, "Do you want to fuck *me*, Loc?"

For a few moments it seemed that Locryn couldn't answer, his breaths hoarse and gasping. Then he nodded, gazing up at Jake through his large, glittering eyes. "I'd love to. But you're so good at it!"

Jake paused long enough to tell him, "I want you to fuck me and whisper *fiddlesticks* in my ear as you do it!" Then he went on, thrust after delicious thrust.

Locryn's lips caught Jake's earlobe and as his hand moved hard and fast, he whispered, "Fiddlesticks and crumbs, Captain Jake."

Those words delivered in Locryn's plummy tones were too much. "Oh…oh, Loc… I can't… I can't hold on!"

And as Locryn's leg tightened just a little more around Jake's waist he added a whispered, "*Gosh*," just to tip them both over the edge.

Pleasure burst through Jake and he cried out Locryn's name. Then he lay still, the sweat on their bodies cooling as he gazed at Locryn through heavy-lidded eyes.

"Fuck it, you're amazing," Jake whispered. Locryn smiled softly, then shook his head.

"You make me feel…I don't know. *Wild*."

"Wild?" Jake chuckled. "You're so passionate."

Locryn lifted his head a little, just enough to kiss Jake. Then he snuggled against him, as cuddly now as he had been abandoned just moments earlier. They were dusted with flour and dabbed with butter but it didn't matter. All that mattered was the contentment of this embrace.

Chapter Sixteen

The table was set for the taster-session. Or, as Jake and Locryn had decided, matchmaking session.

A nice cloth on the table, candles. Nothing too over-the-top, but Jake had decided he'd justify any quibbles with his reasonable argument that they were, after all, making a television series around a wedding, so it had to be just a *little* romantic.

"Just a little arrangement," Locryn told Jake as he crossed the café carrying a vase of flowers in shades of russet and deep reds. "An autumnal mood. Is it too much?"

"No, it's gorgeous!" Jake put his arm around Locryn's waist. "Just like you."

"But no sourdough." Locryn kissed Jake's cheek. "That's just for us."

"Rises nicely when you leave it overnight." Jake opened his eyes wide, feigning innocence. "Right, everything's ready. Tasting platters are go, the runners are primed to fetch Zoe and David on our signal, and...all we need is for Merryn and Petroc to hit it off."

Locryn pulled a hopeful face and held his hands together as though in prayer. "I just hope they do. No running away for Petroc tonight!"

The bell above the café's door tinkled at that moment, heralding the arrival of the couple and their parents. Merryn looked glamorous as ever, all big hair and statement jewelry. Her bracelets jangled as she waved hello.

"Evening, you two!" she called.

"Hello!" Locryn took Jake's hand and together they crossed the café to greet the new arrivals. Petroc was at the rear of the group, ready for the television cameras in a great suit. It was the smartest that Jake had seen him look, more used to cozy jumpers and jeans. "You all look wonderful! Jake's got some amazing treats waiting for you, you're going to love them. Some of our Jake and Locryn pasties too, of course!"

"Best pasties in Cornwall!" David licked his lips. Then he nodded to the table. "I like that, it's well romantic!!"

"Oh, Mum, look at the flowers!" Zoe smiled at her mother, then glanced back at Petroc. "That's got to be your work, Locryn?"

"Guilty." He smiled. "Grab a seat, I'm very much just here as waiter tonight — Jake's the captain. Let me get you all a drink before the crew arrive."

Jake had spoken to his sommelier in Whitstable, and with Locryn they'd decided on a couple of wines. Really nice, special wines that Jake hoped Merryn and Petroc would enjoy.

"We'll be starting with pasties and squabs, then we'll be moving onto puddings. The cameras will be on, and I really want you to be honest, because" — Jake gestured to Zoe and David — "it's going to be your special day. And"—Jake turned to Merryn and Petroc—"Mum and Dad, you're the second most important couple—I mean, *pair* of the day, and we want you to be happy too."

Petroc chuckled bashfully and rubbed the back of his neck. "Well, mother of the bride's the most important one after the happy couple, isn't she? She's the boss!"

Merryn patted his arm affectionately. "It's the father of the groom's big day too! Can't have you put out with dodgy starters, can we?"

The little group settled around the table and Locryn swung into action, filling glasses and putting everyone at their ease. He was a natural, Jake knew, the sort of man who didn't have to playact a welcome. As he watched Locryn laugh with the new arrivals, Jake felt a swell of affection in his breast, affection that he saw mirrored when he met Locryn's gaze.

The cameras started to roll, gathering footage of the two families drinking and happy.

"I'll go and get the first platter." Jake strode off to the kitchen and returned bearing a large slate with mini pasties and squabs on it. "Dive in!"

And to his relief, there was no repeat of the episode on the beach. This time the food was met with nothing but coos and compliments, with even Petroc taking his turn to sing Jake's praises to the camera. As Jake joined the family at the table and went through the ingredients and the inspirations, Locryn hung back in the kitchen to prepare the next platters, an admirable sous chef tonight.

Jake brushed his hands together. He glanced toward the back of the café and saw Locryn ready. It had just hit eight o'clock.

"Are we ready for the —?" Jake was interrupted by the director coming into the café. "Oh, there you are. Hi!"

"Can I borrow the bride and groom?" he asked. "The moon's full over the harbor. It's perfect for getting a few romantic-strolling-honeymoon talking heads."

"And *this* is why I hired you to direct!" Jake gestured to Zoe and David. "Okay, hop it, you two, and that goes for the cameramen too!"

Jake folded his arms as the café began to empty. Merryn picked up her handbag from the seat beside her.

"Maybe I should —?"

"If you could wait that'd be brilliant," was the director's verdict. "We'll be back in twenty minutes or so, and it'll mean an earlier finish if you don't mind hanging around so we can pick straight up."

"Oh, well, okay then." Merryn put her handbag down just as Jake topped up her and Petroc's wine glasses.

"Chill with a nice glass of wine," Jake said. "I'll go and see what Locryn's getting up to."

Jake couldn't resist a quick look back over his shoulder at Merryn and Petroc, side by side in the otherwise empty café.

Could they really turn two lonely lives into a happy ending?

Jake pulled back the seashell-patterned curtain and stepped into the kitchen. Locryn was waiting for him, a cup and saucer in his hand as though posing for an editorial photo.

"How goes the plan?" he asked.

Jake gave a thumbs-up. "Everyone's gone, it's just Merryn and Petroc now," Jake whispered. "And half a bottle of wine!"

"I kept back a little surprise for you." Locryn put his cup and saucer down and opened a cake tin. "The last Porthavel turnover of the day. Simple, local, fresh. I learned that from this sweary chef I know!"

"Locryn!" Jake rushed a kiss to Locryn's cheek. "You *know* how much I love your turnovers. You really are the perfect man."

Locryn handed the tin to Jake, then put his arm around Jake's waist. "You've worked so hard these last few days to get all this ready. It's your turn to be fussed over."

"I don't know about that." Jake put the tin aside before bringing his lips to Locryn's in a kiss. He wasn't used to anyone fussing over him, and before Locryn he would've said he didn't need it. Yet it was nice to have someone there who didn't expect him to be superhuman, someone who told him that it was all right to slow down and breathe the sea air.

When they broke from the kiss, they stood together for a while, Jake not doing anything more than hug his boyfriend. There was no rush, no shouting, only a stillness that Jake wasn't sure he recognized.

From the café he could hear the low hum of conversation, punctuated by Merryn's occasional laughter and, once or twice, Petroc's too. Jake stayed in Locryn's arms as they listened, until Locryn whispered, "Would you like to join me for lunch tomorrow, darling?"

Jake brushed his lips over Locryn's cheek. "Yeah, I'd love that! Here?"

Locryn shook his head. "I'm on breakfast duty in the café tomorrow morning, but come to the cottage at noon?"

"I'm there. Noon. Got it." Jake kissed him again.

As the kiss ended. Locryn cocked his head a little toward the curtain. "Can you hear what they're saying?"

Jake shook his head. "Fancy an eavesdrop? Well, maybe a curtain-drop?"

Together they tiptoed to the curtain and paused. As they did, Locryn whispered, "She really has to broach the Jory question, because Petroc never will. He's one of those men's men."

"Do you think she will?" Jake saw her fluff out her hair, a sign he now knew often meant *Merryn means business*. "I mean, she must know Petroc better than anyone, other than David."

"Zoe said she's had a long talk with her mum about it." He nodded approvingly as Petroc offered the plate of snacks to her. "Come on, Merryn, you can do it."

Merryn fluffed her hair out again, then leaned one elbow on the table.

"Looks like she's revving up," Jake whispered.

"So…" Merryn asked. "Will you have the first dance at the wedding reception with Zoe?"

"Or be the best man," Locryn murmured, shaking his head.

Petroc shook his head too. "I don't know if that'd be right, I wouldn't want her thinking as I'm trying to take her dad's place."

"She wouldn't think that," Merryn said. "She can't dance with a ghost, Pet. And you've been there for us ever since — ever since we lost Jory. He'd've wanted you to have the first dance with her."

"Where's that cameraman?" asked Petroc. "Should I go and look him out?"

"Don't be daft!" Merryn chuckled. "This doesn't need to go on the telly, does it? Oh, Pet, I don't think I've ever told you what a rock you've been. There's times when I thought I'd crumble, and there you'd be. You've always done what you can to help, and I've always admired you for it."

"I shouldn't have let him go back out that night." Petroc looked down at his hands, knitted on the tabletop. "I should've put my foot down and said, *enough's enough. Home.*"

"You know as well as I do what a stubborn bastard that Jory could be!" Merryn laughed even though, inevitably, there was a rueful note in her voice. "He wouldn't have been happy if he *hadn't* gone back out there again."

"But he'd have been here."

"He would," Locryn whispered. "But the half-dozen fellows on that stricken trawler wouldn't."

"Who can say?" Merryn shook her head. "Another storm, another boat sinking out there, and he'd only have gone out again. And you were so brave to go out there with him. And when you dived off the boat—"

Merryn's voice caught. Jake bit his lip. Would Petroc bolt?

He felt Locryn's hand tighten around his and knew he was having the same thought. Then Petroc picked up one of the blue gingham napkins from the table and passed it to Merryn, the gesture undeniably gentle for such a big man.

Merryn nodded to him as she took it. She dabbed her eyes and leaned her head on Petroc's shoulder. "You did what you could, and I just hope that when you lost Bev, I helped you as much as you've ever helped me."

"You're a treasure," he told her. "And a true lady."

"And you, Petroc, you're a gent." Merryn didn't move her head and Petroc didn't appear to have tried to move away from her. Jake gave Locryn a tentative thumbs-up.

"Nearly...nearly..." Jake whispered.

"Me and the boy are going to get our wedding suits tomorrow," Petroc told her, every word careful. "We've got to have the cameras along just for that, but...well, it means I'll be having a day off even though it's not Christmas. Would you like to join me at the pub to drink a toast to the youngsters?"

"I'd love to!" Merryn lifted her head and filled the café with her fruity laugh. "Would it be...would it be a date, Pet?"

"*Yess!*" Jake gave Locryn a fist bump, then he peered around the curtain again, eager to hear Petroc's reply.

"Say yes," Locryn whispered, biting his lip as he waited.

Petroc looked momentarily adrift. Then he asked, "Would that be all right with you?"

"It bloody well would!" Merryn chuckled as she took Petroc's hand. "I've been waiting for you for a long time, Pet!"

"We had our youngsters to raise," the trawlermen told her. "But I reckon we've both done a good job on that score."

Locryn kissed Jake's cheek and whispered, "Your magic nibbles did it!"

"It was your flowers! And your lovely café! And — look!"

Merryn had inclined her head, her brow almost resting against Petroc's. It looked a lot as if they were about to kiss, but Merryn drew away, even though she was still holding Petroc's hand. Maybe deciding to go out on a date was enough for one evening, without a kiss as well.

There was one last gesture though, as Petroc lifted their joined hands and kissed Merryn's hand very tenderly. It seemed to undo Locryn, and he blinked rapidly, then dabbed a handkerchief to his eyes.

"Sorry," he whispered.

Jake put his arm around Locryn. "It's okay — they've got me going as well! This doesn't happen very often!"

"A wedding, and a romance." He offered Jake his handkerchief. "*Two* romances."

Jake took the handkerchief, and smiled at its embroidered, italicized *LT* in the corner. As he wiped his eyes he said, "Porthavel is a magical fucking place!"

Chapter Seventeen

By the time they got back to Jake's house it was past midnight and as well as a burgeoning romance, they had the makings of a wedding menu. From breakfast to sit down to evening nibbles, it now just a matter of finishing the galleon and getting to work in the kitchen.

Jake woke before his alarm but Locryn had already departed for his café. There on the pillow beside Jake, neatly written in his elegant handwriting, he had left a note.

See you at lunchtime, darling! Xxx

It was supposed to be a day off for the production, but in reality it never was. Jake headed down to the galleon, where photographs of old Porthavel were going up on the walls. He was especially pleased when a photograph of a carnival float had been found by one of the locals, showing gap-toothed seven-year-old versions of Zoe and David dressed as pirates.

Once twelve o'clock arrived, Jake took advantage of being the undisputed captain of his galleon and shut down production for the day. Not something that would've happened under Fionn's auspices, but Jake wanted a happy team and that's just what he got as everyone packed up to leave until tomorrow.

And that left Jake free to head up to Locryn's.

He had his own key to the cottage now, but still he knocked on the door anyway. It seemed that Locryn was waiting for him as no more than a few seconds passed before he opened the door and said, "Welcome, Captain, to ye olde smugglers' cottage!"

In his best attempt at a Cornish accent, Jake asked, "Got me some contraband baccy and booze?"

"Think of me more as a dandy smuggler?" Locryn took Jake's hand and drew him into the hallway. Then, his face poker-straight, he asked, "Would you like to explore my tunnels?"

Jake tried not to laugh, but he couldn't hold it in and spluttered with mirth. "It's rapidly become my favorite past-time! Oh, hang on, you mean *the* tunnels?"

"What else?" He kissed Jake's cheek. "So keep that sexy jacket on, because it can be chilly down there."

Jake gave a theatrical shiver before swooping in to give Locryn a kiss. "Go on, then, show me the way!"

They paused for just as long as it took for Locryn to put on his coat and scarf, then Locryn led Jake into the kitchen. Locryn was clearly going for authentic because there on the table was an old glass storm lantern, the candle within already flickering. He picked it up and told Jake, "It was this or a torch and you *are* a pirate captain, so..."

Then, like a magician unveiling a trick, he caught the edge of the rug with his toe and flicked it back, revealing the outline of a trapdoor that was almost invisible against the stone floor.

Jake took a step back in surprise. "Don't tell me, you've got the Famous fucking Five down there?"

"I don't think Enid Blyton ever released that particular spin-off!" Locryn stamped heavily on one of the stones and the trapdoor lifted slowly, revealing a steep flight of steps beneath. The smell of the ocean and the earth rose up from the darkness into the cozy room. "Just imagine the smugglers by lamplight, ready to go out and face the waves. Naughty but romantic, in my mind at least!"

"And your ancestors really were smugglers?" Jake glanced at Locryn, imagining him in breeches and a cravat. The picture was actually rather pleasing, and Jake added an imaginary smudge of dirt to his cheek. *Rakish,* Jake decided.

Locryn led the way down the steps into the tunnel as he said, "I like to think they were dashing. All thigh cuff boots and ruffled shirts."

Jake followed, placing his feet carefully on each step as the light from the kitchen diminished and they were thrown into a darkness relieved only by the glow from Locryn's lamp. "You know there's a fucking great TV special in this, Loc? Can I get you to carry about a flintlock pistol?"

"I'd love that." Locryn kissed Jake's cheek. "Can I wear a cloak too? And look dashingly disheveled?"

"Yes, please!" Jake fanned himself. "I'm getting excited just thinking about it!"

When he heard that, Locryn paused and whispered, "Breeches? A big floaty shirt...bit of sea spray plastering it down? When I was a little boy, I loved it down here. I used to be sure I could hear the smugglers' footsteps behind me or see their lights at night but I was never frightened because—" He smiled. "I had my granny's Cornish pasties, so I decided I'd just give them the pasty corner if they got too spooky."

"And being Cornish, they'd be placated with a pasty, of course!" *Although not by one of mine.* In the silence that followed, he thought he could hear the sigh and rush of the waves on the beach. "Can I hear the sea?"

Locryn nodded. He held up the lantern and the farther reaches of the tunnel were illuminated by its flickering flame. In the darkness Jake listened to the waves and he could understand just why young Locryn had imagined the ghosts of Trevorrows past following in his footsteps. Here the world above was forgotten, generations sloughed off in the bowels of the earth.

Jake stroked the damp stone wall. "Did they carve this tunnel out themselves?"

"They worked with what the land gave them. There's a natural cave system down here, so all they had to do was dig down and put the steps in." They began to walk on toward the sound of the ocean. "And I usually put the table leg on the trapdoor because *nothing* would move that!"

"It's amazing down here." Jake saw tiny fringes of stalactites clinging to the some of the ceiling, and all around them the sharp tang of salt and seaweed, like the smell of the ocean's breath. He felt as though being brought into this secret place by Locryn meant something more than a simple sightseeing tour. This was a place where his lover had dreamed of ghosts and romance, and a place that he had heard no one else in the village mention at all. Perhaps they didn't even know it was here.

"When my grandad first showed me it, he said that I must never, ever come down here alone." Locryn smiled. "I was only four, so it was probably sensible. But eventually the gramps decided that I wasn't going to get swept into the sea, never to bake again, and I turned it into my den. When they were asleep, I'd pack up a midnight picnic and come down here. They hadn't worked out the table trick, but I was too little to stamp on the release stone, so I used to put a cushion down and wallop it with Gran's rolling pin until it opened. I still roll dough with that pin too!"

Jake pulled his jacket closer around him. There was a draught down in the tunnels. "A smugglers' rolling pin! Growing up in London, we never had anything like this. The only den we had was under our nan's kitchen table when we stayed over."

"But I bet you had hundreds of friends, didn't you?" He lifted the lantern, illuminating an incline in the path. "Be careful here, it's a little bit steep."

Jake slowed his pace, picking his way along the incline. He reached for Locryn's sleeve. "Yeah, I had loads of friends. We'd go off down the park, or we'd play by the gas-monitors or the empty garages by the flats. Kids have adventures in all sorts of places. We were a big gang!"

"I would've loved that," Locryn admitted. "Don't get me wrong, I had friends, but I was in boarding school— Oh, it's dull, let's not! So, Chef, can you hear the smugglers yet?"

"Smugglers?" Jake wasn't surprised that Locryn had been to boarding school, but there was something missing from the anecdotes he'd heard about his childhood. There were the adoring grandparents in the smugglers' cottage, and now boarding school, but what about his parents? Jake tried to return to their conversation. "Yes, I think I can hear their footsteps. Each time we take a step, I can hear *theirs,* just behind."

Of course, Jake meant the echoes of their own footsteps, but it was just the sort of thing he'd have said as a child to make the other children jump.

Locryn laughed. The lantern's flame illuminated what looked like a cul-de-sac and Jake wondered where they could go from here. That was, until Locryn angled the lantern just a little differently and he saw that the tunnel turned sharply, almost going back on itself.

"Take the lantern," Locryn urged, standing aside. His voice was filled with excitement, as though he was handing out Christmas gifts. "I want you to get the full impact of my childhood den when you go round the corner!"

Jake gripped the handle. Locryn tapped his bottom, a playful prompt to see what lay around the tantalizing corner. Jake trod carefully, having no idea what would be there. Maybe a mountain of *Beano* and *Dandy* comics from Locryn's youth?

But what he saw instead made him gasp in wonder.

Locryn had set out an afternoon tea inside a cave. There were cake stands everywhere Jake looked, loaded with delicately cut sandwiches and cream horns, eclairs and the sort of fairy cakes Jake hadn't had since his nan had made them when he was little. The walls of the cave were garlanded with fairy lights and bunting and at the mouth of the cave, where Jake could see no sign of life other than footprints in the sand, was a campfire.

"Smugglers' afternoon tea?" Jake set the lantern down on a rock and smiled as he took Locryn in his arms. "You gorgeous bastard."

"I wanted it to be perfect," Locryn told him, his voice gentle. "Something we'll remember forever."

Forever?

Jake was only in Porthavel for a couple of months. Was forever a possibility?

"I will," Jake replied. "No one's ever done *anything* like this for me before!"

"I've never done anything like this for anyone before." Locryn kissed him. "Lovely and cozy with the campfire too, good for cuddling!"

"You—you *haven't?*" Jake was surprised. Wouldn't a bunting-decked afternoon tea in a cave be something Locryn did on a regular basis?

He shook his head. "You're the first person I've brought here."

"I'm touched. I don't know what else to say." Jake ran the back of back of his hand against Locryn's cheek. "I'm not sure what this sweary chef has done to deserve it."

"Do you believe I have passion now?" Locryn asked with a smile. "Because I've never felt so much as I do for you."

"Oh, yes, I do believe it." Jake softly kissed Locryn's lips. "Very much so."

Because passion wasn't only a lot of yelling—it was dedication, too. And Locryn had that in spades. Wheelbarrows full.

"Lunchtime?" he asked, taking Jake's hand. "I hope you've got an appetite."

Jake gave Locryn's hand a squeeze. "After that walk through the tunnel, yes!"

Locryn beamed, then told him, "Then get to it, Chef, because there's a lot to get through!"

Jake chose a spot on the tartan rug laid out on the floor. It reminded him of picnics in the park with his nan when he was little, and he wondered if the rug had once belonged to Locryn's grandparents. He took off his socks and boots and sat them to one side, to enjoy the feel of the wool and the breeze from the sea against his bare feet.

He took one of the sandwiches and peered at the filling. "Salmon? Just like I tried to put in the squabs!"

"Everything here is a Captain Jake favorite." Locryn settled beside Jake, his legs nearly curled beneath him. "I hope I haven't missed anything. An afternoon tea should be special, made to measure, like a good suit."

"I'd never thought of that. A bespoke afternoon tea." Jake slipped his arm around Locryn. When he bit into the sandwich it was, of course, amazing from the first bite, not least because Jake knew Locryn must've baked the bread, and that the afternoon tea had been designed for *him*.

They sat for a while in companionable silence, watching the sea beyond the mouth of the cave, eating the delicate sandwiches and sipping tea from china cups. There was no wonder young Locryn had fallen in love with the place. It was wild and romantic and ancient, filled with magic and mystery.

Jake held up his cup, thinking. "Didn't the smugglers bring in tea? It's fun sitting here, drinking tea where they used to hide the illegal stuff!"

"Tell me more about when you were growing up," Locryn said. "How did you get into cooking? Was it terribly hard to break into?"

"It was a hell of a lot of work," Jake said. "I really put the fucking hours in and learned everything I could. Took every chance that came up. And I was lucky to get a job where a chef decided I had potential and let me cook. After that, I was unstoppable!"

"And world-conquering!" Locryn offered another plate of sandwiches to Jake. "When I saw your programs—once the shouting and swearing was done—I was always struck by how much you cared. These failing restaurants, desperate wonders, bad food…but you really *wanted* to get them back on their feet. It would've been so easy to make it into a circus, but you cared too much to do that."

"I hate seeing people's dreams crumble," Jake explained. "All those places started out like me and the *Lucy May*. Someone throwing every bit of money they have at a scheme, borrowing from their friends, working every hour that God sends, then the whole thing starts to fall apart. I've had some hairy times with my places, I won't lie, and being able to help those other restaurant owners when people had helped me. Well, it's the right thing to do, isn't it?"

Locryn nodded. "It's not all about making money for you. You've got integrity, and so many people don't care about that."

Jake smiled. "Thanks for saying that. I worry sometimes that I've turned into a ridiculous fucking parody of myself. Everyone just wants to see me shout and yell. And I don't want that anymore. I want to cook fab things with great food. I'm close to losing that, Loc."

"You'll never lose that. Since Fionn left I haven't seen much of that bratty chef. I've seen a man who can inspire other people, who works just as hard as they do and who really, really cares." Locryn rested his head on Jake's shoulder. "I wondered how you fit it all in though. Does the TV take away from time in the restaurants?"

Jake nodded. "I've got a fucking brilliant team. I trust them, but... I dunno, when Fionn said you'd turned down that stint on *Good Morning America*, she couldn't understand why, but *I* know why, I *think*. Because you wouldn't be here, baking, would you? And that's the one thing you want more than anything."

Locryn blinked, his gaze filled with affection. Affection for Porthavel, Jake wondered, or — *No*. For Cornwall.

"Whenever I've been away, all I've wanted is to come home. And when I do I shut myself in the bakehouse and I just bake. No amount of money could be better than being here. It's home." He took a sip of tea. "Have you heard of the Royal Cornish hotel chain?"

"Yeah, I've stayed in some!" Jake chuckled "Don't tell me, they wanted to poach you to bake their breakfast pastries?"

"You know it started out as a little B and B here in Porthavel, don't you? The pale blue house up on the clifftop."

"Did it? Fuck me, I had no idea!"

"My mum and dad owned it. They own Royal Cornish." *Bloody hell.* That wasn't just money. It was *money.* "They're worth more money than I can even imagine, but all the lovely personality in that little blue house? Gone. Some people would say they've really made it but I'm not so sure. Bigger isn't always better."

"Your parents? That's —" *What the actual* fuck. "You're right. I mean, those hotels are Cornish in name, but they don't *feel* Cornish. Not as Cornish as your cottage, or the café or even Captain Cod and his fiberglass fucking fish."

"Didn't you know?" Locryn laughed. "Dad thought I should have my head examined when I turned down the US job. He'd love to turn Locryn's into a franchise."

"I bet he would!" Jake shook his head, still amazed. "Royal fucking Cornish Hotels, though? And all from a B and B in Porthavel. Fuck me."

"Not much room for little boys when one's building a hotel dynasty," Locryn said with a shrug. "When I was nine Mum and Dad took me to look at a boarding school and promised if I didn't like it, I wouldn't have to go there. Except when we arrived, they told me I was staying. And my day trip turned into what felt like a prison sentence. Can you believe that, darling? It's almost comical!"

Jake's eyes widened with horror. "That's—that's appalling." And there, Jake saw, was the reason—or at least part of it—for Locryn never mentioning his parents. "That's *cruel*. And you were only *nine?*"

"Character building, if you ask my father." He shook his head and gave a long sigh. "They were off around the world, opening hotels, making money. I spent holidays here with the gramps and that's how things were for a couple of years until at the grand old age of eleven, I ran away down here and decided to live as a hermit in my cave. With occasional trips up for cake and lemonade from Gran, of course!"

"And your grandparents were in on it? Brilliant!" Jake laughed, hugging Locryn. At least there were people in his family who had looked after him.

"They were my saviors really, because I was so terribly unhappy." He snuggled close to Jake. "There's an excellent school about an hour from here, just expensive enough to keep Dad happy and no need to board. The gramps said I could live here but it was up to Mum and Dad. It took a while to convince them, but they said yes after a few tantrums. And I know you're probably thinking that I had a terribly unsettled childhood, but once I came home, it was terrific. And I've lived here ever since."

Jake nuzzled Locryn's cheek. "I'm glad you found a home. I'm glad you found somewhere you were wanted and loved. Where you were happy."

"Maybe I was a mermaid in another life," he said with a smile. "My folks and I get on fine nowadays, because life's far too short for grudges. Dad had a heart scare a few years ago and I think it gave him a bit of a jolt. It was his *perhaps money isn't everything* moment. And it's another reason that I don't want to think of you being stressed."

Jake linked his fingers with Locryn's and held them over his heart. "I'm glad I came to Porthavel. I wasn't at first, but... I needed to chill, didn't I?"

"You were all coiled up like a spring, darling." He lifted their joined hands and kissed Jake's palm. "And I know I was priggish and twee, but I felt abandoned by them. I've made a little nest here, and I was just waiting for you to turn on your cameras and start destroying Porthavel."

Jake shook his head. "I would never have done that. *Never.* But it's okay. I can see why you were being protective. It's your haven, and who'd want some sweary git and his camera crew to turn up and wreck it?"

"But you didn't. You turned up and completed it."

"Completed it?" Jake blinked in surprise. "How the bollocks did I manage that?"

In reply Locryn lifted his head from Jake's shoulder and kissed him. It was the softest kiss he'd ever known,

Locryn's lips as warm as the campfire. Jake kissed him in return, as softly as he could bear. A tenderness was all around him which he'd felt before.

The story Locryn had shared was the last piece in the jigsaw, completing the picture of the man who loved his sanctuary, who needed nothing more than home and hearth and the wild coast of Cornwall. And now Jake needed *him*, and from Locryn's kiss he knew it was mutual.

Jake deepened their kiss and began to unwind Locryn's scarf from around his neck. For a moment, he wondered if the smugglers had ever had afternoon tea down here with a man they were falling for. Maybe so — who could say otherwise?

Locryn rested his forehead against Jake's, letting the kiss turn into a slow smooch. As their lips finally parted he whispered, "I've fallen in love with you, Captain Jake."

"Oh, Locryn." Jake stroked his cheek, his touch light. He hadn't expected this. Not for one moment. Although perhaps afternoon tea in Locryn's den was a strong hint. "Are you sure you want to love a sweary bastard like me?"

"I'm certain of it." He smiled. "And you can swear all you like. Swear enough for both of us."

"I can *more* than manage that!" Jake nuzzled Locryn's neck again, then he said, "I really, really care about you, Loc. More than I have for anyone else. I mean it."

But Jake wasn't sure he could say it. *I love you.* He wanted to, but he didn't want to disappoint Locryn by promising something he wasn't sure he could deliver.

"Thank you," Locryn murmured, wrapping his arms around Jake. "That means more than you know."

"Does it?" *I'm sorry I can't say more.* "Well, that makes me happy. *Very* happy."

Jake breathed in and the scent of Locryn's cologne merged with the sea and the cave and the fragrant tea. He tried to hold the memory in his mind, so that he could go back to it one day and remember the day Locryn had told him he loved him.

In this world away from the world their kisses grew deeper, their caresses more tender. As they slowly undressed each other Jake felt the warmth of the fire on his naked skin, cozy in the blankets and his lover's embrace. The embrace of the man who loved him.

As their bodies combined, Jake knew without the slightest doubt that he loved Locryn too. But he'd never said it before and meant it, and now he didn't know how to. He could show him, though, and Jake was gentle and passionate by turns as their bodies moved as one.

Somehow being in love made his every sense sharper, his every sensation deeper. He couldn't imagine a life without Locryn Trevorrow in his arms, without the strength and sweetness that he'd found in him. Everything he wanted was here.

Chapter Eighteen

Everyone in Porthavel knew that Jake and Locryn were an item, and it pleased Jake more than he could say that they were so accepting.

They wandered the village hand in hand, and during the day Jake would pop into Locryn's café or Locryn into Jake's galleon to catch up — and have a kiss. Jake spent less and less time in his rented farmhouse. Although Locryn had made a stellar effort to make it more homely, Jake preferred Locryn's cottage. Because that was a real home, and Jake knew it was where Locryn was happiest.

It was where Dorothy was happiest too, and she regularly made her way back and forth between the two, as content beside the baker's Aga as she was in front of the chef's fire. Locryn was preparing for the wedding cake in every spare moment now, creating prototypes and test cakes that no one but he and Jake were privy to. Each rehearsal was grander than the last until, on the last trial run, Jake wasn't sure he was looking at a cake at all. Instead it was a trawler, exquisitely detailed, sensitively carved, sailing on a crystal ocean. It was a work of art, a fitting tribute to the land in which the couple lived.

"It's beautiful!"

Jake wasn't sure his words were adequate to capture just what Locryn had achieved. He'd seen a lot of elaborate cakes in his time, but this wasn't showy, it was true to life, created by a man who had grown up surrounded by the sight of the trawlers while learning his craft in the bakehouse.

"It's such a big responsibility," Locryn told him, examining the cake with a careful eye. "When I was a boy, Petroc and Jory got their first trawler together. It was an ancient old thing, but they were so proud of it. That's what I used for my inspiration. Not the trawler Jory died on, but the one that helped him achieve his dream of being a man of business. They worked so hard and Zoe and David have both inherited that. This should be a testament to all of them."

He walked Jake around the cake, like a sculptor showing off his finest work. "I don't know if you can see it, but I've put an M and B into the sea foam. A little secret nod to the ladies."

Jake pointed where the foam bubbled against the prow, so realistically that Jake was half-certain he could hear it. "Yes! I can see it. Just there? What a lovely idea!"

"I feel like I've run a marathon." Locryn stretched his arms above his head. "But I think…dare I say it? I think it's okay. I hope they'll love it."

"Okay? Just okay?" Jake put both arms around Locryn and hugged him tight. "It's the best fucking cake I've ever seen!"

"Do I get a Jake-lin star for it?" Locryn teased, hugging him. "And is eight o'clock too early to collapse into bed? Dorothy was already on the pillow after dinner!"

"You can have three Jake-lin stars. I would definitely make a special journey for that cake. I might even do it by sea—in the fucking cake!" Jake laughed. "Well, I don't mind going to bed at eight, but not for sleeping." He raised an eyebrow, insinuating.

And it worked, because ten minutes later they were snuggled among the mountains of pillows and blankets, cozy on Locryn's vast brass bed. Dorothy had abandoned the pillows with a complaining *miaow*, moving only as far as the rocking chair before she was slumbering again.

Jake toyed with the buttons on Locryn's shirt. "What can we do in bed if we're *not sleeping*? I forgot to bring the crossword up from the newspaper. Damn, Locryn, what *can* we do?"

"It's uncivilized to wear clothes in bed after eight," was Locryn's verdict. "That's the city way."

"So you Cornish lot"—Jake heaved his jumper over his head and cast it aside, leaving his tight T-shirt on underneath—"you just strip off, like this?"

"Exactly like that. We're an earthy bunch, you know." Locryn began to unfasten his shirt buttons. "If I'd been on your show I wouldn't have heard a word of your advice. I'd have been staring at that T-shirt."

Jake smoothed it over his chest, knowing how it clung to every contour. "Staring at what?" he said with feigned innocence.

"Staring at what?" Locryn echoed, returning his fingers to his shirt buttons as he kissed Jake back into the mountain of pillows. These wonderful moments of unbridled lust from Locryn never failed to thrill him, a reminder of all the strength it took to be so gentle.

Jake sank his hands into Locryn's hair, gazing at him, losing himself in the blue depths of his eyes. "I love it when you get toppy with me!" He laughed.

Locryn peeled his shirt off and threw it aside, deliberately taking his time and letting Jake admire his sculpted shoulders before he said, "Toppy? Me? I'm just a mild-mannered baker."

"A gorgeous, passionate artist," Jake said as he ran his fingertips over Locryn's chest.

"Who's all out of Horlicks." Locryn slid his hands beneath Jake's T-shirt, caressing the shape of his body before he teased the T-shirt higher.

"Sod the Horlicks." Jake drew in a hitched breath. Lust and desire were rising in him, and he helped Locryn pull off his T-shirt. As Locryn's mouth fell to his chest, his hands were already at Jake's belt, unfastening the buckle before he moved onto the button of his jeans.

He kissed his way down Jake's torso, teasing soft darts of his tongue against his hardening nipples, and all the time he was unfastening his jeans with a practiced hand. Jake joined his hand to Locryn's, his fingers trembling with anticipation on his buttons.

"I've got the most gorgeous, sweariest top anyone could ever want," Locryn murmured as together they popped each button free, the words a caress against Jake's skin. "You make me feel wild. *Alive.*"

"I need you... All your bunting and sugar and kindness." Jake moaned Locryn's name before brushing his lips over Locryn's, their kiss rapidly turning into a sloppy snog. They barely broke the kiss as they stripped each other's clothes and slipped beneath the quilt, bodies and mouths pressed together.

Jake tangled their legs and closed his hand around Locryn's erection. For a moment, his hand was still as he enjoyed the firmness and size of his lover. When Jake began to stroke, his rhythm was determined. He wanted nothing more than to give Locryn pleasure, and they had enjoyed so many delicious interludes now that he knew just what Locryn liked.

He loved the way Locryn's naturally quiet manner gave way to moans of pleasure, the way his hands moved against Jake's body, how he could conjure up so much wonder so easily. They know how to please each other, how to draw out gasps and groans, because they were in love.

And Jake was sure that Locryn didn't have to hear the words to know it.

Jake always knew the moment when Locryn's climax began, and he kissed his neck, willing Locryn on, wanting the joy of feeling his body against him as he tensed and writhed with pleasure. It swept through him in an irresistible combination of moans and kisses, his hand moving harder against Jake's erection to bring them over the edge together.

Jake moaned an incoherent jumble of swear words as his body, still wrapped around Locryn, seemed to glide up to the ceiling as his climax hurtled through his blood.

Afterward they lay together in dreamy, drowsy happiness, limbs entwined and lips softly touching. Jake noticed moonlight spilling through the open curtains, throwing a hint of glitter over the bed and silvering their naked skin. London might have been a million miles away.

"Love you," Locryn murmured, his eyelids closing just as a knock sounded on the front door.

Jake pressed a kiss to Locryn's cheek, then he lifted his head and glanced at the luminous dial of Locryn's alarm clock. "Who is *that?*" But then, it wasn't all that late to most people. At least, to most people who hadn't gone to bed at eight o'clock. "Shall we find out?"

"Let's" — Locryn kissed him — "not."

But the knock sounded again, and from outside Jake heard Zoe's voice float on the breeze as she said to someone, "Let's try the bakehouse."

"The cake!" Locryn exclaimed. He jumped out of bed and hurtled to the window, holding the curtain around his naked body like a toga as he lifted the sash and called, "I'll be there in a moment. *Don't* go to the bakehouse!"

Jake wheezed with laughter and rolled over, trying to muffle himself with the pillow. "We are *so* busted."

"Is Jake here too?" David called.

"I think he might be here somewhere," Locryn replied innocently, as though he wasn't so obviously naked behind his chintzy curtain. Then he glanced back toward the bed. "Yes, there he is!"

"Come down!" Zoe told them through her laughter. "And close the window, you'll catch a cold!"

Locryn nodded. "Let yourselves in and pop the kettle on. We'll be down in a mo!"

Jake got out of bed and grabbed a dressing gown and threw it to Locryn. He slipped into another and tied the belt. "Quick wash and brush up then our public awaits!"

Five minutes later the men descended the staircase, leaving Dorothy to happily occupy the bed in their absence. Locryn had fussed and worried a little about meeting his colleague in nothing but a dressing gown, but since she had just seen him in nothing but a curtain, he eventually decided that there was little point in worrying about it. Besides, he reasoned, he was regularly seen in even less when he undertook his sea swims.

And the thought of Locryn in swim shorts, his arms scything through the ocean, was one that Jake wouldn't easily forget.

Jake scrubbed his hand back through his hair. "Evening," he said, as casually as he could. It was so obvious that they'd been up to saucy shenanigans, but Jake didn't care. It didn't help that Zoe and David were seated at the kitchen table which, though comprehensively cleaned and tidied since he had romped there with Locryn, would forever be the place where they had made love after midnight amid clouds of flour and slicks of butter. Now all that was on the table was a bright blue teapot and four mismatched cups and saucers, as well as a little plate of shortbread fingers from which Zoe was stripping the clingfilm.

"I baked!" she told them, beaming with pride. "And you're both...sort of naked."

"Hardly," Locryn told her, tightening the belt of his cozy dressing gown a little more. He settled onto a chair and said, "Hello, bride and groom! How're the parents getting along?"

Zoe looked to David and said, "Tell him about your dad, Dave. He's like a new man!"

Dave paused, a piece of shortbread almost in his mouth. He lowered his hand and said, "He's had his hair cut. He's bought a new shirt. He took me to Plymouth to go shopping for new aftershave. He sings to himself. Not just them old sea shanties, but modern stuff too. And he keeps laughing. And...well, we're calling it The Merryn Effect, aren't we, Zo?"

"Yes we are." She laughed. "And he even went shoe shopping with Mum and *didn't* complain! It's early days, we know that, but...fingers crossed. And that's down to you two and your lovely food!"

"Petroc went *shoe shopping?* Fuck me!" Jake laughed as he picked up a piece of shortbread. Its aroma was amazing, and Jake wondered how Porthavel had managed to produce so many excellent bakers. "Well, they needed a nudge, didn't they!"

But Zoe didn't answer. Instead she was watching Locryn closely and chewing at her lip, her eyes unblinking as he lifted a piece of shortbread to his mouth and took a bite. She was waiting, Jake realized, for his verdict.

Locryn chewed thoughtfully and swallowed, taking his time, like a connoisseur sampling a fine wine. Then he announced, "That is *excellent.* Someone's been practicing!"

"Yes!" Zoe bumped fists with David. "At last!"

"She's been working on them for *ages!*" David said, affecting a world-weary tone. "And I've been doing all the washing up!"

Locryn poured tea into the two empty cups, taking another bite of shortbread as he did. Jake could see from Zoe's expression that she hadn't come here just to give biscuits though. There was a slight shadow in her eyes, and when she began to talk, the reason for it became clear.

"So, we're getting married in a week and it's been wild. Thanks to you two. I know this is just a telly program to you, Jake, but it's been amazing to be part of it. And you've hardly shouted at anyone!" She reached out and took David's hand. "And, Locryn, after we lost Dad, when it felt like the world was ending, just knowing you were there kept us going. Your café was a haven for us."

"And that won't ever change," Locryn told her. "You're the family I got to choose."

David smiled at Zoe. "That's it. Family. That's what we want to ask."

"I'd like you to give me away," Zoe said to Locryn. "Would you think about it?"

But Locryn shook his head, his expression kind. "It should be Petroc. I know he's already refused but he'll regret it one day. I'm honored that you'd ask me, Zoe, and it'd be a true privilege, but he's the only man for the job."

"What if he says no again?" David asked, trepidation in his voice.

"He won't," Jake said, as he bit into the shortbread. "Fuck me, this is good!"

Locryn knitted his hands on the tabletop, the hitch in his breath at Jake's words one that only Jake would hear. To their visitors he was nothing but Locryn, as proper as ever despite his state of undress. He looked to his lover and asked, "Do you think there'd be any mileage in making it a joint endeavor? Couldn't Merryn *and* Petroc do it?"

"Either side of the bride?" Jake took another bite of the shortbread. Yes, it was still just as good. "Yeah, why not? Zoe, would you like that?"

"If I ask them together..." she murmured, then she turned to her groom. "Dave, would you *dare* say no to Mum? Would your dad?"

David chuckled, his cheeks turning red. "No, I bloody wouldn't. And nor would Dad! I dunno, I reckon he's in a romantic sort of mood at the moment. Bet he could be convinced now, especially if Merryn's doing the convincing!"

"I'll make you a deal." Locryn unknitted his fingers and took another piece of shortbread. "If they still say no, I'd be honored to do it. But I've got an offer for you too. You don't have to say yes, but I want you to promise to consider it."

He rose from the table and crossed to the worktop, where a neatly handwritten envelope addressed simply to *Zoe* waited. Jake knew what it contained. It was the offer of a promotion to café manager, with all the attendant benefits that would bring, which were more generous than Jake could ever remember an employer offering *him*. But he'd never had an employer like Locryn.

"What's this?" Zoe frowned, intrigued as she tore open the envelope and took out the similarly handwritten letter within. She and David read it together, their eyes growing wide as they did. Locryn said nothing but simply returned to his seat and took Jake's hand, offering him a smile as he settled.

David slapped his leg, his knee jigging up and down. "It's not April Fool's Day, Locryn. What are you up to?"

"The café needs a manager because I want to spend more time baking and less time managing." He bit into the shortbread, chewing and swallowing in his usual leisurely way. "Nobody else in the world would be half as good as you at the job, Zoe, but take all the time you need to consider the offer."

"Can I just say yes now?" She laughed, then glanced at David, who was clearly as keen as she was. "I don't need to think about it, Locryn. I want to do it!"

"Go on, say yes!" Jake insisted.

"Yes!" Zoe exclaimed. "Massive, massive yes! But only if you promise to keeping teaching me baking too.

I've got a taste for it now, I don't want to stop at shortbread."

Locryn laughed. "It's a deal. We'll start *both* after the new year!"

Chapter Nineteen

Jake was halfway through a thick, toasted slice of Locryn's homemade bread and jam when his phone rang. Even though it wasn't quite nine in the morning, he was expecting one of the electricians working on the galleon to call about light fittings, so he put down his toast and answered without checking the caller's name.

And wished he'd had.

"All right, tiger!" Fionn sounded as though she had already smoked her way through a pack of Woodbines. "How's life in the back of beyond?"

"Bloody good," Jake said. He reached across the table for Locryn's hand and squeezed it. "How's your leg? Hobbling about yet?"

"Yeah, squeezing my pot into my Jimmy Choos, you know how it is." She laughed again, the sound deep and throaty. "So have I got a biiiiig announcement for you. You ready for it?"

Jake glanced back at his breakfast. *This had better be good.* "Did I get nommed? No, wait, you're giving up the smokes?"

"My American wants you, with or without the monkey. He's talking two hundred thou an *episode*, twenty episodes to kick off. They're even willing to compromise on the electrocution angle if it brings you on board." She coughed again. "The network can't get enough of you losing your shit. You could probably get them to write a blank check!"

Jake tried to make a quick calculation but the numbers spun too fast for him to grasp them. They wanted him, they would spend vast amounts of money to have him, and... "They'd cut the electrocution?" With a grin for Locryn, he asked, "And I *can* have the monkey?"

Locryn silently applauded, guessing the gist of the conversation.

"They'll cut the electrocution *if* you'll give them the full-bore, big-bollocky shouting chef. They want to see tears and trembling. It's all about the circus." He heard Fionn take a drink and pictured the thick, treacle-like black coffee he knew she would be quaffing. "We need to get things bolted down and signed while they're still hard for you, sweetie. How soon can you get here?"

"But I'm..." *In Cornwall.* Jake saw the numbers spin again. Maybe he could do it, just one series of yelling and bawling and carrying on, then he'd grab the money and run. "I can spare a day. If I get in the car now, I can be in London just after lunch."

"And make sure you've got your passport in London. If it's a yes, they want to jet over to the States on Friday night to meet the big bosses before they all fuck off for the Christmas break." *America? The wedding –* "And before you mither me about the wedding, I've thought of it. Do the nosh on Thursday and fridge it ready for Saturday. Fly out Friday night and we can do a staged shoot when you get back. Nobody'll know you weren't there and we'll get the guests to sign a non-disclosure. Okay? When you hit town, head straight for my office. And start dreaming of how you're going to spend those dollars!"

Jake already was. He'd seen an old yacht stores building on the quayside in Porthavel, and he wanted to buy it and turn it into an open kitchen training college. And he couldn't do that on fresh air. And there was the old technical college he'd trained at, needing new kitchens. And the animal sanctuary down the road from Porthavel needed a new roof and a new van. If he did the series, he'd have the money for all of that and more.

He didn't want to miss Zoe and David's wedding, but they'd only known him five minutes. They wouldn't miss him. He'd assembled a great team on the galleon and the day would work perfectly even if he wasn't there. He didn't need to be in Porthavel.

"I'll do it," Jake decided, his heart thudding in excitement. He gave Locryn's hand one last squeeze and let go.

"Brilliant." She laughed. "They're talking about a three-year golden handcuff deal. If the first twenty take off, you're looking at a long and happy life in the sun. If they don't, they'll be giving you a hefty goodbye payment. Catch you soon, gorgeous! Love to baker!"

"Three years?" Jake's elation turned into a panic, but it was soon replaced by those spinning numbers again. He could just pop over to America every so often, shout at people with tomato-juice stains on their whites, slam pots and pans about and come back with enough money to do tremendous things. And he could open a restaurant on the Isle of Wight, too. And that one on the

River Dee. And the Clyde had an appeal. Fuck it, he could open one on Shetland if he felt like it.

Jake Brantham could do anything.

The phone went dead. Locryn said nothing but instead waited for Jake, his face still wearing that little smile.

Of course he was happy for his boyfriend. Who wouldn't be?

"I've got to go. Can't bloody believe this is happening, but it is, so can you hold the fort today? I'll drive back tonight. I'll be fucking knackered, but all the shit'll be worth it! They're chucking a fucking shitload of money at me, and the things I'll be able to do. Fuck me!" Jake took a deep breath. His thoughts were rushing. Cornwall's stray cats and dogs were swirling in a giddy carousel with dream restaurants and smiling college students wielding frying pans and icing bags. "I'll give you a bell from the car once I'm on the motorway. Sorry. I didn't expect this, but it'll be fucking amazing!"

Jake was out of his chair and he kissed the top of Locryn's head. Then he grabbed his leather jacket from the hook on the door and his car keys jangled in the pocket.

"You can't drive back tonight, you'll be shattered!" Locryn told him as he followed Jake through the house. Dorothy wound around Jake's feet too until Locryn stooped and gathered her into his arms. "What about the wedding? You'll miss it if you fly on Friday, darling."

"I'll prep all the food in advance. Don't worry. I don't need to be there, and we can film it all again once I'm back from the States. No one'll miss me. They'll be too busy gawping at your fucking amazing cake!" Jake gave Locryn a quick kiss and fussed Dorothy at the same time.

Can I fucking multitask or what?

"Well, I'm sure they'll pop on the wedding togs and plaster on a smile when Fionn tells them to." That could almost be snippy, Jake thought, but Locryn was never snippy. And he was still smiling. Besides, he knew the villagers better than anyone, so if he thought they'd be happy to recreate the big day for the cameras, then he'd be right. "Good luck, darling, we'll miss you."

"You two have a great day!" Jake beamed. "See you both soon, and I'll bring you a crappy souvenir, Loc! A ceramic London bus!"

Jake patted his pockets and, satisfied he had his keys, wallet and phone, bolted out to his car. The weather had taken a turn for the worst, the clouds dark and lowering, but it would brighten up once he was heading away from the coast.

"Cheerio!" Locryn lifted one of Dorothy's paws and together, they waved Jake off. "We love you!"

"You two keep out of trouble!" Jake blew them a kiss, then he tooted as he drove away.

Jake changed the selection on his stereo. He wasn't going to drive all that way listening to a babbling brook, so he chose his over-the-top 1980s power ballads selection instead.

And sang along.

Until, twenty minutes into his journey, he met the world's slowest tractor.

"Fuck me," Jake muttered. But ire was burning in him again and he hit the steering wheel with both hands. *"Fuck me! Ride me fucking sideways, don't you have a fucking second gear on that rusty heap of shit?"*

But the tractor driver was a Porthavelen, he knew, and they weren't given to rushing. Jake would have to wait until the flat-capped man in front decided that he was ready to relinquish the road.

After a couple of miles soundtracked by Steve Winwood, the tractor accelerated at last — and turned off into a field.

"Fuck's *sake!*"

But at least the road was left clear, except for a lorry full of pasties ahead. Jake found a place to overtake and he sailed ahead once more.

It wasn't a bad route, quite picturesque really. Maybe Jake would always associate winding lanes and rocky hillsides with Locryn.

Jake already missed him. But Locryn didn't mind. He understood what it was like, being at the beck and call of *telly people*.

Jake settled into his drive, singing along, occasionally shouting at other drivers and unleashing the occasional *toot-toot*. It didn't seem long at all before he could see the Tamar Bridge in the distance. And once he drove across it, he'd be leaving Cornwall behind him.

Jake turned down the music. The clouds, as dark as a fresh bruise, unleashed their promise of rain. Jake put the windscreen wipers on and as they squeaked back and forth, he had the panicky feeling he'd forgotten something.

He felt with one hand for his wallet, and found it in his pocket along with his phone.

So he hadn't forgotten *anything*.

Tool.

But the feeling wouldn't shift. Until Jake got nearer and nearer to the bridge and he finally remembered.

I haven't told Locryn I love him.

Without taking a moment to think, Jake took the last turning off the dual carriageway, leaving a chorus of enraged hoots in his wake.

And now he was leaving the bridge behind him, heading back to Porthavel.

What a prat he'd been. What a fucking idiot. He *couldn't* go to America. He couldn't yell and scream on television. He didn't want to. He'd only pass out again, maybe worse.

And besides, he had Locryn waiting for him in Porthavel. And Jake loved him.

Jake drove through pouring rain, his thoughts filled with Locryn. Every kiss, every smile, every moment they had spent in each other's arms. He thought of Locryn's cottage and the café and the galleon, he thought of Locryn's bed and Locryn's kitchen table. He thought of selling his warehouse flat and spending *that* money on animal sanctuaries and colleges and more. But most of all, he thought of Locryn because he loved him.

Once again Jake was on the coast road, the sea displaying its full fury. The rain near Porthavel had brought ferocious wind and waves like towering dark-glass mountains.

The goats were sheltering when Jake arrived at Locryn's cottage, and when Jake made the dash from his car to the front door, he had to hold his leather jacket over his head like a cape.

He let himself in, the rain pattering on the floorboards as he went into the darkened kitchen. It was silent, save for the steady tick of the kitchen clock.

"Loc? Loc, it's me."

But as Jake went from room to room, each neat and clean and everything in its place, a dull sense of loss took over Jake.

I've really fucked up this time.

He braved the rain again to check the bakehouse, because didn't Locryn say that baking made him happy?

But he wasn't there either. The place was as lifeless as an unused film set.

So was Locryn down in the village?

Once he was out of the rain and back in the kitchen, Jake took out his phone, but before he glanced at the screen, he noticed something he hadn't before. There was a rug rolled up, leaning against the wall.

Then Jake saw it. The trapdoor down to the smuggler's cave was open.

Jake used the light on his phone to help him navigate the dark stone tunnel, until he slipped in his haste and his phone burst apart on the rocks. He felt the rest of the way, his senses alert to the tang of the sea air and the soft roar of the waves, as distant as a shell held to his ear.

"Locryn!" Jake shouted.

His voice echoed and echoed and died. So he pushed on, sliding in the dark, swearing when he banged his knee, until finally he turned the corner and was in Locryn's cave.

And there at the mouth of it, standing beside a blazing campfire, was Locryn. Dorothy was snuggled close to his chest and together they were watching the rain that hissed noisily against the choppy ocean. Jake could hear Locryn's voice, soft and heavy with emotion, as he told the little cat, "We'll look after each other, won't we? And we'll get lots of treats ready for Daddy when he comes to visit."

"Locryn?" Jake's voice was small, a hoarse, pathetic squeak after all his bellowing. He came a step closer. "Locryn, I...I..."

For a moment Locryn was unmoving then he turned, his expression disbelieving, as if he wasn't sure that Jake was really there.

"Jake—" He smiled, but his blue eyes were filled with sadness. "You silly thing. What did you forget?"

Jake took another step, but didn't come any farther. He wasn't sure he deserved to.

"I...I forgot to tell you something."

"I know where Dorothy's treats are, don't worry," he teased, taking a step toward Jake. "Because what could be more important than Dorothy's tummy?"

"Well, there *is* something. Although Dot won't agree." Jake smiled as he ran his hand through his wet hair. "Loc, I never said I love you. And I do. I really do."

"Only say it if you mean it." Locryn's smile wobbled and disappeared. "It's all right if you don't. Caring about me's lovely enough."

"I got to the toll at the bridge, and I—I couldn't leave. I don't want that job. It's a bloody joke. You said I have integrity, and what integrity would I have going off and doing that? What integrity would I have going off and leaving you?" Jake strode over the gap between them and held out his arms to Locryn. "I love you. I'm not telling you a fib, it's true, Locryn."

"It's all right to love me *and* want the job." Locryn put his arm around Jake's waist as he snuggled into his embrace, Dorothy still safe in the crook of his other elbow. "Dorothy and I will wait for you. We love you, we're so proud that they want you for the show."

"I can't do it. I would've, before I met you. Before I came to Porthavel. I would've chewed their arms off to do it. But I'm not that person anymore. I don't want to bellow in people's faces. I want to—" Jake held Locryn and the cat. The sound of the waves, and their embrace, were calming him, and Jake said, "I want to be here, with you. I want to be happy, and I want to make *you* happy."

Locryn lifted his head and kissed Jake. "You do, darling. I love you. Whatever you decide, wherever you want to be, that's not going to change."

"I want…" Jake glanced up at the rolling waves as they hit the shore and sent foam into the air. He pressed his lips to Locryn's cheek, then he whispered, "Can I stay here?"

"Oh, Jake," Locryn whispered. "Welcome home."

Chapter Twenty

The galleon restaurant was festooned with flowers and bunting for the wedding. Jake had put on his crispest chef whites, and caught Locryn's eye with a smile as the strains of the wedding march began to play. Dorothy, a large bow around her neck, batted a paper table decoration up the aisle and was scooped into the arms of one of the locals who'd helped to work on the ship. And the groom, waiting patiently with his best man, could only laugh.

Locryn, resplendent in a deep-blue shirt with just the right number of buttons unfastened, squeezed Jake's hand. Then he dabbed at his eyes with his handkerchief and rested his head lightly on Jake's shoulder for a moment, suddenly shy again.

"She looks stunning," he whispered as he sat straight and the bride swept past in a cloud of delicate perfume. "There were moments when I thought we'd never get here, but it's been worth it."

Jake tightened his entwined fingers around Locryn's. He'd had to improvise and was using a stiff napkin from the linen cupboard to dab at his eyes. "I'm not crying. I was chopping onions until five minutes ago."

"I know, darling, I just don't believe you." Locryn kissed Jake's cheek as the bride finally reached the groom, safe on the arm of the only person who could have given her away. When Zoe turned to leave Merryn safe beside Petroc, she gave the congregation a thumbs-up and an affectionate murmur of laughter went through the ship. It had taken long enough, but they'd gotten here in the end.

"First Zoe and David, now Petroc and Merryn." Locryn dabbed at his eyes again. "I wonder who'll be next."

Dorothy escaped her captor and wound herself around Jake's and Locryn's legs. With the slightest hint of a tremble, Jake brought their joined hands to his lips and said, "I think Dorothy's dropping a hint, don't you? What do you say, Mr. Trevorrow?"

For a moment Locryn simply gazed at him. Then he whispered, "I say yes, Captain Jake. And, because I haven't said it for five minutes, I love you."

"I love you, too," Jake murmured in reply. "My adorable, passionate baker."

Want to see more from these authors? Here's a taster for you to enjoy!

The Captain's Ghostly Gamble
Catherine Curzon & Eleanor Harkstead

Excerpt

John Rookwood peered through the grimy leaded windows and saw lights approaching along the driveway. It was the same every year—uninvited guests always arrived on their anniversary.

"Captain, they're nearly here! Stop preening, man!"

"Guests!" Captain Cornelius Sheridan didn't look away from the ornate mirror where he was admiring his own reflection. He beamed at himself before pouting, then placed one hand on his hip. As John watched, Sheridan turned a little to the left, a little to the right, admiring his own form, clad as he was in a suit of shimmering gold silk.

He frowned and adjusted one of his lace-shrouded cuffs very slightly, then considered his reflection again, turning his shapely calf a little before he leaned down to brush an imaginary smut from his white stocking. "Does one need more powder, Rookwood? One doesn't want to look *gauche* for one's chums!"

"You have natural pallor enough, Captain. Besides, they're not our chums."

A large conveyance had drawn up to the front door. John turned up the collar of his greatcoat, watching as two passengers, a man and a woman, climbed out.

"The damned impertinence of it, turning up uninvited every year. Wandering about my house, disturbing our peace. They're lucky I haven't taken a pistol to them."

"*Natural?* Lord preserve me from *natural!* More powder and a touch more rouge on the lips, I think." Sheridan put his elegant hand to his silken cravat and slightly adjusted the diamond pin there. An even larger diamond was housed in the ring he wore, and it glittered as brightly as his eyes. "*My* home, Mr. Rookwood, lest we forget."

At the sound of their guests letting themselves in at the front door, John sighed. "Rookwood Manor has been in my family for generations, as well you know, you damned dandy interloper!"

"Indeed, sir, *Sheridan* Manor was once home to your people, but one believes there was the small matter of a duel and now it is *mine*." Sheridan glanced at John and beamed, his handsome face now fashionably pale. He bowed low, a cloud of rose perfume billowing from the decadent cuffs. "Let us go and say hello to our newest friends, Mr. Rookwood!"

John bowed in return, doffing his tricorne hat. "That duel was unfair—therefore, in default, Rookwood Manor is *still* mine, I think you'll find."

As John's heavy boots thumped over the floorboards, a woman's voice echoed up from the entrance hall.

"Did you hear that? I *swear* I heard footsteps!"

"Ooh, the young lady sounds so terribly nervous!" Sheridan hugged himself in amused excitement then clapped his hands together. His grin was positively wicked as he added, "What *fun!*"

"Should be easy to get shot of them, then!" John looked over the bannister as the couple began to set up their equipment. He'd seen quite a lot of this caper over the years, gadgets galore ranged through his house with nary a by-your-leave. *How terribly rude.* "Well, then, Captain, as my footsteps have served to scare her witless, would you like to go next? I'd wager you shan't terrify them in the least, but I'm happy to watch you try!"

The two men peeped down into the baronial hall below, where the enormous studded oak door stood open on the autumn night. Leaves swirled in around the feet of the second visitor, a young man with a large bag slung over his shoulder. He threw it down and looked up at his splendid surroundings, his face set into a scowl.

"Oh, now what a handsome gent!" Sheridan touched his hand to his breast and quirked one eyebrow. "If my heart had not already stopped, it would *certainly* have just skipped a beat. Who have we here?"

He began to descend the staircase, polished shoes shining in the light of the chandelier, the diamond buckles on his toes twinkling. With a glance back at John, Sheridan hopped down the last two risers and landed neatly in front of the couple, who continued to unpack their infernal equipment. Then he blew a sharp blast of rose perfume into the young lady's face.

She stumbled back a step and nearly lost her footing on the uneven floorboards. "What—what was that? Dan, can you smell it? Roses. They say that the highwayman who haunts this place smells of roses. I'm not imagining it, am I? And it's suddenly *so* cold in here!"

"You do *know* that it's all bollocks, don't you?" Dan tutted and shook his head. "I can't believe you've even talked me into this. The sooner it's on the market, the sooner some big hotel chain buys it and the sooner I get to buy that Ferrari I've always wanted, so let's get the night finished and lock the bloody door on this dusty old hole."

"Can you please not say *bollocks* when I've got the EVP recorder on, Dan?" The young woman crouched down to rummage about in a trunk. "I can't believe you want to sell this place—my family lived here too, you know. And anyway, a haunted house is much cooler than a Ferrari."

"Oh, he's one of yours!" Sheridan called upstairs to John. "A Rookwood, which makes him suddenly far less attractive! A Rookwood who intends to sell *my* bally house!"

"Balderdash—it's Rookwood Manor, after all, and will you just look at that handsome face!" John followed Sheridan downstairs. Could the young lady hear him, or even see him? She had glanced in his direction and was gawping at the stairs.

"Dan! I can hear footsteps again!"

But Dan had turned his back, so John prodded him on the shoulder to get a better look. Was this impertinent young man worthy of the name Rookwood?

"Stop pissing about, Jenny," Dan huffed. "Funny isn't it, really? Here we are, a Rookwood and a Sheridan, spending one last night in the place where our great-whatever-uncles however far removed supposedly rattle their chains and flap their sheets? And by tomorrow the For Sale board will be *up*!"

PUBLISHING

Sign up for our newsletter and find out about all our romance book releases, eBook sales and promotions, sneak peeks and FREE romance books!

About the Authors

Catherine Curzon

Catherine Curzon is a royal historian who writes on all matters of 18th century. Her work has been featured on many platforms and Catherine has also spoken at various venues including the Royal Pavilion, Brighton, and Dr Johnson's House.

Catherine holds a Master's degree in Film and when not dodging the furies of the guillotine, writes fiction set deep in the underbelly of Georgian London.

She lives in Yorkshire atop a ludicrously steep hill.

Eleanor Harkstead

Eleanor Harkstead often dashes about in nineteenth-century costume, in bonnet or cravat as the mood takes her. She can occasionally be found wandering old graveyards, and is especially fond of the ones in Edinburgh. Eleanor is very fond of chocolate, wine, tweed waistcoats and nice pens. She has a large collection of vintage hats, and once played guitar in a band. Originally from the south-east, Eleanor now lives somewhere in the Midlands with a large ginger cat who resembles a Viking.

Sign up to receive their newsletter at
https://curzonharkstead.co.uk/newsletter/

Catherine and Eleanor love to hear from readers. You can find their contact information, website and author biographies at https://www.pride-publishing.com.

www.ingramcontent.com/pod-product-compliance
Lightning Source LLC
Chambersburg PA
CBHW050730180626
46814CB00002B/682